Dixie Fish

Dixie Fish

Andrew Geyer

ISBN: 978-0-9835968-8-2
Library of Congress Control Number: 2011936071

Cover art by Eric Beverly
Manufactured in the United States of America

Ink Brush Press
Temple and Dallas, Texas

Acknowledgments

Grateful acknowledgment is made to the following publications, in which a portion of this novel previously appeared:

The Georgia Guardian 2.24 (June 1993): 11. Print.

Whispers in Dust and Bone. Lubbock, Texas: Texas Tech University Press, 2003. 150-156. Print.

I would like to thank Emily Geyer, Judy Geyer, Frank Geyer, James Dickey, William Price Fox, Keen Butterworth, Ina Rae Hark, Eric Beverly, and Jerry Craven, without whose guidance and generous assistance this novel would not exist.

I am especially grateful to the South Carolina Arts Commission and the *South Carolina State* for the South Carolina Fiction Project grants that provided me with time to write and recognition for work already done.

Other Books By Andrew Geyer:

Siren Songs from the Heart of Austin

Meeting the Dead

Whispers in Dust and Bone

For the ones who chase rainbows

Through the middle of broad fields,
The rainbow returned with me.
To where my house is visible,
The rainbow returned with me.
    —Navajo Night Chant

All families lie together, though some are burned alive.
    —James Dickey

1. Potential Bliss

W.W.W. caught the unmistakable scent of potential bliss the minute he walked into the Dixie Fish. Somewhere among the homey smells of deep-fried fish and frying starches, amid the slightly sweet odors of beer and steaming oysters, in the middle of the rank aromas of cigarette smoke and sweating bodies, he caught a whiff of the scent he'd spent his whole life searching for—a hint so strong it made his soul water.

As the three strangers W.W.W. was staying with until he found a place of his own wound their way through the weird glow of too few fluorescent lights toward a table, he picked his way through an olfactory maze, trailing potential bliss like a bee homing in on a bed of roses. The four of them sat down at a six-top in the center of the waitfloor underneath a rainbow-colored canopy slung between two wooden oars. There was Hank Williams on the corner jukebox wailing "Lovesick Blues." There were white Styrofoam mannequin heads in Confederate caps high up on a wooden rail over a faded green fish net. There were porthole windows on the walls and pictures of ships and Confederate soldiers. The smells of food and beer, and of common folks enjoying both, kept growing stronger in layer upon layer of tastebud-tempting, belly-baiting, soul-seducing splendor. His excitement grew with them. And with it all grew the wonderful, certain feeling that just the process of elimination lay between himself and potential bliss.

It was potential bliss he smelled, W.W.W. knew, rather than bliss itself. True bliss was a cold weather scent—a wood-smoky, worn-leathery, first-pot-of-coffee, eggs-in-bacon-greasy kind of mélange that there was no forgetting. At its heart was the smell of breakfast cooking while you were lying in bed and listening to the voices of people you loved. Regular as sunrise after first light, rock-solid as motherlove, true bliss had a lot to do with the feel of home.

The scent of potential bliss had a more sultry tang. It was a first-day-of-springy, cheap-perfumey, hot-body-odory kind of smell that was more exhilarating, but less fulfilling, than the real thing. It was warm, moist air and bee pollen. It was skirts coming up. It was necklines going down. Its lush bouquet made certain parts of W.W.W. sit up and take notice—and of course, excitement aside, true bliss wasn't possible without it.

The potential for bliss must be realized before true bliss can be achieved.

This was one of the maxims his daddy lived by, and that had begun shaping W.W.W.'s life even before he was born. As much as he loathed his daddy, W.W.W. had to admit that the old man was one sharp son of a bitch. True bliss—and the home that went with it—was W.W.W.'s ultimate goal, the reason he had come to South Carolina. But before he could feather his nest, he had to find a mate.

W.W.W. was almost certain that the source of the potential bliss scent was their waitress. He wouldn't have called her beautiful exactly. But he liked the way the red-brown curly hair framed her plumpishly pleasant face as she walked up to their table almost as much as he liked the way the brownish-green shorts framed her plumpishly pleasant hinder parts as she walked away toward the bar with their drink order. Her legs were long and lovely. But her smile looked a little ragged—as though she had one smile she shared with every table, and every table frayed it a little more around the edges.

"Hello," she said, "and welcome to the Dixie Fish."

Despite the threadbare smile, it sounded to W.W.W. like she really meant it.

"Hello there," he said.

"Can I get y'all something to drink?" she asked, her voice low and raspy.

W.W.W. felt, despite the "y'all," that the invitation had been directed at him alone. He barely managed to order a beer.

The table was long and narrow, but she stayed on the far side of it as she took their drink order. Try as he might, she got away before W.W.W. could catch a definitive whiff of her. Which made him just that much more horrified, when he looked down from the threadbare smile and discovered that the Strangers were coloring on the tablecloth with crayons.

Somehow, whether by the grace of God or sheer fatigue, the waitress seemed not to have noticed yet. But they were still coloring as she walked away from the table—three short-haired young professionals with ties around their necks, crayons in their hands, and satisfied looks on their faces. W.W.W. could see by the way the white area was shrinking like the last frontier that there was no way she could help noticing the Strangers' handiwork when she came back with their drinks.

W.W.W. didn't know what to do. He thought for a second about really laying into them. It seemed to him that the Strangers needed a good laying-into; that just because a body, or bodies, could afford to buy and sell every tablecloth in the place didn't mean they had a right to act like it. But, he figured, he wasn't their mother. Or their father, for that matter. And he couldn't afford a hotel. If it wasn't for the distant friend in Atlanta who had hooked him up with the Strangers—and more importantly, W.W.W. reminded himself, the Strangers' couch—he would be sleeping in the street. The $18.61 in his pocket was all the money he had in this world, and it would barely cover his dinner and beer.

He decided to go to the restroom. He figured if the waitress didn't see him actually talking to the tablecloth-colorers, she would be more inclined to believe the truth: except for the fact that he was sleeping on their couch, he didn't know them from Adam. And it was plain that the Strangers couldn't have cared any less whether he stayed or went. They were so busy coloring hearts with arrows through them, mutilated fruits, and the acronyms of corporations it was their souls' dream to help make multinational, the Strangers didn't even notice when the long-haired guy with no job, no tie, and no home got up and left the table.

W.W.W. sniffed as he went. With the half-formed intent of being surreptitious, he tried pretending that he had a bad head cold or a mild case of the flu. But the scent kept getting stronger. Potential bliss swirled all around him now, so thick it was almost visible. It drifted up off of people at tables. It floated down from the banks of fluorescent lights above his head. It wafted up off of the jukebox in the corner. He felt suddenly like the half-starved coyote his daddy had once told him about who, after finding a hole in the henhouse, wound up starving to death because he couldn't decide which hen to eat first.

W.W.W. could barely find the bar, much less the restroom. "W.W.," he said and smiled, sticking a hand out in the bartender's direction.

"Tommy," the bartender said and smiled back. But instead of shaking, he raised both his hands so that W.W.W. could see they were covered with soap suds. The suds were pink.

"Tommy," W.W.W. said, "I'd appreciate it if you could point me toward the restroom."

Tommy was tall, friendly, around twenty-two or three. He not only provided W.W.W. with the necessary directions, but also gave him the waitress's name, which turned out to be Bonnie.

"Bonnie . . ." W.W.W. said. It rolled off his tongue. "Bonnie . . ." It eased between his lips.

"That's right," Tommy said.

"Bonnie . . . What a sweet ring that's got to it. Can you hear the ring that's got to it? Doesn't it sound like bliss?"

Tommy nodded slowly, still smiling helpfully and holding up his hands that were covered with pink suds.

"Do you know what *Bonnie* means in Scotland?" W.W.W. asked, hoping that Tommy wasn't as slow-thinking as he was slow-talking and slow-moving.

Tommy nodded slowly. "No," he said.

"It means *pretty*," W.W.W. said.

"Pretty engaged."

"Engaged? Engaged how?"

"Engaged to be married," Tommy said. "To a diesel mechanic by the name of Blue."

"Blue . . ." W.W.W. said. "Blue and Bonnie . . . Bonnie and Blue . . ."

He bumped into a Trivia Whiz machine as he staggered away from the bar, then lurched on down a dark hall toward a red neon sign that read: REBS. The sign over the other door at the end of the hall read: BELLES. It wasn't until he opened the restroom door that W.W.W. realized the scent of potential bliss was as strong on the bartender as it had been on the jukebox.

He stumbled into the men's room—a powder blue one-holer the size of a closet with a sink an elbow's reach from the toilet—and latched the door behind him. He felt himself sweating. He tried to tell himself that he was just confused. But when he caught a whiff of potential bliss wafting up off of the hot water heater in the corner, W.W.W. began to wonder if he was losing his mind.

He turned on a faucet and splashed cool water onto his face. And then, pasted into the bottom corner of the mirror just above the sink, W.W.W. caught sight of the red and yellow sticker that he knew in a flash was the answer to all his questions and his prayers for achieving bliss:

> STOP!
> Wash Your Hands:
> before starting work,
> after visiting toilet,
> when soiled by work,
> after a smoke break.
>
> Protect Your Fellow Worker,
> Your Customers, Your Job.
>
> HELP PREVENT DISEASE!

2. Bloody Chicken Feathers

W.W.W. stood at the sink, feeling the cool tapwater on his face and staring at his reflection right next to the red and yellow sticker that reeked of potential bliss like a blue-haired retiree reeks of spray-net. *Work, work, break, worker, job.* Those five words leapt off of the yellow at him again and again, razor-cut red. *Work, work, break, worker, job.* As they fixed themselves in his head, he felt his life click together. And he understood at last why the bartender smelled like the jukebox.

He dried his face and walked out of the restroom feeling like the world was his laundry load, and he'd just washed and bleached it. The beer lights were brighter, the tablecloths whiter, and he noticed for the first time the crayons that had been placed on all the tables. They glowed like rainbows in clear plastic cups. W.W.W. also noticed that the tablecloths were paper. When he sat back down at the table—where the Strangers still sat coloring hearts with arrows through them, mutilated fruits, and the corporate initials of their dreams—he picked up a crayon of his own. But he couldn't make up his mind what to draw.

He was having a hard time making up his mind about a lot of things. After a couple of swallows of the beer Bonnie had brought while he was in the restroom changing his outlook on life, even the Strangers looked better to W.W.W. Despite the close-clipped blonde hair that was concreted into place with as much mousse as there was starch on their buttondowns, despite the buttondowns that were as dazzling a white as the veneers on their teeth, they looked less like junior corporate raiders and more like human beings. Their ties were as bright as their crayons.

He made up his mind to try and make friends. The idea, he decided, was to try and look beneath the buttondowns, behind the teeth; to try and see them as something more than just the distant friends of a distant friend of his from Atlanta; as more than just guides, rides, and a couch to sleep on for free. W.W.W. sipped his beer and watched them talk, following the conversation as it moved from face to face, waiting for a break he could squeeze himself into.

But they sat and talked—and talked, and talked—three dreamy Strangers, one wistful voice, about "leveraged buyouts" and "bank foreclosures." They dreamed out loud about "bargain-basement real estate" and "gentrification." They stared through W.W.W. with eyes as green as golf courses at country clubs.

"It is the initial capital investment that is the latchkey to the entire operation."

"What about the hike in property taxes? The property tax hike is the best part."

"No, you have to wait for that. The tax hike only comes after the tax assessor has raised the property values."

"But the tax assessor can't help you until you've made the initial capital investment. You first have to buy up a couple of properties in the slum . . . um, excuse me," he looked at W.W.W.'s faded blue-jean jacket, "underdeveloped neighborhood, and renovate, or raze and rebuild, said properties."

"And then comes the property tax hike."

"No, then comes the reassessment."

"Right. First the reassessment, which drives up the property values, which drives up the property taxes, which forces the riffraff . . . um, excuse me," he looked at W.W.W.'s faded flannel shirt, "the present occupants of the underdeveloped neighborhood, to sell their properties at bargain-basement prices."

After a while W.W.W. gave up on the human angle, and started coloring bloody chicken feathers.

"What's that you're coloring there?" one of the Strangers asked, finally, as Bonnie delivered another round of beers to the far side of their table—and W.W.W. tried yet again, without success, to get a whiff of her.

"Bloody chicken feathers," W.W.W. answered.

"Chickens? That sounds like one of the things that drives down the property values of the riffraff in slums," one of the Strangers said. He looked W.W.W. straight in the eye. "Or should I say . . . rednecks?"

It was the final straw. "Actually," W.W.W. said, "it's just the bloody feathers that I'm drawing. The smell of them is a sure sign of impending misfortune . . . especially for those whose pockets are deeper than their perceptions."

"Is that a fact?"

"Why don't we try a little experiment?" W.W.W. asked, remembering the Trivia Whiz machine that he'd bumped into as he left the bar. He looked from one set of golf-course green eyes to the other, to the other, and back again. Potential bliss would have to wait for another day. "Y'all ever play any games of chance?"

"What do you have in mind?"

"How about a friendly game of trivia-for-beer?" W.W.W. asked.

Two bars, thirteen free beers, three free shots of tequila, and a free seafood dinner later, he lay stretched across the bed of the Stranger who lay passed out on the living room couch. W.W.W. had the same $18.61 in his pocket he'd started out with that night. But he still felt every bit as soul-lonely and friendless as he'd felt since the ride he'd hitched to Columbia, South Carolina had let him off at the Strangers' door.

One of the bars the Strangers had taken him to was called Group Therapy—but he'd never in his life felt so alone in a crowd of people, and he'd always thought real therapy meant someone you could talk to who cared. He lay awake for a long time, thinking about his daddy. W.W.W. thought about what a damned intelligent man his daddy was, and about what a shame it was that the old man had never cared a day about W.W.W. in all the twenty-four years of W.W.W.'s life.

But almost before he knew it, Sunday morning had come, and W.W.W. was giving the Strangers a chance to get even by betting on football for the beers, shots, and seafood they'd lost by betting on trivia the night before. They sat around the sports page, the three of them—a clump of silk print kimonos and designer bedroom slippers on a Persian rug in front of a big-screen TV—trying to plug the point-spread into some kind of mathematical formula.

"What's the margin of error?"

"It's right there."

"This thing?"

"No, that thing. That thing right there."

"Two."

"Plus or minus two points?"

9

"Yeah. That."

"How can the margin of error be two, when the point spread is only ten?"

"The line is only ten?"

"We need more points."

"Can we have more points?"

"I'll give you seventeen," W.W.W. said. "All of you. A one-time offer of seventeen points. Take it or leave it. It's almost kick-off time."

"I'll take it."

"I'll take it, too."

"We'll all take it."

"Alright," W.W.W. said. "Now. How much?"

He gave them the underdog and seventeen points. He took their bets, despite the fact that he was about $281.39 short of the amount he'd have to pay out if he happened to lose. Then W.W.W. sat back and enjoyed the second most lopsided victory in playoff history. The Strangers mostly ignored him. So he stared for a while, out the French windows of the Strangers' spacious two-story red brick house, at the windows of all the other spacious two-story red brick houses in their exclusive neighborhood. Then he picked up the sports section and ignored them back.

He went through it slowly, lingering over the prep basketball results like he gave a damn. But in reality, he was afraid to turn to the want ads in the back. W.W.W. was searching for the answer to all his questions and his prayers for achieving bliss that—ever since seeing his reflection next to that red and yellow sticker in the Dixie Fish restroom last night—he had been certain he would find in the want ads today. He turned, finally, to the employment section and looked up the food and beverage listings. His hands shook as he read through listing after listing, column after column of WAITRESS, WAITRESS, COCKTAIL, WAITRESS. He felt sicker and sicker. The world seemed to be turning as black as the ink on his fingers. And then there it was, suddenly, in the last column of the want-ads, all the way at the very bottom:

> WANTED. WAITSTAFF. DIXIE FISH.

On the Monday afternoon that was two days after the Saturday night on which W.W.W. had first caught the unmistakable scent of potential bliss at the Dixie Fish, he was back again. It was after one o'clock; and despite the fact that it had just turned January, the sun was out and the temperature was well up into the seventies.

W.W.W. sat out front on the new/used 700 c.c. maroon metal-flake and chrome motorcycle that he'd practically stolen, at twelve hundred and fifty dollars, less than an hour before. He thought of the bike as both new and used because, although it must have seemed used to the man who'd been fool enough to sell it, it was as new to W.W.W. as Easter morning. It had been that kind of a day.

"Hell," he said, right out loud and alone, to every puffy spring cloud that had the unexpected good fortune to grace that January sky. "It's been that kind of a weekend."

You can't lose when you're on a roll.

If there was one thing his daddy had told W.W.W. that had stuck out, head and shoulders, above all the other things the old man had said over the years, it was that you can't lose when you're on a roll. W.W.W. felt at that moment like he could outwrestle Jacob's angel three falls out of three. Since he'd seen his reflection next to that little red and yellow sticker in the restroom of the Dixie Fish, W.W.W. had been on the kind of roll that people like the Strangers—whose house he'd been sleeping at, but that he was moving out of as soon as he got done at the Dixie Fish—scarcely dreamed of. It was the kind of roll that would've done even his daddy proud.

W.W.W. shifted his weight in the seat of his motorcycle and looked over the outside of the Dixie Fish. He decided that he liked it, even though it didn't remind him of anything. W.W.W. usually liked things best that reminded him of something else, especially something from his childhood in Southwest Texas—during which he had been completely happy like he'd never been since, but which had gone by so fast all that remained of it was a blur of rolling plains and scrub brush.

He was sure he liked the look of the place. But W.W.W. couldn't say why, exactly, apart from the fact that it smelled right. He liked the collection of gray concrete letters that spelled out DIXIE FISH less than he did the assortment of rusty nails that held them up. He liked the walls. The walls were put together with red bricks that seemed to have come from the same brickyard as every other brick that had ever been laid in the South. But instead of that just-washed look all the other bricks seemed to have, the bricks at the Dixie Fish looked dingy. They didn't look dirty, though, as much as comfortable, like the favorite pairs of jeans his mother used to hand-wash to keep from having to throw them in the trash.

Jesus, he thought.

W.W.W. stopped looking at the bricks and tried to concentrate on the windows. Maybe it was the plate glass windows that he liked—the way there were no bars across them; the way they took up more wall space than the bricks took up; and the way a person would be able to climb right out of them, if she had to, in an emergency. He liked the bright red fire hydrant on the corner. He liked, even better, the fire station that was right there across the street. He would be safe here. Safe from flames, and bars, and from hands on bars in burning windows. Safe from the sickeningly sweet smell of burning flesh.

Jesus Christ, he thought. Not again.

W.W.W. loosened his borrowed tie and checked his borrowed watch. 1:55 p.m. He'd applied for enough waitstaff positions to know most places only interviewed from 2 to 5 p.m., in the dead space between lunch and dinner. The ad for the Dixie Fish hadn't said any different. And W.W.W. didn't want to look desperate about getting the job.

The man who looks like he needs a thing worst is the man least likely to get it.

If there was a thing his daddy had told him that stuck in W.W.W.'s mind, besides the fact that you can't lose when you're on a roll, it was that need always lost out to greed when it came to business. His own experience had shown W.W.W. that the old man (as sorry an excuse for a human being as the son of a bitch was) knew human nature. W.W.W. had been worried enough about making an impression to practically beg the Strangers to lend him the pricey watch and tie.

So he pulled the day's receipts out of his backpack and started checking through them. Even though they were just thin pieces of pink and white and gray and yellow paper, they felt heavy—concrete confirmation of a chance at achieving bliss. Of course, W.W.W. would have to accomplish a great deal more than he'd managed so far today to get himself to a state of true bliss. But he'd made a start. He'd gone early that morning to the Confederate State University Coliseum to register for graduate courses (pink legal-sized scantron sheet with colored-in computer dots). Not that W.W.W. was any too keen on school, graduate or otherwise. But one of the most important reasons he'd come to Columbia was to sample the fruits of academic freedom. Academic freedom, according to all that W.W.W. had been told, was the freest state a person could be in without being independently wealthy—a condition his chronic impoverishment seemed to preclude. Just as long as the federal government was willing to hand him a student loan check (white perforated check stub), he was eager to explore the world of Graduate History at five percent interest.

The same Stranger who'd driven W.W.W. down to the Coliseum drove him over to the bank where all the Strangers did their banking. This was handy. W.W.W. wrote his football winnings in on the same deposit ticket (gray dollar-bill-sized slip with neat black boxes) as his student loan money, and maybe saved a tree. He found a roommate through the secretary in the Graduate Director's office—a fellow incoming student named Reese with a two-bedroom duplex (torn-off piece of legal pad with an address and phone number scribbled in pencil) and a rent within W.W.W.'s budget. He called up and took the place without even bothering to go and look at it. Then he bought the first motorcycle (yellow legal-sized carbon with a little black motorcycle on top) he saw, at the first place the Stranger took him to, thanked the Stranger for everything, and drove himself to the Dixie Fish.

It was a little after 2 p.m., but W.W.W. wasn't in a hurry. He came not as a customer, but as a prospective employee.

3. What's in a Name

W.W.W. edged his way into the between-shifts gloom of the Dixie Fish like an intrepid explorer into the Amazon Jungle.

His aim was simple: to get a job here in this place that had seemed on Saturday night like the hidden source of the bliss he'd been seeking his whole life.

His plan was simple: just to wander in sort of nonchalant, like maybe he was the tail-end of the lunch rush, and then make absolutely certain it was him that got in the first word.

His reasoning was simple: getting in the first word was a sign of strength and goodwill, qualities necessary to both intrepid explorers and food and beverage employees.

Meeting managers, at least in W.W.W.'s experience, was a lot like what he'd seen on television about encountering primitive tribes. One minute, you were trading them pocket combs for golden idols; the next minute, they sensed a weakness and used your head for soup stock.

The Dixie Fish had a different feel to it in the afternoon than it had in the evening. All that light gushing through all that window space made the place look huge and empty, like some kind of restaurant graveyard where intrepid explorers and their sea knick-knacks came to die. The covers and condiments had been stripped off the tables, leaving them looking like naked bones on a dead-flesh concrete floor. The only sign of life was a doughy guy in a dirty red apron who stood over at the register, looking to W.W.W. like a burned-out cook who'd made up his mind that a cashier job was as good a ticket out of the kitchen as any, and who was hanging around after hours to study up.

W.W.W. noticed Dirty Apron looking him over. If W.W.W. was going to make the first move, like he knew he had to, the time had come. He breathed in once—quick—through his nose, seeking the sultry tang of potential bliss. Nothing. He sniffed again, retesting the air. And he almost panicked. Then he caught that hint of spring and sweat and cheap perfume, and he felt something start to stir. It wasn't excitement exactly. At least, nowhere near like on Saturday night. But there was potential bliss here. The scent drew him toward the cash register, and it grew stronger the closer he went.

"Could I please fill out an application?" W.W.W. asked.

Dirty Apron ducked and rummaged around under the cash register for a while, but came up applicationless. He had a thoughtful kind of measuring look about him. His eyes darted back and forth between W.W.W.'s head and chest as though the entire weight of his opinion hung balanced on an imaginary line that ran midway between W.W.W.'s long blonde hair and his black silk tie.

"Where did you hear about the job opening?" Dirty Apron asked.

"The Sunday paper."

"There were an awful lot of job listings in the want ads yesterday."

"Yeah," W.W.W. agreed. Then he regretted the monosyllable, which he'd just kind of grunted out, and which Dirty Apron responded to by moving his eyes in the direction of the long blonde hair.

"Just what was it, exactly, that made you pick the Dixie Fish?"

"The way it smelled."

The look on Dirty Apron's face, which had been neutral, seemed now to slide toward doubtful. His eyes seemed to focus only on W.W.W.'s long blonde hair—on the way it slid over his collar, past his shoulders, all the way to the middle of his back.

"I came to the Dixie Fish the first night I was in town," W.W.W. said. "And I went kind of haywire over the smell of the place. Have you ever really smelled this place?"

Dirty Apron shook his head.

"Bliss," W.W.W. said.

Dirty Apron's eyes slid back in the direction of the black silk tie. He looked almost interested. "Kent," he said, extending a hand across the cash register in W.W.W.'s direction. "Kent Bronstein."

"W.W.," W.W.W. said and shook hands. Kent's grip was firm, but doughy. It left a greasy feel on W.W.W.'s hand.

"W.W. what?"

16

"W."

"That supposed to be funny?" Kent asked. "I mean, I know about the Internet and all, even though the technology here at the Dixie Fish ain't exactly 21st Century."

It was just then that W.W.W. noticed the way Kent was fondling the cash register. It looked like between-features time at the drive-in movies; and instead of the register, Kent had a back-seat date. He ran his fingers over the shiny black buttons. He touched the lean, smooth flanks of the register with the palms of his hands. W.W.W. didn't need the sudden hot-body-odory aroma of potential bliss that struck him so hard his knees buckled to finally figure out the way things stood.

"Hell, Kent," W.W.W. said. "You own the place. Don't you?"

There was a confused look on Kent's face now, but he looked interested again. Maybe even a little proud of himself. The eyes shifted back midway between the hair and the tie.

"How could you tell?" Kent asked. Both hands still stroked the register.

"Trick of the trade."

"How many years you been working in restaurants?"

"Five, and about a half."

Kent pointed at a table that had three chairs on either side of it. "What would you say that was?"

"Six-top," W.W.W. said.

Kent pointed at a table that had just two chairs.

"Deuce."

Kent pointed at the area behind the faded green fish net that was mostly counter space and refrigerators.

"Waitstation."

Kent pointed at an open square space in the wall between the kitchen and the waitstation that had a ledge at the bottom of it wide enough to accommodate plates.

"Waitwindow."

Every answer planted Kent's eyes a little more firmly on the tie. W.W.W. was sure he was as good as on the waitstaff, when Kent poked a forefinger at some Godawful apparatus that not so much sat as lurked on the bar.

"Well?" Kent asked when W.W.W. hesitated. "What's that?"

17

It looked more like an instrument of torture than a restaurant appliance. It had a knobby black handle like a hunting knife and a wedge-shaped blade that pointed down out of a set of stainless steel innards at a cupped metal plate that looked designed to hold body parts. W.W.W. felt completely at a loss. But just then, what he could only call pure animal instinct took over.

Instinct pulled his eyes up above the torture-dingus to the wall above the bar. A set of photos hanging there showed Confederate soldiers in different kinds of uniforms and with different kinds of equipment. The photos looked authentic. But he was thinking that they didn't seem likely to help out very much when instinct pushed his gaze up a little higher. And just above them, arms firmly crossed beneath the firmly set face, W.W.W. saw a white-haired gentleman staring down out of a silver frame. The gentleman stared down past a firm jaw, past silver-white whiskers—past that awful courthouse in Virginia and the national Union cemetery that used to be his front yard—straight at the bar, and at the torture-dingus, and at the Dixie Fish.

W.W.W. said, "Robert E. Lee."

Kent went teary-eyed. Then he reached underneath the register and started rustling papers. The scent of potential bliss was now so strong in the Dixie Fish that W.W.W. could taste it. It had a salty-musky tang that put him in mind of the taste of victory.

"You're a good man, W.W.," Kent said. "The way you hesitated when I pointed at that mechanical oyster-shucker threw me for a minute. Well, that and the hair. But you're as right as rain. There's just one more thing that I need to know."

"What's that, Kent?"

"Your full name." He handed W.W.W. a piece of white paper that had black typing on it.

It was a federal tax form. At the sight of it, the tang of victory went a little stale on W.W.W.'s tongue.

"It's just for tax purposes," Kent said.

W.W.W. hardly heard him.

"Don't you have a name?" Kent asked.

W.W.W. hardly heard that either. He had a picture in his mind of the son of a bitch responsible not only for his name, but for his attitude toward taxes, the federal government, and just about every other so-called organized activity that was supposed to prop up the individual, but that always seemed to wind up grinding W.W.W. down. He saw his daddy standing in a field (it seemed like the old man was always standing in some field or other). He was facing west (it was one of the main reasons W.W.W. had come east). He was talking about taxes.

Walt Whitman, the old man said. (The son of a bitch always addressed W.W.W. by his first and middle names: what else could you expect of someone who, at the age of eighteen, had changed his name from Alexander Hamilton Woodcock to Thomas Jefferson Woodcock and left the city for the semi-desert Southwest Texas plains so he could get right with the ground?) *Income tax is just a term that the federal government came up with to make organized thievery sound legal.* The old man looked at the ground and spat speculatively. Then he looked back west. *The day of reckoning will come. One day we will cleanse this once-great nation with fire and take back what is ours.*

The memory made W.W.W.'s gorge rise. But right now, he told himself, the important thing wasn't feelings, income tax, or the federal government. In order for him to be able to take the first shot at bliss he'd had in he didn't know how long, the name he'd spent his whole adult life keeping private was going to have to come out in public.

"Well?" Kent's eyes were beginning to focus back in on W.W.W.'s hair.

Like it or not, there was no way around it. W.W.W. put the tax form down on the counter. He picked up the pen. Then he scratched, letter after awful letter: WALT WHITMAN WOODCOCK.

4. New England Lobsters and Angel Food Cake

W.W.W. took a deep breath and smiled contentedly. It was his first night at the Dixie Fish, and the air was thick with the scent of potential bliss. He was supposed to have spent the whole night in training, but it turned out busy. So around 8:30, when the restaurant started to crowd up, the waitstaff just kind of huddled up behind the faded green fish net that closed off the waitstation from the waitfloor. And then, right there in front of him—just as though there had never been a single word spoken on this earth that anybody needed to hide—they made a group decision about cutting W.W.W.'s training short.

"He's okay," Alisha said. "We're slammed. Wanna let him take some tables?" Alisha was the waitress who'd volunteered to show W.W.W. the Dixie Fish ropes. But once she found out about his being enrolled in the Graduate History program, she spent her time leading him around from table to table, staring hard at him through bushy dyed-black bangs and grilling him about authors whose books he'd never read. "Okay, Sartre," she'd said, whipping a ticket out of a soiled red apron pocket and writing down a drink order for a family of four, "let's start with Sartre. What do you think about *No Exit*?"

"Never read it."

"Never read *No Exit*?"

"Never read Sartre."

"Oh." She led W.W.W. back to the waitstation. "How about Camus?"

"Nope." They poured two sweet teas, an unsweetened tea, and a coke into Styrofoam cups, then hustled the drinks out to the table. "Okay, how about Simone de Beauvoir?" Alisha asked, whipping the ticket back out and taking a dinner order of two flounder plates, a child's shrimp, and a kiddie burger with only ketchup and mustard. "We'll start with Simone de

21

Beauvoir."

"I don't know him either."

"He's a her. The lover of Jean-Paul Sartre. Who the hell do you know anyway?"

"I've read some of Plato and Aristotle; all of Whitman, Emerson, and Thoreau; most of Garland and Steinbeck; a lot of Hemingway; some Faulkner. And history. I've read a ton of history."

"Let's just stick to learning the ropes at the Dixie Fish, shall we?" They'd spent the rest of the time up to the huddle doing just that.

"Hello Bonnie? Hello Brave? Hello Gladys? He's okay," Alisha said. "It's getting busier. Wanna let him take some tables?"

"Okay by me," Bonnie said. The threadbare smile she gave W.W.W. looked every bit as lovely as it had on that first night when she'd welcomed him to the Dixie Fish.

"Okay by me," Brave said and patted W.W.W. on the back. Brave, the only other male on the Dixie Fish waitstaff, also seemed to have a weak spot for the lovely Bonnie. But if he was bothered by the addition of W.W.W., Brave hadn't shown it.

"Okay by me!" Gladys said in a baritone voice. Then she gave W.W.W. a cheek-stinging slap on the butt.

It was one of the most beautiful things he had ever seen—at least, in the workplace, anyway—and W.W.W. made up his mind then and there to stay at the Dixie Fish forever. There hadn't been a true democracy in the world since the fall of Athens in 404 B.C. But the folks here at the Dixie Fish seemed to have reestablished one.

Freedom is the cornerstone of bliss on earth.

Wiser words, it seemed to W.W.W., had never been spoken—even if the son of a bitch who had spoken them happened to be the genocidal agrarianist who'd named him Walt Whitman. And a true democracy, a partnership of equals, was the only rock the cornerstone of freedom could be carved from.

True democracy was certainly bedrock firm here at the Dixie Fish. Which was good, because life had otherwise been on shaky ground since the weekend. Especially in school, where he'd been given the due dates for a good bit of paperwork, but hadn't learned much; and what little academic freedom he'd experienced wouldn't prop up a dollhouse, much less the lofty marble Parthenon of true bliss. Things at the new duplex he'd rented weren't exactly rock-solid either. W.W.W. had walked into the Dixie Fish hoping for a change.

His post-referendum transition from trainee to equal partner on the waitstaff had been as smooth as the polished concrete of the Dixie Fish floor. His customers were happy. Tips were good. He'd learned the entire beer list, plus every one of the entrees, and it was almost closing time. But as he walked up to his thirteenth—and, he hoped, his last—table of the night, there amid the scent of potential bliss that had enveloped him all evening, he caught the stultifying stink of bloody chicken feathers that meant misfortune lurking near.

"Howdy," W.W.W. said and handed out three powder-blue paper menus. "Can I get y'all something to drink while you're thinking food thoughts?"

Nobody at the table paid him any mind. As time drew out and W.W.W. kept standing there smiling, politely waiting for someone to place a drink order, it struck him that the people who were so pointedly ignoring him were dressed in tuxedos and an evening gown. A queasy feeling seemed to creep up on him out of the concrete. He wished he could take back the "howdy" and the "y'all."

The table was peopled by three gray-haired persons, all of whom looked to W.W.W. like they'd walked straight out of an opera box. One of the men sported a goatee. They had a high-brow kind of air about them that W.W.W. knew could mean nothing but trouble in a place like the Dixie Fish—which would serve anyone with shoes, a shirt, and his privates covered, and whose waitstaff dressed like the clientele.

It was the man without the goatee who finally asked W.W.W. to tell them about the wine list. "Tantalize us. Tease us. Fill us," he said, "with lust for the grape."

W.W.W. looked from the bare concrete floor to the tablepaper. The bloody-chicken-feather stink of misfortune wafted up from all around. "I don't know anything about the wine list," he admitted. "But I can tell you all about the beer list. Our selection of domestic beers is quite extensive."

"I have no doubt, whatsoever," the Man Without the Goatee said, "that your beer list is quite as extensive as it is impressive. Our exclusive interests, however, lie with the wine list."

At this point W.W.W. was forced to admit that he wasn't sure there even was a wine list. "And if there is a wine list," he went on, "I don't think it will prove to be an extensive wine list." Then he said that he would go and ask the bartender.

Before W.W.W. could start that way, though, the Man Without the

Goatee said not to trouble the bartender, "who is undoubtedly as familiar with the wine list as certain others are unfamiliar," but just to tell him to send out a bottle of his best champagne, and that Dom Perignon would be preferable, of course.

W.W.W. started for the bar, glad to get away from the Opera People—who even though they were sitting, and he was standing, made him feel like it was them that were looking down at him. Just then, though, the Man Without the Goatee reached over and slipped something into W.W.W.'s hand.

W.W.W. thought at first it was a tip. He thought next about throwing the tip back into the Man Without the Goatee's face, job or no job. But then W.W.W. got hold of himself and decided to see how much it was.

It was then that he discovered it was not a tip, but a note. It read:

> Waitress:
>   My name is Dr. Bob Allen. I am eating with
> the Rev. Dale Sessions (bearded guy) and his wife,
> Norma. When you come back to our table, please say
> to me the following: "The fresh New England lobsters
> are being prepared, champagne is being chilled, and
> fresh peaches will be served with angel food cake."
> Thanks,
> Dr. Bob Allen

The note was scrawled on white stationery with a bright red logo across the bottom of the page: SOUTH CAROLINA DEPARTMENT OF MENTAL HEALTH.

5. Purple Private Parts

When he read the logo at the bottom of the page, W.W.W. got over his initial hostility at the contents of the note. But lunatics or no, it galled so in his guts being called *waitress*, even on paper, that he was all the way to the bar before it struck him that the Opera People might be dangerous.

If there was one thing W.W.W. knew less about than rich folks, it was mental disorders. But he remembered his daddy telling him once that the rich never went insane, they only got eccentric. W.W.W. wasn't sure what *eccentric* meant exactly, behavior-wise. But it didn't sound particularly hazardous—and anyway, he'd never heard of the high-brow yet that would do anything so low-brow as walk into a restaurant and open fire. He decided to call Tommy over and ask about the wine list.

"Tommy," W.W.W. said when Tommy finally made it over from the other side of the bar, where he had been standing and doing nothing. "Tell me about the wine list."

The confused look that W.W.W. had yet to see leave Tommy's face deepened until his eyes looked as blue and empty as the Southwest Texas autumn sky. "Wine list?"

W.W.W. nodded encouragement.

"Well," Tommy's forehead crinkled. His eyebrows moved slowly toward each other. "We have red, and . . . white."

Out of the corner of his eye, W.W.W. could see the Opera People. They looked every bit as oblivious as Tommy—except for the Man Without the Goatee, who was staring in the direction of the bar in what was obviously an attempt to catch W.W.W.'s attention.

"Champagne, Tommy, do we have champagne?"

Not only Tommy's face, but his entire body had grown so completely still that W.W.W. wondered if Tommy's heart were beating.

"Tommy!"

The Man Without the Goatee started making hand signals.

"I think there's a bottle of . . . something . . . left over from . . . somewhere. You'd better go and ask Kent."

"There is champagne, then," W.W.W. said quickly, managing somehow not to reach across the bar and rattle teeth.

Tommy's head bobbed up and down.

The Man Without the Goatee was now waving both arms in the direction of the bar.

W.W.W. started back toward the Opera People, satisfied well enough as to the existence and availability of a bottle of champagne to go and announce it to the Man Without the Goatee.

The Man Without the Goatee, when he saw W.W.W. moving back in their direction, gave up the arm waving and the hand signals and settled back into his chair.

W.W.W. was too busy studying back over the note to be able to see what Tommy was doing, if anything. But he hoped that, whatever it was, it was painful.

W.W.W. stuck the note into his pocket as he reached the table. Then he cleared his throat and started through the Man Without the Goatee's speech. "The fresh New England lobsters are being prepared . . ." At least, he had assumed that the Man Without the Goatee was *Dr. Bob Allen*. But it struck W.W.W. suddenly, as he studied the people in tuxedos and an evening gown—who weren't paying the slightest attention to anything that was going on around them, himself included; and who, it seemed, had discovered their crayons while he was searching for champagne—that the first thing an escaped lunatic would pretend to be was a doctor. ". . . the wine is being chilled . . ." The Woman in the Evening Gown, who the note called *Norma*, had just finished beating the pants off herself at tic-tac-toe for what looked like the eleventh or twelfth straight time. And right next to her, the Man With the Goatee, who the note called *the Rev. Dale Sessions* and who was supposed to be her husband, was drawing yellow stick men that had huge purple private parts and that were engaged in some of the most amazing acts W.W.W. had ever seen. ". . . and fresh peaches will be served with angel food cake."

He rushed through the last part of the Man Without the Goatee's speech. For all W.W.W. knew, the Opera People might be serial-killing psychotics. He had never seen an honest to God psychotic before—outside of TV and the movies anyway, where it always seemed like they were not so much vicious as misunderstood, and where the good-looking young nurse could almost always talk them out of killing anybody else once they'd knocked off whoever it was that tied them up as children and kept them locked in the attic—but he was absolutely certain that he wanted to put some distance between himself and the people in tuxedos and an evening gown.

Just as W.W.W. turned to head for the waitstation, though, the Man Without the Goatee—who all through the speech had been staring at *the Rev.*'s stick men and crushing purple-private-colored crayons into purple-colored crumbs—reached over and slipped another piece of paper into W.W.W.'s hand.

W.W.W.'s first instinct was to drop the thing on the concrete and run across the street to the fire station for whatever help they might be able to provide. But then he felt the texture of the paper. It had that magic raspy thickness to it that had changed the way he thought about so many of the people he'd waited on over the years. It wasn't ragged, or crumpled, like most of the more common denominations. It had a high-dollar smoothness that made him peel the edges back slow and sweet.

When W.W.W. saw the banknote was a fifty, he decided that a little harmless eccentricity might be good for the soul.

But the Dixie Fish wasn't TV or the movies; and it wasn't his restaurant, it was Kent's. So W.W.W. headed off to the kitchen for a second opinion. He had to ask about the champagne anyway. And it struck him, as he slipped the fifty into his pocket and felt the Man Without the Goatee's note, that W.W.W. had no clue as to whether the Dixie Fish served lobster or not.

6. Cold Duck and Billy Clubs

W.W.W. looked through the waitwindow. In the kitchen, over the order of deep-fried sea creatures and deep-fried starches waiting to be prepped and carried out, he saw Smiley standing over the deep-fryer in a dirty red apron, looking like a grease-covered gingerbread man. Smiley, Kent's fry cook and all around dirty-job-doer, handled the fry-baskets with what looked almost like love. He didn't so much clutch as fondle them. It was exactly the way Kent had looked on that Monday afternoon three days before when W.W.W. had walked into the Dixie Fish as a prospective employee—except that instead of a fry-basket, it was the cash register Kent had been fondling.

Kent was manning the steamer. He spun the pressure-lock wheel on the big stainless steel door, and a cloud of superheated water vapor belched out into the kitchen along with the taste-tingling aroma of steamed oysters. Once the steam had cleared, Kent scraped the dark-gray, partly opened oysters into blue-and-white plastic buckets and slung the buckets into the waitwindow with the other order waiting to be prepped and served.

W.W.W. caught Kent's eye and handed him the Man Without the Goatee's note. As he read it, Kent's complexion paled to as dry a white as bleached wheat flour.

"They look dangerous?"

"Look like customers to me. Personally, I think we ought to serve them."

Kent had the kind of call-cops-first-ask-questions-next look on his face that W.W.W. had seen so many times before. But it was a look that he had learned to identify more with the waitpeople who had to actually serve every axe-murderer or serial killer who didn't feel like cooking, than with the managers and owners who sat safe in the back and made the wait-people go out and do it.

"The customer," Kent said, "is always wrong."

It made W.W.W. almost want to kiss Kent, hearing him say those magic words. It was the first time W.W.W. had ever heard them come out of an owner's, or even a manager's, mouth. But in this particular case, it seemed like profit potential had to outweigh principles.

"But these are rich customers, begging to be served."

"The customer," Kent repeated flatly, "is always wrong."

"They're wearing tuxedos and an evening gown."

"The customer," Kent said again, "is always wrong." But this time, his voice sounded almost hopeful.

W.W.W. held out the fifty-dollar bill that he'd gotten from the Man Without the Goatee. "They gave me this."

The call-cops look faded from Kent's face when he saw the banknote. Then his features twisted around into a slit-eyed smile of greed that W.W.W. thought of as more natural to managers, and especially owners, than to waitpeople—although he guessed no waitperson was ever really immune, once cash touched hand. W.W.W. remembered one night in New Orleans, walking into work at this bigtip-shitjob Cajun place called the Crawfish Boil just as Heather, the last lunch waitress, was figuring up her tips. She wasn't so much counting the money, though, as just running her fingers through it. She stopped fingering her bills long enough to smile, slow and sly, up at W.W.W. "You look, um. . ." he started; but he hadn't wanted to say "horny," so he said "happy" instead. Heather narrowed her eyes and said, "Greed, baby. Greed."

"Lobster and champagne . . ." Kent said wistfully. "How much you think they'd pay for the stuff?" His eyes never left the fifty.

"Almost anything."

W.W.W. was sure he and Kent were on the same page when Kent said, "We have a problem."

"What problem?" W.W.W. asked. "Tommy said he was almost sure he had a bottle of champagne."

"Yes, there are a couple of bottles of champagne left over from New Year's that we could peel the labels off of and mark up a couple of thousand percent."

"That doesn't sound like much of a problem."

"Well, no, that isn't much of a problem. The fact that we don't have any lobster, though, much less New England lobster, is the problem. But we've got an assload of Alaskan king crab. W.W., do you think they would take Alaskan king crab instead of lobster?"

"I don't think they'll know the difference."

When they met at the bar, Kent was busy scraping the label off a bottle of Cold Duck. "You're sure they're not dangerous?"

W.W.W. already had the ice bucket ready to go. "Where would a bunch of escaped lunatics, dangerous or otherwise, get this kind of cash?" he asked, re-flashing the fifty he had just re-pocketed. And although the body of *Dr. Bob Allen* leapt immediately to mind, he kept his mouth shut.

W.W.W. managed to keep his mouth shut, but there was no way to shut off his mind. The more the thought of *Dr. Bob Allen*'s body worked around in there with the thought of the bloody-chicken-feather stink of misfortune, the more the thought of serving the Opera People turned sobering. By the time he got back to the table, W.W.W. was starting to worry kind of seriously. What would the Man Without the Goatee—who might or might not be *Dr. Bob Allen*; and more importantly, who might or might not have done *Dr. Bob Allen* in—do if he noticed that his $120 bottle of Dom Perignon was really a $5 bottle of Cold Duck?

But when W.W.W. set the ice bucket and glasses down on the table, none of the Opera People even seemed to notice. He popped the cork, and none of them even looked up. *Norma* had given up on beating the pants off herself at tic-tac-toe and seemed now to be completely absorbed in losing anything that might be left to herself at hangman. The stick men that *Norma* kept hanging by their stick necks among the X's and O's looked a lot like the ones *the Rev. Dale Sessions* was still drawing. But while *the Rev.*'s stick men were still busy engaging in some of the most amazing acts of perversion W.W.W. had ever seen, *Norma*'s seemed not to have any kind of sexual apparatus at all. Much less the huge purple private parts that *the Rev.* seemed so intent on and that *Dr. Bob Allen* was still so busy staring at while crumbling purple crayons into purple-colored crumbs.

So despite the smell of bloody chicken feathers that was so strong now in the air W.W.W. could hardly breathe, he went ahead and filled their glasses to the rim. He wrapped the napkin a little tighter around where the label should have been. He ground the Dom Perignon that was really Cold

Duck down into the ice bucket. Then he headed back to pick up the Alaskan king crab, which he was now fairly certain he could pass for lobster—so certain, in fact, that he was thinking he might even cover it with peaches and try to pass it off as angel food cake—when he got back to the waitwindow and Kent said that they had another problem.

"But not a big problem," Kent said. "Don't worry, W.W. It's really nothing at all." Kent held up what looked like a billy club. "This is all we have as far as cracking tools go."

W.W.W.'s face must've put into words what his mouth couldn't. At least, not into the kind of words that didn't cause immediate unemployment.

"It's a crab bat," Kent said. "Ain't you ever been crabbing?"

W.W.W. shook his head.

"Look," Kent said, "you just got to trust me on this. It's a tradition, that's all. Those people will probably know what to do with them."

"And if they don't?"

"I'll take care of it myself."

So when W.W.W. carried out the tray, he carried out—in addition to the three plates of steamed crab, steamed produce, steamed rice, and toasted French bread—three billy clubs and some serious doubts. He was careful to put the billy clubs down last, and to jump clear of the table just as soon as they were on it. Which was good, because before he took two steps, he heard the whacking start up behind him. It sounded hollow. Ugly. The hollow kind of ugly sound he connected somewhere in the back of his mind with an axe breaking, not so much through bark into soft pulp, as through bone into soft flesh.

W.W.W. retreated all the way to the waitstation—not running flat out, exactly, but not exactly taking his time—and ducked behind the faded green fish net. He pretended to roll forks up into paper napkins while he kept an eye on the goings-on.

Kent had been right about the Opera People knowing what to do with the crab bats. W.W.W. would have said, though, as he watched them beat the dead lobsters that were really crabs with the crab bats that were really billy clubs, that it had more to do with killer instinct than with tradition. As the hollow whacks went on and on, the rest of the waitstaff—who had been moving around behind the fish net taking care of closing duties W.W.W. hadn't learned yet—left off what they were doing and huddled in close, watching meat from the dead crabs splatter onto tuxedos and an evening gown, onto the tablepaper and floor. and even onto the plate glass windows where the reflections of the crab bats rose and fell.

It felt good to be a part of the huddle.

7. Seventies San Francisco Disco Queens

"But I can't screw Reese," W.W.W. said, thinking of his new room-mate at the duplex he'd rented. And looking down at W.W.W. through the red glow/white flash/red glow of the Dixie Fish beer lights, the heroically suffering—and very tastefully framed—face of General Robert E. Lee seemed to agree.

Instead of arguing, Tommy poured W.W.W. another draft beer. Ever since the close of W.W.W.'s triumphant first shift at the Dixie Fish, Brave and Tommy had been trying to convince him to break his lease agreement with Reese and move into a three-bedroom house with them instead. The combination of Tommy's silent beer-pouring and Brave's soft-spoken logic was growing harder and harder to resist—twisting W.W.W.'s thoughts and values into a bewildering knot where up seemed like down and wrong seemed like right.

"What about those disco queens?" Brave asked again, sensing a weakness.

Brave's beerbreath whisper echoed in W.W.W.'s ears, over the George Jones croon of the jukebox, like the base throb of disco from the Seventies San Francisco Disco Queens had echoed through W.W.W.'s body for the three days and nights since he'd been idiot enough to move into a closet-sized duplex without first checking out the tenants on the other side of the wall.

The duplex. Reese. The disco queens. Looking up again at Robert E. Lee, W.W.W. wondered how Lee's suffering during Grant's Siege of Petersburg compared with what he himself was going through. He wondered whether he could handle his own siege as heroically.

It had started out with such promise—all the pieces of W.W.W.'s new life falling into place in a perfect line that pointed straight at true bliss. He'd ridden his new/used maroon metal-flake and chrome motorcycle straight from his triumphant hiring at the Dixie Fish to a triumphant lease-signing at Cratchett (Don't Get Scrooged, Get Cratchett) Properties. The lease-signing had left W.W.W. 190 rent dollars and 190 deposit dollars poorer, but would leave him 100 percent free of the Strangers just as soon as he'd picked up his things. Then he headed straight over to what he'd thought would be a triumphant entry into the house he would soon call home. But he squeezed through the front door and ran square into an upright piano that was the color of dried blood and that took up the remaining seven-eighths of the living room that wasn't already taken up by a dried-blood-colored leather recliner and shelf after shelf of hardback novels, hardback books about novels, and hardback books about books about novels. And just as the claustrophobia started to set in, the disco started banging its earsplitting way through the duplex wall.

Thinking about it all now, in the red glow/white flash/red glow of the Dixie Fish beer lights, W.W.W. felt overwhelmed. And he realized, with bitterness as deep as the bass throb of disco through paper-thin duplex walls, that the perfect line stretching straight between his new life and true bliss had gotten twisted up into the same kind of Gordian knot that Brave and Tommy had tied in his head.

"Hello? W.W.?" Brave beerbreath whispered. "What about those disco queens?"

W.W.W. looked from Robert E. Lee to Brave to the disco ball perched atop the Dixie Fish jukebox, whirling white flashes into the afterhours gloom. He found himself wishing, once again, that disco hadn't made a comeback. Even here at the Dixie Fish, he couldn't seem to escape it. The Seventies San Francisco Disco Queens, W.W.W. knew, would love the disco ball on the jukebox. Even their little brown lapdog with fuzzy blonde bangs—that the Disco Queens let out morning and night to crap on Reese and W.W.W.'s half of the lawn, and that howled every minute the Queens weren't home and the disco didn't—would eat it up.

"It isn't just the Disco Queens. Even if I hadn't signed that lease," W.W.W. said, "which I did, I gave Reese my word."

Not to mention 190 rent and 190 deposit dollars, he thought. But when he saw the puppy-love look that Brave and Tommy gave him after the part about giving his word, W.W.W. was glad he hadn't mentioned the money. Ever since becoming a hero earlier that evening at the Dixie Fish, he'd had to watch his mouth.

36

The watching his mouth part was turning out to be a lot tougher for W.W.W. than becoming a hero, especially with Brave and Tommy buying him at least as many free beers as he'd won the other night off the Strangers. The hero thing had been about nine-tenths managing to wind up in the wrong place at the wrong time—it always seemed to come so easily—and about one-tenth managing not to get beaten to death with crab bats.

And not getting beaten to death with crab bats had been child's play. Just a matter of keeping an eye on the Opera People until the thunking stopped and the last of the crabmeat that wasn't on their tuxedos and an evening gown was in their stomachs. Once the bottle of Cold Duck was empty enough to have slowed them up some, if not completely settled them down, all W.W.W. had to do was edge up to the table, snatch up the crab bats while at the same time slapping down the check—in one long lunge that fell somewhere between grace and desperation—and then say over his shoulder as he didn't exactly run away from the table, "I'm sorry, but we've run out of fresh peaches and angel food cake."

No, W.W.W. guessed it was his getting—and splitting—the $100 tip that was the real root of Brave and Tommy's trying to freebeer him out of his duplex deal with Reese and into a plush three-bedroom house with separate living and dining areas. And for W.W.W., it was the tip-sharing that had been the hardest part of the evening's struggle by far.

Even harder than keeping his mouth shut.

The first thing Kent had told W.W.W. after his triumphant hiring was that the waitstaff split tips at the Dixie Fish. It was the kind of thing that even a true democrat like W.W.W.—being more accustomed to the moneymaking philosophy of every man for himself rather than some commie collective—wasn't sure he liked the sound of, potential bliss or no. True democracy was one thing; communal earning was something else. It smacked to W.W.W. of communism, which had to be the most ill-advised attempt at government mankind had yet conceived. It always seemed to degenerate into anarchy the minute guns stopped being pointed at heads. But seeing the tip-sharing in action, and the way everybody pulled together and worked the restaurant like it was one big section instead of five little ones, had changed his mind. Well, that and being a part of the huddle. When W.W.W. had gone back to the Opera People's table—once he was sure they were good and gone—and discovered that on top of the fifty-dollar bill he'd gotten to start with, they had left him an additional pair of twenties and a ten, he'd taken the whole $100 tip straight to the group tip jar and dropped it in. He'd felt, at that moment, like Robert E. Lee at Chancellorsville: a conquering hero winning a great victory against all odds.

But now, looking back up into the eyes of the larger-than-life, still-suffering face of Robert E. Lee hanging over the Dixie Fish bar, W.W.W. felt small. Weak. Unheroic. Besieged by Grant at Petersburg. And incredibly tempted to break his lease agreement—and his word to Reese.

He kept trying to fight it. But the more beers Brave and Tommy pumped down him, the more intently W.W.W. found himself listening to Brave's beerbreath whispers about a "spacious three-bedroom home" with a bathroom of his own, not to mention Tommy's "state of the art entertainment center." A breathing-room-filled, free-standing house with a lush, crap-free lawn for a buffer zone against all the anti-bliss forces the world could muster—instead of a duplex besieged by disco, the Seventies San Francisco Disco Queens that came with it, and their lapdog-shit artillery.

Brave leaned toward W.W.W. again and in that same beerbreath whisper, started giving him the specifications on Tommy's entertainment center. Tommy stood by like he didn't know any better and nodded at W.W.W. across the bar. By the time Brave had worked his way through the "digital receiver," the "compact disc player," and the "remote control DVD/VCR combo," to the "widescreen TV," W.W.W.'s word to Reese was hanging by the same flimsy thread as the Confederacy while Grant's trenches closed in on Petersburg.

"But," W.W.W. said and salvaged at least a piece of conscience, "I can't screw Reese."

8. Hope Street

*I*t was the entertainment center that most held things up, moving-in-wise.

"The entertainment center goes all the way in the back corner of the living room," Tommy said to W.W.W. They stood out in front of their newly rented house on Hope Street surrounded by Brave, Reese, and Gladys; two cars loaded with boxes, lamps, and nightstands; and Gladys's furniture-laden truck. "So the entertainment center has to go in first. The cabinet is solid walnut, easily two hundred pounds. The electronic components are fragile. They need to be handled with care, placed into the cabinet immediately, and wired together as they go in. Since I could never ask anyone else to be responsible for carrying in these delicate and costly components, and since I'm the only one who knows how to hook up the wires . . ."

It was the most W.W.W. had heard Tommy say at one clip. And W.W.W. knew, when he heard it, that it would be himself on one end of the cabinet—all two-hundred-plus solid walnut pounds of it—and Gladys on the other end; while Tommy carried in the components, piece by origically boxed, carefully padded piece. Putting Gladys on the other end of the cabinet, rather than Brave or Reese, was one of those choices that W.W.W. thought of as *unspoken* rather than *democratic*. There was barely room for one person on either end of the thing to squeeze up between the rails on the front steps and through the front door that looked like it had come off a closet. So when W.W.W. took hold of the back end of the cabinet as it slid off the truck, it was Gladys—who stood a head taller than Brave; and who had a good thirty pounds on Reese, not much of it fat—who took hold of the front.

Gladys was a juggernaut. When W.W.W. ran out of steam after the

39

first of five front steps, it was Gladys who hauled the cabinet—and, he was ashamed to admit, himself along with it—up the remaining four steps and into the green-carpeted entry room. After Tommy edged past them with a fifteen-pound component at what didn't seem to W.W.W. could've been more than about half Tommy's usual speed, it was Gladys who craned the cabinet around and manhandled it through the living room door, across the hardwood living room floor, and into the far corner. As she grunted and strained, centering the cabinet between the fireplace and the big living room window, W.W.W. felt another pang of shame at being outworked by Gladys. Truth be told, the twinge of conscience took him completely by surprise.

I find that the harder I work, the more luck I seem to have.

This was a phrase W.W.W.'s daddy had borrowed from Thomas Jefferson, one the old man repeated often (usually as the son of a bitch stared away at the western horizon while W.W.W. worked like a dog at some dirt-grubbing task or other), and one with which W.W.W. had always strongly disagreed. It seemed to him that those who most loudly extolled the virtues of hard work were those who had people to work hard for them. W.W.W. had spent the years since he'd left Southwest Texas wringing the most possible benefit from the least amount of work he could get by with. During a waiting or bartending shift, he made the most of each trip out to the waitfloor or down the bar, finessing his customers rather than fawning all over them. During a move—and all other types of heavy lifting—he generally timed his trips so that he ended up, if not with the light loads themselves, then at least on the lighter side of the heavy ones.

Today, though, W.W.W. found himself looking for the heavy stuff—searching out what was biggest and thickest from among the boxes, nightstands, tables and chairs, headboards and footboards, recliners, and love seats that Brave and Reese pulled from the back seats of cars and the back of Gladys's truck and set down on the front lawn—and none of the stuff was even his. When W.W.W. couldn't find a load that looked heavy enough, he stacked up the light stuff and made a heavy load. He didn't even look twice at the lamps. He found himself in a combination footrace and powerlifting competition with Gladys, who looked to be in the same kind of competition with Brave and Reese. The more they carried and the faster they went, the more in-whack the moving-in process seemed to get; and the more the five of them moving into the house on Hope Street together seemed like working at the Dixie Fish. Everyone was doing his or her own thing, at his or her own pace. And yet, by some miracle, everything was getting done. W.W.W. hadn't felt this good since he'd been very young, and very warm, lying awake in bed at night and listening to his mother singing.

Timing had been the key to everything. Well, timing and Tommy, W.W.W. guessed. He thought back to late Thursday night at the Dixie Fish bar. Just after Brave had made his last beerbreath-whispered pitch for he and W.W.W. and Tommy to move into a three-bedroom house together, and just after W.W.W. had said for the last time that he couldn't screw Reese, Tommy—who up to that point hadn't done much more than pour draft beer and nod his head—suddenly said, "Then why not just look for a four-bedroom house instead?"

It was a revelation. There in the red glow/white flash/red glow of the Dixie Fish beer lights, W.W.W. had a vision: a rainbow-colored blaze of social inspiration. He'd been thinking about the true democracy and collective effort, the tip-sharing and communal earning at the Dixie Fish. And when Tommy made his comment about all of them sharing a house together, the thought arced across W.W.W.'s mind in a spectrum of beautifully intermingled colors that people, possibly even the kind of people he knew, could live that way as well as work it. It was a vision of home and of happiness that W.W.W. watched unfold. It looked a lot like a training program, but for achieving contentment on earth instead of just excellence in sports: a program for bliss. He saw the Gordian knot his new life had become—school, transportation, job, a roof over his head, friends, something to do—being untied and perfectly aligned so that it pointed, once again, straight at true bliss. He saw Brave, Tommy, Reese, and himself cleaning together, shopping for groceries together, eating together. He saw Reese helping him out with some of this mysterious graduate schoolwork that W.W.W. still couldn't get a handle on the reason behind. And he felt sure that he was as close to achieving true bliss as he'd been since he was a child.

All they had to do was convince Reese to break his lease and join them.

To that end, W.W.W. and Brave and Tommy had gathered up an armload of beer, piled into Tommy's convertible, and driven over to the duplex to recruit Reese. They billed it to Reese as a co-op. W.W.W. guessed that a commune was a little closer to what they had in mind. But it sounded an awful lot like *communism*—which still seemed to W.W.W., collective effort aside, to be the most ill-advised attempt at government mankind had yet conceived. And it wasn't just W.W.W. No, if there existed a word that Americans tended to be as touchy about as *communism*, except maybe *marijuana*, it was one W.W.W. had never heard. He wasn't about to risk his Program for Bliss on a definition.

It was the co-op idea, plus two or three of the beers they'd brought, that had lured Reese over to Tommy's one-bedroom efficiency to, in Brave's words, "be baptized in the full wash of the entertainment center effect." It was the co-op idea that brought them all on Friday—a little hungover and with the addition of Gladys, who it turned out was moving in with Tommy—to Cratchett (Don't Get Scrooged, Get Cratchett) Properties, to work out a deal with Bob Cratchett. Cratchett himself, not a member of the co-op but eager to make a deal that would pay him more rent money, had suggested the house on Hope Street: "extra-high ceilings, finished attic and basement, roomy front and back yards, not to mention the Grecian-style garage."

With the exception of the thirty seconds or so it had taken them to choose up bedrooms, the transition of the co-op from a mere concept to a concrete reality at the house on Hope Street had gone so smoothly as to surprise and satisfy everyone. But most satisfying of all for W.W.W., as the move-in drew toward a close, was the fact that there was a certain someone coming over later that evening to help him arrange the bedroom set he'd rented and that the furniture rental company had delivered earlier that afternoon to the house on Hope Street—a certain someone W.W.W. hoped would prove to be the pivotal piece in his new Program for Bliss.

W.W.W. beat Gladys to the last box left in the front yard. Then he picked it up and carried it into the house that, even though it was still only January, smelled like the first day of spring.

9. A Little Piece of Rainbow

*M*ake the most of the Indian hemp seed, and sow it everywhere.

This instruction from George Washington to his gardener in 1794 was one that W.W.W. was still following 206 years later. Like the Father of Our Country, who grew cannabis at Mount Vernon for thirty years, the first thing W.W.W. always did when he moved into a new place was plant a marijuana garden. The reason he called it a *garden*, rather than a *crop*, was that his motives for planting the marijuana were the polar opposite of commercial. W.W.W. knew that over the course of human history, people growing green things together had been one of the greatest promoters of social harmony. And now that the five of them had moved into the house on Hope Street, he planned to promote domestic harmony by cultivating cannabis they could all help grow and whose fruits they could all share equally come harvest time.

W.W.W. always planted each new garden with seeds that he had saved from his previous harvest. In this way he could trace the history of his quest for true bliss backward in space and time to Atlanta, then back to New Orleans, and then all the way back to his daddy's place in Southwest Texas where the original cannabis plants had been grown. For W.W.W.'s daddy, marijuana was strictly a cash crop. W.W.W.'s old man and his fellow agrarian revolutionists—unlike George Washington, who used the fruits of the cannabis plant to fight his chronic toothaches; and unlike W.W.W., who used the fruits of the cannabis plant to fight domestic discord—were growing pot for sale and using the proceeds of their crops to buy the weapons that they planned to use to overthrow the U.S. Government come Judgment Day.

Every generation needs a new revolution.

This was another favorite phrase of W.W.W.'s daddy that the son of a bitch had borrowed from Thomas Jefferson. And it was another of those by-proxy proclamations about which W.W.W. had decidedly mixed feelings. What W.W.W.'s old man had in mind when he said *revolution* was something inherently violent, a combination bloodbath and firestorm from which no one but agrarian revolutionists would escape alive. For W.W.W., *revolution* meant something inherently nonviolent, a combination of civil disobedience and the ballot box rather than murder and mayhem—something more along the lines of Thoreau, or Gandhi, or Martin Luther King, Jr.

This was what W.W.W. was thinking when he brought out the gallon-sized baggie he'd been carrying since Atlanta, held it over a cookie sheet, then broke the ziplock seal and sprinkled nine months' worth of pot-seed savings onto the wax paper he'd spread across the bottom of the sheet. He studied the seeds; shook them; then carefully studied again, cataloguing the colors in his mind. Whites; pale, medium, and dark greens; black greens; and green-black speckled potseeds stood out against the yellow-brown wax paper. The seeds blended nicely, though, with the carpet W.W.W. sat on while he worked. The carpet was the color of new spring leaves. W.W.W. eyed the seeds, putting rough numbers to the various colors. Then he shook the cookie sheet and rough-numbered again. Finally, having decided with an intense satisfaction that the darker shades outnumbered the lighter shades—the darker the seed, the more viable the seed; the lighter the seed, the less viable the seed—he started picking the white seeds off of the wax paper and tossing them into the trash.

To make a good yield, a man must plant good seeds.

The most important thing, his daddy had always told W.W.W., wasn't the fertilizer or the herbicide or even the tender loving care that went into making green things grow. Without good seeds, none of the rest of it mattered. *Every time you harvest*, the old man always said, *you save back some good seeds. That way, can't nobody ever take the ground out from under you.*

When he couldn't find any more white seeds to cull, W.W.W. started picking out the pale green ones. The going was slow as always. But the thought that the residents of the house on Hope Street would all enjoy the fruits of his labor come springtime was enough to turn the tedious process of hoarding and sorting, sprouting and planting, culling the males, clipping the top bud, harvesting, slow-drying, weighing, and bagging into a kind of slowly unfolding Easter Sunday. Even the fact that cannabis was illegal couldn't put a damper on his good spirits. After all, how could you outlaw something green that grew? It was like outlawing nature. You might as well try to legislate the rain.

Sitting there on the leaf-colored carpet reminded W.W.W. all of a sudden of sitting in the middle of a field of growing greens underneath the wide Southwest Texas sky. Whether it was a field of dark green peanuts or winter oats, or of light green coastal Bermuda, this was one of the few things from all those years of farming and ranching that W.W.W. sometimes missed. There was nothing quieter, or more peaceful. Growing greens never seemed to need much besides herbicide, hoeing, a little fertilizer, and some pesticide now and then. They demanded nothing at all.

He tossed the last of the pale green seeds into the trash and took a long, hard look at the medium green seeds. Should they go or stay? It was a question W.W.W. had agonized over before, both in Atlanta and New Orleans. On both those occasions he had thrown them out for reasons ranging from prejudice to practicality.

W.W.W. despised medium green potseeds. He hated them almost as much as he loved watching green things grow. It was more than just the fact that half of the medium green seeds would lie there and never even think about germinating, and it was more than just the fact that the half of the medium green seeds which did sprout would have to be culled as runts before he even culled the males. W.W.W. liked things best that were clearly one way or the other. And the medium green potseeds never seemed to be able to make up their minds.

On the other hand, W.W.W. loathed waste. It was, in his opinion, the second greatest sin of the modern age. Waste, hand in hand with materialism—which was, of course, the modern age's greatest sin—posed the gravest threat to humankind in the history of the species. It was against this two-headed monster that W.W.W.'s own nonviolent revolution was focused and against which he hoped to lead humanity to victory by personal example. True bliss, he wanted to shout from the rooftop of the house on Hope Street, must be achieved by other means than piling up personal possessions and then throwing them away and piling them up again.

In his *Nicomachean Ethics*, Aristotle formally defines bliss—from the Greek *eudaimonia*—as a complete and sufficient good. In W.W.W.'s painstaking interpretation of Aristotle's treatise, this implied that bliss:

1) was desired for itself alone;
2) was not desired for the sake of anything else;
3) satisfied all desire and had no evil mixed in with it; and
4) was stable.

W.W.W. and Aristotle were on exactly the same page about bliss up to that point. But then Aristotle took a turn and started going on and on about how an individual could only achieve true bliss through the development of his own personal intellectual and moral virtue. And this is where Aristotle and W.W.W. parted ways. In W.W.W.'s experience, bliss had less do with personal virtue—whether intellectual or moral—than with companionship. The only true bliss he'd ever known had come as a result of close contact with someone he loved.

W.W.W. sat and soaked up the Hope Street atmosphere, daydreaming about bliss and trying to decide what to do about the medium green potseeds. The muffled thuds of people opening and closing boxes, drawers, and closet doors; the swooshes and groans of people sliding bedroom, living room, and dining room furniture; the pounding din of people hammering six, ten, and sixteen penny nails into ceilings, doors, and walls echoed and re-echoed so that it sounded like his new roommates were renovating the house instead of just moving in. Those renovation sounds were music to W.W.W.'s bliss-starved ears. Unlike his daddy, whose answer to the gross inequities of modern society was to burn the house of society down and rebuild on the ashes, W.W.W. held out hope that a good renovation could remake the house of society so all people could call it home.

It was the renovation sounds that finally decided the fate of the medium green potseeds. W.W.W. determined that he would make the effort to save and grow them, even though it might be a lost cause. After all, he had always shared the American weak spot for underdogs and lost causes.

"Hell," he said to every medium green potseed that had the good fortune to be on his cookie sheet at that moment, "I guess I'm kind of a combination underdog and lost cause myself."

No sooner than the words were out of his mouth, W.W.W. glanced up through the bank of windows on the eastern wall and caught sight of a piece of rainbow. It was one of the most amazing things he'd ever seen: a little section of the rainbow, almost like a rainbow seed, an arc of maybe ten degrees. The piece of rainbow seemed so close that W.W.W. felt sure he could reach out and grab it, if he just opened up a window and stretched out his arm. But he didn't, and the reason he chose not to reach out that window had nothing at all to do with being afraid of clutching air. No, it was the entire arc of rainbow he was after—the whole 180 degrees.

It came to him, suddenly, that the path to true bliss didn't run in a straight line after all. Instead, it ran in a perfect curve. And looking up into that splash of beautifully intermingled colors in the eastern sky, W.W.W. saw the seed of the Program for Bliss that he'd first glimpsed at the Dixie Fish sprout and grow in his mind's eye into the form of a whole and perfect rainbow. Like the rainbow arch, the Program for Bliss was doubly grounded in his wants and needs for the present; but it also stretched skyward to encompass his hopes for the future. And like the rainbow spectrum, there was a point of the Program for Bliss for each of the seven colors.

It was another revelation. No, he thought, looking up at the piece of rainbow; it was instead a renovation of the vision of home and happiness he'd watched unfold at the Dixie Fish.

What he saw was a seven-point plan for achieving true bliss:

2) SCHOOL, which meant savoring academic freedom and the other fruits of higher education, and maybe the chance to learn a little bit about life off a farm/ranch and outside a restaurant/bar;

3) TRANSPORTATION; a

4) JOB, which meant money; a

5) ROOF OVER HIS HEAD that he could shape into a home; and

6) FRIENDS; which, combined with 2) SCHOOL, 3) TRANSPOR-TATION, and a 4) JOB meant:

7) SOMETHING TO DO.

Reaching out for that piece of rainbow would have been like picking potential bliss over true bliss, like picking body odor and cheap perfume over worn leather and the smell of breakfast cooking—okay for the short term, but nothing doing for the long haul. And it was only the long haul that he was interested in. Out the window, the piece of rainbow started to fade. W.W.W. started picking medium green potseeds off of the wax paper and lining them up on damp sponges, taking stock of the present state of his renovated Program for Bliss as he worked.

He had 2) SCHOOL. Even though he hadn't gotten a whole lot out of it yet besides a headache and a bunch of homework, 2) SCHOOL had been worked out well enough, before W.W.W. even got to South Carolina, so that all that was left for him to do was register for classes and pick up a check.

He had 3) TRANSPORTATION. 3) TRANSPORTATION had been just a matter of a student loan check, a ride from a Stranger to a motorcycle dealership, and most of one morning.

But he wasn't happy. Despite the 4) JOB, 5) ROOF OVER HIS HEAD, 6) FRIENDS, and 7) SOMETHING TO DO, all of which he had, W.W.W. wasn't satisfied. The words of his daddy echoed again in W.W.W.'s ears: *the potential for bliss must be realized before true bliss can be achieved.* The one thing he needed to complete the whole and perfect rainbow of the renovated Program for Bliss was a:

1) WOMAN.

But a good woman, and a slow one. He was sick to death of fast, short run women. And his last long haul had done W.W.W.'s soul almost to death, what seemed like a lifetime ago, when he'd been young and so very foolish.

10. Shine

W.W.W. had just started picking the green-black speckled potseeds off of the wax paper and placing them onto the sprouting sponges when Shine walked in. She had gold eyes. Not amber, not butter-colored, but eyes that were the color of Southwest Texas sunlight on a late summer afternoon through the haze of dust that rose up off of the fields. He couldn't help but sit still and stare.

Stare, and remember the first time he'd seen her over at the Strangers' place three weeks before. It was Sunday night. He'd just finished taking the Strangers for a hundred bucks apiece at betting football and was sitting in the living room going hungry while they sat in front of the television eating filet mignon. Shine walked in, and W.W.W. forgot about his empty belly and the bitterness of being alone in a room full of people and even the three hundred dollars he'd won. He noticed the way her gold shoes set off the ivory flesh of her feet. He noticed her muscled calves and the ivory thighs beneath her short gold skirt. He noticed the way she held her head a little to the left when she looked at him, the way Alexander the Great held his head in the history books. Then she met his eyes; and the living room air went from a mélange of broiled steak, bitter bile, and easy money to a bouquet of potential bliss. Before she left, W.W.W. asked her name— the Strangers being as stingy with introductions as they were with steak— and she said, "Shine Solomon." He echoed it. "Shine Solomon." It rolled softly off his tongue. "Shine Solomon." It eased between his lips. He ached to ask for her telephone number; but he figured that might be a bit much, seeing as how the reason for her coming over to the Strangers' place had been to break things off with one of them. So he followed her outside and asked for her telephone number on the Strangers' perfectly manicured front lawn.

They had been out three times since. But seeing Shine again in the Green Room of the house on Hope Street was like seeing her for the first time. The cheap-perfumey, hot-body-odory scent of potential bliss was even stronger than it had been that first night at the Dixie Fish. W.W.W. felt the skin on the back of his neck start to tingle with the expectation that potential bliss would soon be achieved—and that Shine would untie the Gordian knot of his new life and guide him along the perfectly curved path that led to true bliss.

Then he remembered the cookie sheet full of potseeds in his lap, and W.W.W. felt the cool tingle on the back of his neck burn across his face to end in a cheek-scalding blush. Shine wasn't supposed to have been there for another hour.

"Hello," she said.

"Ah . . . hello," W.W.W. started. But where on earth was there for his mouth to go after that? They hadn't talked about much outside of the usual Crap About Music, Crap About Movies, and Crap About Majors in School. He hadn't much more than kissed her goodnight. How in God's name could he even whisper the word *marijuana*, much less ask her if she'd like to help sort potseeds? It would be about like asking her to join the Communist Party. "I'd have been done sorting," he managed, but saw her gold eyes come up off of the potseeds to where they could just sort of melt into his blue ones, "if I'd known you'd be . . ."

"No problem," Shine said. She walked over and sat down beside him on the leaf-colored carpet, and started picking out green-black speckled potseeds and placing them onto the damp sprouting sponges. "This looks like one of those times when four hands would be better than two."

Surely, W.W.W. thought, this was the 1) WOMAN who would fill the gaping hole in his Program for Bliss. He felt like he was back in the men's room on his first night at the Dixie Fish, staring at his reflection next to that red and yellow sticker in the mirror and realizing that all his questions and his prayers for achieving bliss had been answered at last. He believed, maybe for the first time ever, that he had found a female kindred spirit. He believed that he had found a fellow-traveler. He believed that he had found a woman who was pure long haul. Mary, he thought, would have been back out the door before he finished up "Hello"—Mary being the woman who had done his soul almost to death, what seemed like a lifetime ago, when he'd been young and so very foolish. The one thing Mary could never abide, besides the slaughter of anything that ever had eyelashes, was marijuana.

But the here and now of the Green Room was all Shine. Shine, and talking. Really talking, for the first time. As the green-black speckled potseeds went onto the sprouting sponges, W.W.W. found out about Newport News, Virginia, where he'd never been.

"It's a wonderful place," Shine smiled. "Home."

He liked the way she said *home*. She poured the word out sweet as Tupelo honey and made *home* sound like the most important and the loveliest word in the world. She talked about the Causeway, how it went all the way across the brackish water at the mouth of the James River; and *home* lay in the way she made W.W.W. see the sun rise and set in the water on either side of the bridge as she talked. "Out of saltwater on the sea side in the morning," she said. "Into freshwater away upriver in the afternoon." She told him about her family's three-story Southern-style house that was built of red brick with white trim and had a back lawn that sloped right down to the James. "You can sit under the mimosa tree my father planted when I was born and see the Causeway," she said, "on a clear afternoon." *Home* lay in the way she made W.W.W. feel the cool river breeze brush against his skin.

Newport News seemed to W.W.W. like a piece of ground where things could spread and grow—green and wet instead of dry-brown, watered by rain instead of irrigation, and with creeks and rivers that never ran dry. The James River, the long sward of down-sloping lawn with its birth-commemorating mimosa tree, Shine sitting in the shade and staring out over the water. He could hear the 1) WOMAN in all of it and smell potential bliss rising up off of Shine like a morning mist off of the James.

All of which made his skin shrivel that much tighter when the next thing out of her mouth was, "All my old boyfriends there are dead."

"Boyfriends?" W.W.W. sputtered. "Dead? What do you mean?"

"Guys I went out with," she said. "Not breathing. You know? Dead."

She said it kind of off-hand, like: *we mostly had eggs for breakfast.* This left W.W.W. floundering someplace between the back yard on the James River and a graveyard full of boyfriends; but Shine just whistled past and started talking about Virginia Beach, where he'd also never been.

"I've been there a lot," she said.

At least, W.W.W. thought she said it. And maybe something about living there summers. It was tough to catch hold of what Shine was saying about living when he was suddenly so preoccupied with what she'd said about her dead.

"Umbrellas," he thought she said.

"Dead umbrellas?" he asked, trying to focus.

"Colored umbrellas," she said and laughed.

But he wasn't joking. W.W.W. felt as though the ground had been yanked out from under his feet. He imagined himself sitting under the mimosa tree in Shine's back yard, staring at the Causeway across the James and wondering how her boyfriends had died. Car pile-ups? Overdoses? Worse? He felt the entire 1) WOMAN search process grinding down all around him. From long haul straight through to short run. From short run all the way down to dead stop.

"I remember sitting under colored umbrellas and staring out to sea," she said. "I remember watching the sun rising red over the water. It was like a poem: in wave after wave, gray-blue surf whispers and sighs, beneath blue-gray skies. The ocean speaks in rhyme."

"No," W.W.W. said. "It's the desert." Or had he only thought it? "The desert speaks in rhyme. My mother said so."

"Excuse me?"

"Jesus," he croaked, suddenly engulfed in a memory of the fire. The memory centers on sound. Everywhere, flames roar out of control as smoke crinkles his nose like the touch of fire shrivels the skin. Nearby, horses scream. And he can make out, fainter and farther away, the screams of a woman.

"W.W.?"

"Jesus Christ." For a moment he sees his mother—the woman who taught him to hear the poetry of the desert he grew up in—shoving with all her might against the bars on her bedroom window. But in the next instant, the house is swallowed by flames.

"W.W.?" Shine said again. Then she took his hand. "Are you all right?"

"I don't know."

He felt Shine take his other hand, and felt her fingers cool against his. He felt himself pulled by the coolness of her touch back into the here and now. He wanted to touch more of her; wanted to run his hands up her arms to touch her shoulders, her cheeks. But Shine was wearing long sleeves. Green sleeves, he noticed, that ran all the way from her cool and lovely hands to her pale and delicate neck. He noticed her dark hair. He noticed her scent that was like . . .

". . . like I was saying," she said, "I've never been in the desert. Was it terribly lonely there?"

"Lonely. Dry. So hot in summer you could hardly breathe." He was, he noticed as her green sweater brushed against his blue-jean jacket, hardly breathing here and now. He felt the 1) WOMAN selection process cranking back up again, from dead stop to short run, from short run all the way back to pure long haul.

"You grew up there?" she asked.

"Yes." He edged close enough so that his boots nudged her high-heels. "In Southwest Texas, on the northern edge of the Chihuahuan Desert." Looking at her, W.W.W. felt sure that whatever had happened, dead-boyfriend-wise, couldn't possibly have been Shine's fault. How could anything in this life have been her fault—the way the fire that caused his mother's death had been his daddy's fault, and his? W.W.W. gently disengaged his hands from Shine's and put the last of the potseeds onto the yellow sprouting sponges, placing the sponges end to end on the cookie sheet so the seeds were lined up in long straight rows. "Would you mind helping me carry some of these things up to my room? Then you can turn your superior interior decorating skills to the contents of my attic-turned-bedroom."

"Of course." She followed him through the dining room, around Reese's table and chairs, past the attic stairs, and into the kitchen.

W.W.W. opened the refrigerator and pulled out two longnecks. "One good thing about living with Gladys and Tommy is that we'll never go thirsty for beer."

"I hope that won't be the only good thing," she said.

"I hope that, too." They mounted the straight flight of stairs that climbed steep as a ladder, almost, up into the finished attic. The glare of the bare overhead bulb that dangled from the ceiling made the room seem even sparser than it was. W.W.W. set the beers on his rented nightstand, flicked on the rented lamp, and sat down on the edge of his rented bed. "Would you mind putting the cookie sheet on my desk?"

"No problem," she said. Then she pulled the cord on the overhead bulb.

In the absence of overhead glare, the lamplight threw long soft shadows that made the walls seem less bare. The soft light turned Shine's pale skin to gold as she sat down beside him on the bed. When she turned to face him, the look in her eyes was pure long haul.

"What do you think about the layout of the furniture?" W.W.W. asked.

"I think everything looks fine right where it is. I'm much more interested in this blanket." She patted the rainbow-colored quilt folded across the foot of the bed. "I've never seen anything like it."

"My mother patchworked this quilt from material that her mother sewed into squares. The pattern is based on Joseph's coat of many colors."

"It's beautiful." Shine kicked off her shoes and leaned in close enough so that their legs rubbed. "They must love you very much."

"My mother did. I never met my grandmother."

"Did?"

"My mother did love me, I mean," W.W.W. said. "Very much."

"Then your mother is—"

"When I was seven years old," he broke in softly, meeting Shine's eyes that glowed now in the lamplight, "our house burned. My mother didn't . . . she didn't make it out."

Shine kissed him then, the taste salty and sweet at the same time. Then she reached over and turned off the lamp.

She seemed so much paler in the half-dark, but so much less delicate than in the light. Her skin that had felt so cool downstairs now felt warm. He caught the sound of Shine's breath coming sharp and shallow, his world narrowed now to the silk-smooth feel of Shine's skin and the warm wetness that covered his fingertips.

She eased his hand up.

He pretended not to notice . . . maybe didn't notice . . . the hand maybe moved itself back inside her panties.

"Those aren't coming off."

He didn't even slow up . . . then he heard her breath catch, felt her moving . . . and was all of a sudden alone on the bed.

"I said," he heard Shine say, "those aren't coming off."

"I'm sorry," he said, breathing heavy and wondering when it was, exactly, he'd gotten naked. "I guess I got a little carried away. It won't happen again, I promise."

W.W.W. held his breath and heard Shine breathing softly in the dark. He lay still. Waited. And was quiet.

After a long while, he felt her climb back onto the bed beside him. And lying there on his rented bed, he was afraid to touch her.

He felt, after another long while, Shine touch him.

He ran his hands gently across her silk-smooth skin and felt her breasts firm, but not too firm. And warm. He kissed her again, slowly. Gently.

He felt her return the kiss, felt her hands warm against his skin.

He lay there in the dark with Shine still in her panties. He stroked her skin and tasted the promise of her mouth against his. In the darkness near the bed, he could almost feel the seeds they had laid out together beginning to germinate. He could almost hear the newborn plants pushing through their shells.

Downstairs, he could hear the sound of people, his people, settling into the house on Hope Street. Feathering their nest.

The potential for bliss had been realized. It only remained to be seen whether true bliss could be achieved.

11. Grecian Garage

When W.W.W. woke up, he was warm. The bed held him like a womb. The darkness smelled of Shine. His chest, his belly, his thighs felt warm where she spooned into them. Her hair brushed against his face soft as the breast feathers of a dove.

A cold front had blown through in the night, chilling the air that surrounded the bed. He lay on his left side, facing the window that faced east and basking in the warmth of flesh contact. Over the dark mass of Shine's hair that was deeper black than the darkness, he watched the bottom edge of the window turn red. Dawn crimsoned the window, pane after slatted pane. It bled out into the attic. It blood-haloed Shine's raven hair.

There was nothing W.W.W. wanted more than to lie there with Shine. But something didn't feel right. He eased his arm out from underneath her and rolled away, easy-careful, then edged out from under the covers and stood up.

Shine murmured in her sleep and rolled over into the warm spot he'd left. The first-day-of-springy, hot-body-odory scent of potential bliss wafted up off of the bed so strong it was all he could do not to climb back in. He breathed deep and savored the scent of sap and new leaves, the luscious aroma of hormones and possibilities.

But something, somewhere, felt amiss.

W.W.W. stretched his legs, stretched his arms that had gone stiff from holding Shine. He stretched his senses, trying to catch at least a hint of the wrongness that had woken him.

Maybe just the dawn, he guessed, the tingle-skinned anticipation of first light. Feeling his heart beat fast and his breath come shallow, W.W.W. wrapped himself in the quilt his mother had patchworked and walked over to the window.

Outside, the dawn was a sideways rainbow laid out flat against the eastern sky. The bands of color spread wide against the horizon as the sun rose. The orange band spread as the sun rose into it, then the sun strengthened into yellow as it mounted higher. The pale green band lightened for a moment. But the orb of the sun, fiercer and more powerful now, burned the green, blue, indigo, and violet bands away, fading them along with the stars into sky blue.

The sun paced white-hot across the back yard now like an angel of the apocalypse whose pale fingers scorched everything they touched into ashes. The touch of the sun whitened the Grecian garage, whitened the rusty swing set, whitened even the heavy old cottonwood with its bare arms spread to the sky.

Looking at it, W.W.W. was all of a sudden five years old, staring out over a field of peanuts that had just been cropdusted with DDT. There was no sound now that the drone and buzz of the airplane had faded. DDT glinted on green rows like dew on back yard grass. No creature stirred. Only the wind moved among the dark green leaves. There was nothing left that could move except for the green, nothing but the wind left to move it. *If a man could spray DDT over the whole Earth*, his daddy said, *only the green and the ground would survive*. Towering over W.W.W., the old man spread his arms wide as cottonwood branches. *The green, the ground, and the good few who knew what was coming . . .*

In the back yard of the house on Hope Street, the only thing moving was the sun over the Grecian garage. The garage, with its Doric columns and its frieze of plaster gods, lay dead on the winter-white grass. The whole scene looked so much like the fulfillment of his daddy's genocidal agrarianist vision that W.W.W. couldn't help but shudder.

It was nothing at all like the afternoon, only a week and a day before, when they had all driven up in Tommy's import convertible—five separate people, one tight-packed mound of flesh—in front of the house on Hope Street. There had been people in the street, children playing in yards, cats in the grass, and birds in the trees. W.W.W. had just finished saying how much he liked the neighborhood and how the name of the street spoke pretty well for itself, when Tommy pulled into the driveway and Reese went insane over the garage.

"My God," Reese had said, "look at it. Look at that exquisite garage!"

"Exquisite my ass," Brave said. "It looks more like some kind of Greek temple than any kind of practical car shelter."

W.W.W. could see both sides. The garage was indeed an exquisite replica of the Parthenon, complete with perfect right angles and Doric columns and white plaster statues of gods in a frieze over the double front doors. But it wasn't even connected to the house. And they would be hard-pressed to fit Tommy's tiny convertible into it—much less three cars, a truck, and a maroon metal-flake and chrome motorcycle.

While Reese charged up the drive, leapt the fence, and disappeared into the back yard, Gladys, Tommy, Brave, and W.W.W. walked up to the house itself. Built out of limestone, it looked to W.W.W. like a white rock island in a red-brick sea. They burst through the front door like kids into Autumn's first crisp pile of leaves. Then like the leaves, they scattered. But while the rest of them ran from room to room, going on and on about the various fabulous features of the place, W.W.W. settled down to inspect for flaws.

For W.W.W., home was something not found, but made—through a slow, sometimes soul-wrenching process of selection, renovation, acclimatization. It was like birds nesting. The mother feathered her nest with down she pulled from her own breast. He studied the living room fireplace until he was absolutely sure the fire screen didn't have any gaps in it and that the stone lip in front was wide enough to catch any stray sparks. He looked hard at the floor tile and appliances in the kitchen, and found loose tiles coming up in rows; an old refrigerator; and a stove that he would call *antique* at best, if not *outright dangerous*. He opened every window in every room of the house to make sure no one could get trapped in case of fire.

It wasn't until he climbed up into the attic that W.W.W. felt sure this was the kind of house they could make into a home. He stretched out on the hardwood floor. He stared up at the slanted roof that was arched like the roof of a barn. He sat up and looked out the huge attic window. *Home*, he mouthed to himself, not even daring to whisper it yet. They wouldn't be housemates until they managed to choose up bedrooms.

And that, he thought, promised to be a problem.

W.W.W. knew for a fact that no one but himself would want to sleep in the attic. It was a long way from a bathroom, it didn't have a closet, and the narrow set of steps leading up to it was about as accommodating as a chimney. The chief attraction for W.W.W. lay in the fact that this chimney of a staircase climbed straight up from the kitchen into the attic. So the first-pot-of-coffee, eggs-in-bacon-greasy scent of true bliss would waft right up into his waiting nostrils—if they could manage to bring all the pieces together here on Hope Street and make a home.

No, W.W.W. choosing the attic as his bedroom wouldn't pose a problem. The problem was that there were two big bedrooms downstairs on either side of the corner bath, both with hardwood floors. And then there was a third downstairs bedroom that was not only smaller than the other two, but farther away from the corner bath—the corner bath being the only bathroom in the house—and smack up against the living room wall. With five of them living there, this tiny bedroom promised to be noisy. Even worse, the third downstairs bedroom had a pink shag carpet.

When W.W.W. got back downstairs, he found Brave, Gladys, and Tommy standing in a ring just outside the third bedroom door. They were all trying to put as much choosing distance as possible between themselves and the pink shag bedroom.

"I'm not gonna sleep in that son of a bitch," Brave said.

"Well, I'm not gonna sleep in that son of a bitch," Gladys said.

Tommy just kept shaking his head back and forth, back and forth.

Then they all looked at W.W.W.

"Don't look at me," he said. "I'm sleeping in the son-of-a-bitching attic."

It made the prospects for the house on Hope Street ever becoming home look kind of dim. But just then, W.W.W. saw Brave's face light up. He saw Gladys's face light up, and Tommy's. Their eyes, W.W.W. noticed, were fixed on something behind him. He turned and peeked over his shoulder. And through the single window in the tiny pink shag bedroom that Brave, Gladys, and he himself had been trying to son-of-a-bitch themselves out of laying claim to, W.W.W. caught sight of Reese.

Reese was still in the back yard. And he was sniffing around the Grecian garage like a dog around a strange set of tires.

"Look at him," Brave said. "He'll sleep in this son of a bitch."

"Yep," Gladys said. "He'll sleep in this son of a bitch for sure."

Tommy looked from Reese back to W.W.W. and started nodding his head up and down, up and down.

"But . . ." W.W.W. said.

"Come on, W.W.," Brave leaned in and whispered. "He'd sleep in the toilet, if he had to, to be close to that garage."

"But . . . we can't screw Reese."

Eight days and a move-in later, the January sun that was streaming now through W.W.W.'s wide attic window—situated just above Reese's tiny pink shag bedroom window—had softened to yellow. It looked less like an avenging angel and more like the nurturing sun of spring arriving two months early. The potseeds lay on W.W.W.'s rented desk, almost sprouting. And the house on Hope Street, only a day after they'd moved into it, was beginning to feel like home. All it needed was some wood-smoke and worn leather, the smell of eggs frying in bacon grease while coffee was brewing, and the sound of voices he knew.

W.W.W. breathed deep, feeling the morning sun start to warm his skin at last, and sighed a silent prayer of thanks to the providential power of bliss—and Reese's Grecian garage fetish—for getting him this far. He looked at Shine, her body half uncovered in the strong morning light. She had ivory gooseflesh on her delicate shoulders and on her perfect breasts. He pulled his mother's patchwork quilt from around his shoulders and spread it over Shine, feeling relieved now that things last night had stopped when they did. They had almost gone too far, too fast. He and Mary had started out like that. It seemed like a lifetime ago, when he'd been young and so very foolish.

It was less than two weeks now until Valentine's Day. He planned to make good and sure that he and Shine would wait.

12. Young and So Very Foolish

*H*e was waiting, but it wasn't raining.

There were stars out, even though with all the light coming up off of the city W.W.W. could hardly see them. He was feeling okay through the first hour, but then it turned into an hour and a half. He had driven six hours northeast from his daddy's place to get to Dallas, and a half hour west to Valley Ranch—a full eight hours of unmet expectation.

She claimed she was playing softball.

That's where she said she'd be. And while Mary was out God knew where, doing God knew what all, here he was stuck waiting in a parking lot square in the middle of God knew how many other parking lots—sober—but stone-drunk in love, listening to beer-drinking music and holding out hope that she would come rolling up with a crumpled fender or a flat tire in the trunk.

He was still sitting underneath the area light outside her apartment when the two hour mark went past. It was midnight, and W.W.W. swore to himself that, love or no love, he would start the long drive home at 12:15 a.m. She said she'd leave a key there in the window, but there was none. And when she said that she'd be home by ten o'clock, he'd assumed that ten o'clock meant 10 p.m. But at 12:15 that window was every bit as dark as the empty place he could feel swallowing his insides. He was wishing more than ever, if not for an honest-to-God collision, then for a whiskey-drunk. There was nothing like a whiskey-drunk to kill the pain.

He extended his deadline to 12:30. And sitting there on the truck hood at 12:45 a.m.—engine running—listening to his third "just one more" Willie Nelson song in a row, W.W.W. had long since given up on bourbon and bad luck, and gone to wishing for a little necessary resolve.

When she pulled into the parking lot at 12:55, it was only two songs and one eternity later. The car had not a single scratch on it. Mary slipped out like a little girl who had dressed up in Father's softball suit and snuck out for a spin in Mother's midnight blue Cadillac Eldorado. W.W.W. was fairly certain, truth be told—although he'd never seen the pink slip—that the name the car was in was really Mary's and not her mother's. But he was willing to bet the name inside that softball suit wasn't her father's. And W.W.W. knew damn well that it wasn't his.

He steeled himself with the promise to be cold as a February 5 a.m.; deaf to all due apologies; man enough, when they came, to dry her tears. But she walked away from the Eldorado with her head held high; and instead of rushing right up so W.W.W. could cut and wilt her, that wayward flower headed straight for her apartment without a nod in his direction.

Forgotten. She'd forgotten.

He managed to catch up to her at the foot of the stairs without ever quite breaking down enough to bust into a run. He saw the beer in her hand. He smelled the beers on her breath. He eyed the blue and red softball uniform. It looked to have been made for two or three of her.

Foremost, he wanted to know what had happened, just exactly, to the year's worth of "missing" and "needing" that she'd cried about on the phone. "Trusting," W.W.W. didn't even want to think about. But the only thing there was, once he was close enough to feel the stitching, was the way Mary seemed to fold into the flannel.

The next thing he knew, they were drinking screwdrivers.

"O.J.'s in the fridge. Vodka's in the freezer." And could he mix the drinks, Mary wanted to know, while she handwashed just a couple of dirty dishes? Dishwashers took "such a toll on the environment."

"Glasses?" W.W.W. asked.

She was "crushed" that he'd forgotten. Her nice glasses, she said, were over the sink where they had always been.

"The apartment looks smaller than the one in San Antonio."

The apartment was so "teeny," Mary said, she could hardly stand it. Did he need just a little more vodka in his screwdriver? She could hardly taste the vodka for the O.J.

"Okay."

She was glad she'd moved to Dallas, though. It was almost three hundred miles farther away from the "armpit" of mesquite and cactus they'd grown up in together. She would never understand how W.W.W. could stay there. The drive in to work from her new place took forty-five minutes if she got up early and missed the rush hour; and she had to set her alarm, every morning, for six o'clock. But she loved her job. She had her "own little cubicle" with windows for walls—all the cubicles were like that, for teamwork, everybody seeing everybody else and knowing they weren't alone—and her own desk, the one in the middle of all those other desks, with her own phone. He could go ahead and make himself at home. She was almost done with the dishes.

"The furniture in the living room looks familiar."

"Threadbare," she said, was more the word for it. She was counting on Father for a brand new suite; but in the meantime, she would have to "make do."

W.W.W. sat on the floor, eased his back against the couch, and listened to her clink dishes together. He'd doctored calves all morning long, right on through lunch into the white-hot afternoon, and watched the sun go down out the driver's window of his pickup. He could still feel the weight of every wormy calf he'd thrown and held and vaccinated without pause, and the bruises from every kick that had connected. But there were worse things than working with cattle. One of the boys he and Mary had grown up with had broken his neck instead of the cowhorse he was trying to train, and another had gotten electrocuted turning on an irrigation motor. W.W.W. guessed all the ones with any sense had moved off to the city, gotten their own little cubicles, and stayed gone. Through the window in the partition, he saw fluorescent light catch the shine in Mary's hair.

"That San Antonio apartment sure looked to've been neater," he said.

Mary had "no concept."

"The clothes," he said, "laying all over everything."

"Are Rebecca's," she said. Her hair moved out of the window. He heard the icebox door.

"Rebecca?"

The girl she was thinking about moving in with, which was why she was counting on Father for the new suite of furniture. Although Father, she said, was against the move. Father was always against everything. What did W.W.W. think?

He knew for a fact that he didn't want to talk about Mary's father. What W.W.W. wanted was to talk about Mary and about the two of them

65

being together. He wanted to talk about San Antonio. About why on earth she'd called him up and cried and said what she'd said. About why she'd asked him all the way up here if all she wanted to do was dishes. About how much she'd changed. But what he told her was that he'd have to hear more about Rebecca before he could say.

It was the most awful thing, Mary said. Rebecca had driven down from California to live with "Cokie."

"Cokie?"

Cokie. She came down to live with him, and he seemed like a really "neat guy." But, well, it turned out that Rebecca had driven all the way to Dallas just to find out that she "needed room." Which was why she'd told Cokie that she would be spending the night with Mary, but was really going out with Michael, who Rebecca had met her first day at work.

"Poor Rebecca," he said.

"Excuse me?"

"Nothing. How did y'all meet?"

That part was "hilarious," Mary said, laughing and talking now at the same time. She was the one who had introduced Rebecca and Michael. Rebecca had walked into Mary's office looking for "temporary secretarial" not five minutes after Michael had phoned for a secretary/receptionist for his real estate firm who was "attractive," but "level-headed" and "a real go-getter." Anyway, she and Rebecca "did lunch," had "one or two too many," and "went on for hours." And here it was only two weeks later, and she and Rebecca were talking about moving in. That was the best thing about her job. There was always someone close for her to talk to.

W.W.W. was about to stand up and walk into the kitchen just to get a little closer to her—and God knew how much he could use another drink—when he heard water start to drain, then heard the icebox door again, and in Mary came carrying two more screwdrivers. They looked more clear than orange.

It was so hot, she said as she handed him a glass, she could hardly stand it. She needed a change, that was what she needed. She needed to go for a swim.

"I don't have any shorts."

"No problem," Mary said and went into the back. She came out wrapped in a blue-green towel that he remembered and tossed him a pair of polka-dot swimming trunks that she said were her brother's. But when

W.W.W. was finished in the bathroom—filled with other blue-green towels that he remembered and a box of dried rose petals he would never forget— the shorts hung loose around his waist. He was twice the size of Mary's brother.

The only stop they made was at the icebox; and when W.W.W. dove into the pool, all the way to the bottom, the water felt as cold as the screwdrivers Mary had made. It was hushed, the water smooth and quiet, and all along the bottom there were lights that were warm. When he surfaced, the outside air that had been hot and dry felt cool. Mary sat on the edge of the pool as he swam over, on a towel that she had folded, and dangled her feet in the water.

"There looks to be a good bit less there of you," he said, "than I remembered."

The pace, she said, had been a little "fast" lately. She finished her drink and started in on his. She could hardly stand it. Things in San Antonio, Mary said, had been so much nicer before they started "speeding up." Did he remember that time, when? And that other time, when? And the zoo? The Fiesta? All the parades?

"Yes," W.W.W. said. But he didn't remember.

She kept on remembering things. Things that never happened—or else, never happened with him—and the empty place that had opened up in the parking lot kept swallowing more and more of W.W.W. inside it, all the way back upstairs into her room. It was the same bed. And Mary was tired, she said, up since six o'clock and worked all day. But not that tired . . .

Somewhere things kind of faded out. When they faded in again, it was almost daylight.

He lay there and felt her head on the empty place in his chest and thought about the last time he'd felt the softness of her hair against his neck. It was on the couch at his daddy's house, on a Saturday morning almost a year ago, eighty miles and more from the San Antonio city lights. She was supposed to have been there the night before. And W.W.W. had been lying there fearing flat tires, crumpled fenders, worse. Until the rain started coming down hard from the northeast where she was supposed to be driving in from and he figured, what with the bad roads and all, she'd turned back. So he lay there kind of dozing, thinking about the sound of rain and the way it smelled like security, and not having to work until the ground was good and dry. He figured he would call her in a couple of hours or so. But just as it was getting light, in Mary came and put her head on his chest and said she'd just "been with" some other guy. He felt her hair damp against his neck and felt his chest empty underneath it, and said, "You're nothing but pain." Then she was gone, and his chest was wet, and he smelled the rain.

It seemed to W.W.W., lying there six hours northeast and a million miles distant from the only life he'd ever known, that he was as empty as the sky before stars. All her time she didn't spend saving the environment, Mary put toward causing pain. There was no way around it. It was time for a change.

When he walked down her stairs, it wasn't raining. He opened the truck door and the sky was empty, the sun just starting to pale the horizon, the city lights.

13. Rainbow Trout and Mountain Oysters

W.W.W. stared up into the red glow/white flash/red glow of the Dixie Fish beer lights, gathering himself for the effort that lay ahead. It was Saturday, Valentine's Day, a day he'd spent most of the last two weeks agonizing over and preparing for, and a day on which the success of the entire Program for Bliss depended. If he was going to avoid letting what had happened with Mary happen again with Shine, he knew that this Valentine's evening had to be perfect.

W.W.W.'s mistake with Mary had not only been that he'd moved too fast, but that he'd aimed too low. They had sex the first night they were alone together, on a blanket in the bed of his beat-up old ranch truck beneath a canopy of mesquites so thick he couldn't see the stars. He'd been young enough—sixteen years old, a virgin, fumbling his way into the sweat-soaked harbor that had sheltered so many others already—and foolish enough to believe that love was a physical thing alone. At nineteen, in the Dallas apartment where he'd seen Mary for the last time, he realized that true love, like true bliss, was in equal parts spiritual and physical—a thing of rainbows and stars as well as sweat and hormones.

It had been a life-changing epiphany. He knew at that moment that his ideas about love, learned mostly from Mary, and his ideas about bliss, learned mostly from his daddy, would have to be completely rethought. The dark vision of bliss that had been burned into W.W.W. over the nineteen years he'd lived with the old man was a mix of the ancient Greeks, Thomas Jefferson, and the Transcendentalists. But as he'd lain there in Mary's apartment feeling as empty as the sky before stars, W.W.W. had finally understood that instead of a bitter visionary his daddy was crazy and blind. He'd driven back to the ranch, gathered up his things, and headed east. Along with some clothes, a bag of potseeds, and a silver bracelet that had been his mother's, W.W.W. carried with him Aristotle's formal definition of bliss from the *Nicomachean Ethics* and Jefferson's admonition to pursue happiness from the *Declaration of Independence*. His aim was to build a new life in much the same way Thoreau had done in the woods of Walden—except that W.W.W. wanted to renovate the house of his life by living deliberately with other people, instead of building a new house all alone.

He'd come up short in New Orleans and again in Atlanta, having lost the ranch truck and a couple of new attempts at love along the way. And here and now, on Valentine's night at the Dixie Fish in Columbia, South Carolina, W.W.W. faced the most crucial test of this third—and almost certainly final—shot at finally reaching true bliss. He didn't have enough human capital left in him to try and build a life again someplace farther east; and anyway, it wasn't much farther east to the sea.

W.W.W. climbed up onto the stool that Bonnie always stood on to chalk the specials and looked out across the waitfloor, surveying the terrain like a veteran field commander before a major engagement. He decided that they would need to triple the usual number of condiment set-ups to meet the onslaught of Valentine's couples that he was certain would come pouring through the double front doors once the rest of the staff arrived and they opened for the evening. Then he climbed down and ducked into the waitstation to mix a vat of cocktail sauce. As he poured and stirred ketchup, horseradish, lemon juice, and hot pepper sauce into the five-gallon plastic cocktail bucket, he remembered with a mix of triumph and trepidation the progression of events that had led up to this Gettysburg moment in the Civil War of his life.

He'd spent the last week and a half agonizing about how he could possibly achieve Valentine's perfection on his meager budget and while working his shift at the Dixie Fish. As the new hire, W.W.W. had about as much chance of getting Valentine's night off as he had of coming up with the cash to take Shine out to a dinner complete with champagne, hors d'oeuvres, and the heart-shaped carat-and-a-half ruby ring he'd been dreaming of buying her since the first night she'd spent at the house on Hope Street. Instead, he would have to come up with something perfectly creative. But as the precious days and nights had passed, and creativity had failed him, he'd prayed to bliss for inspiration—bliss being the highest manifestation of things spiritual that W.W.W. believed in—lying in bed at night and whispering, "Bliss, bliss, bliss," and listening hard for an answer to come out of the dark. But bliss had chosen not to reply. Until suddenly, seven beers into the final Thursday evening drinking-and-bull session at the Dixie Fish bar prior to Valentine's, he'd heard bliss whisper its long-awaited answer in a voice that sounded very much like his mother's.

Rainbow trout and mountain oysters.

"Run rainbow trout as the Valentine's special and sell the mountain oysters as an appetizer," W.W.W. had said, echoing aloud the words that bliss had just whispered in the lovely voice he remembered hearing during the most perfectly happy moments of his life, as he lay in bed and listened to his mother singing.

"Do what?" Kent asked, eyeing W.W.W. They'd been talking about the approach of Valentine's Day, Kent's uncle's upcoming hog castration, and the phone call Kent had just gotten about the shipment of redfish and Chesapeake Bay oysters he'd planned to sell on Valentine's having doubled in price due to increased demand.

"Run rainbow trout as the Valentine's special and sell the mountain oysters as appetizers instead of regular oysters," W.W.W. said, echoing again the words that bliss continued to whisper in his mother's lovely singing voice. "Price the mountain oysters at $3.95 a dozen. Offer them regular and Cajun-style. They'll sell and sell."

"But what about the women?" Kent asked. "I mean, we're talking about hogs' balls here, W.W. I don't want to offend our clientele."

"The women are exactly the ones who'll order them. Especially if you make them sound like some kind of mysterious Valentine's treat." W.W.W. took a long swig of draft beer. He was trying to remember a single time his daddy had given his mother anything special on Valentine's, despite her singing and her pale ivory skin—that it came to him, suddenly, looked very much like Shine's skin—and the fact that she'd given up everything she loved in lush New Orleans to follow the old man to the arid Southwest Texas plains. "Women understand that love is a thing of mystery, of rainbows and stars and sweat and hormones all tangled up together."

"So?" Kent leaned against the bar and stared doubtfully back across it, sipping a non-alcoholic beer. As a combination gut-check and clean-out period, the Bronstein men never touched a drop of alcohol between New Year's Day and Valentine's.

"So you serve rainbow trout and mountain oysters, and you cover

71

both bases."

"I still don't know about the women."

"You just have to do Valentine's right," W.W.W. said. He could sense his own need for a special Valentine's evening for Shine, and Kent's need for a Valentine's special that he could make pay, working together in perfect harmony—exactly like he'd always wished, as a child, for his mother and daddy to do. "Hire music. Advertise. They'll sell and sell. I guarantee it."

"But—"

"What the hell else are you going to do with those hogs' balls, besides throw them in the trash and take a loss on them?"

"I don't know that I'd necessarily call it a loss," Kent said. "That is, unless I was one of the hogs. My uncle's hogs have got to be castrated, regardless."

"Waste is the worst kind of loss," W.W.W. said. "Something that should've been, but wasn't. If you do this right, it will be the biggest night in the history of the Dixie Fish. I give you my personal guarantee."

Two nights of frantic Valentine's preparations later, they were getting ready to serve the mountain oysters. W.W.W. had finished mixing cocktail sauce and was now engaged in pouring the results of his labor—a tangy and aromatic concoction that set his taste buds atingle—into plastic squirt-bottles that he carried out to the tables.

Perched atop her stool like a beautiful exotic bird, Bonnie chalked the hogs' balls up on the special board in all capital letters that were as bright a red as her dress: MOUNTAIN OYSTERS $3.95. It was RAINBOW TROUT $8.95 that did the headlining. But W.W.W. could see right off by the way the mountain oysters stood out, even stuck square in the middle of the rest of the list—underneath the RAINBOW TROUT $8.95 in rainbow-colored letters, in between the banana yellow BANANA PUDDING $1.25 that held the second spot and the various domestic beer specials variously priced at the bottom in various browns and golds—that those hogs' balls would see a lot of action.

"W.W.!" he heard Kent say. "Get over here, dammit! I've got a surprise."

W.W.W. dragged himself away from his Valentine's preparations and headed over to the waitwindow. Through it, he saw Kent standing in the kitchen and chewing something. Steam rose up off of a plate of fresh-cooked food that sat in the window. The mound of fried stuff on the plate looked a lot like hushpuppies. It smelled a lot like chicken.

"What is it?" W.W.W. asked.

"Mountain oysters," Kent mumbled around the mouthful he was still chewing. "What else? A half-dozen fried regular and a half-dozen fried Cajun-style in spicy batter."

W.W.W. felt himself start to gag. He pressed his lips tight-shut.

"Well?" Kent said.

"Well, what?" W.W.W. managed, trying to find something to look at besides Kent, who seemed every bit as excited to be chewing—and chewing, and chewing—mountain oysters as a kid smacking saltwater taffy.

"How do they look?"

"They look . . ." W.W.W. stared down into the plate of mountain oysters that were still steaming, but that were starting to look less like hushpuppies and smell less like chicken. "They look, um . . ."

"Try one," Kent said. "Try one, now."

W.W.W.'s gaze was fixed on the Cajun-fried mountain oysters. The spicy batter that covered them was the color of dried blood. He could feel his gorge start to rise.

"Umph," was all he managed to say.

"We'll talk about this later," Kent said in a voice that made it plain the conversation could well involve unemployment. "Smiley! You try one."

With a mighty effort, W.W.W. tore his eyes off of the blood-colored batter and gazed back up into Kent's face. In it, he saw that same eyebrows-together, tight-lipped, owner/manager *it's your ass* glare that he had seen so many times before. W.W.W. looked away from the glare—and away from the mountain oysters—into the kitchen, to where Smiley stood over by the deep-fryer. Smiley's face, very black under the brand new white chef's hat he was wearing, was twisted up so it looked like someone had squeezed a lemon into his mouth.

"Sweet Jesus!" Smiley said. "Don't look at me. I done told y'all I ain't about to touch those damn nasty things."

W.W.W. had to agree—and agree he did, but silently. Kent didn't say anything either. But W.W.W. could still feel that owner/manager *it's your ass* glare as he picked up the order of mountain oysters and carried it out. "Kent has a little surprise," W.W.W. said to the rest of the waitstaff. Sporting the brand new white aprons that Kent had bought especially for Valentine's, they were all huddled up around table 51 where W.W.W. set down the tray. "Eat up."

"You eat up,"Alisha said. "It was your idea."

W.W.W. could make out Kent watching them through the wait-window. But despite the fact that the whole thing had indeed been W.W.W.'s idea—and despite the fact that if the mountain oysters didn't sell, it could cost him his job—just the sight of those bloody-battered balls, with steam coming up off of them, made W.W.W. break out in a cold sweat.

And suddenly, fight it as he might, he felt himself carried back to Southwest Texas. It was an early morning in February, dry-cold, the first time W.W.W. had ever helped his daddy work cattle. His daddy and some of the other genocidal agrarianists that W.W.W. would later come to know had just finished cutting the bull calves away from their mothers. The cows, penned on the far side of the chute W.W.W. sat on top of, lowed back at the calves that crowded close to the chute. Two men threw the first calf and held him, stretching apart the back legs while W.W.W.'s daddy reached in, grasped, and cut. W.W.W. saw the calf scrotum contract in the old man's hand and watched steam rise off the bloody testicles as the old man held them up for W.W.W. to throw to the dogs. But W.W.W. couldn't bring himself to touch them. His daddy looked up at him and waited while the big men laughed. Then the old man's face twisted into a mocking half-smile that made it clear he thought W.W.W. was the weakest, most cowardly, most worthless thing alive.

Half in/half out of the here and now at the Dixie Fish, W.W.W. felt cold sweat trickling across his goose-pimpled skin. But just when it seemed like things might go as badly in the here and now as they had gone that February day back in Southwest Texas, he saw Gladys elbow her way up to the table. She popped one of the regular-fried mountain oysters into her mouth, screwed up her face a little as she chewed—and chewed, and chewed—and then gulped it down, belched, and popped in a Cajun-fried mountain oyster.

"Fantastic!" Gladys mumbled around a mouthful of spicy-fried hogs' balls. "Freaking out of this world."

It started the whole waitstaff going. Brave popped in a regular-fried mountain oyster. Alisha popped in one fried Cajun. Gladys never slowed down.

But W.W.W. still couldn't bring himself to touch them.

Bonnie reached out, finally, to try one fried Cajun; and W.W.W. felt his gorge rising again, even though he knew the result would most likely be his termination. He watched Bonnie pop the mountain oyster into her mouth—at the same time smelling fresh blood and seeing that mocking half-smile on his daddy's face.

Bonnie chewed—and chewed, and chewed—the mountain oyster as W.W.W. watched. She swallowed. Then she picked up another, fried regular. "Delicious," she said and gave W.W.W. that threadbare smile he remembered from the first night he'd walked into the Dixie Fish.

And looking at Bonnie smiling at him in her red and white Valentine's outfit, W.W.W. felt himself fully grounded, once again, in the present moment.

Bonnie took a long look at the special board, then climbed back up onto her stool and started chalking a border of hearts and curlicues along the sides. By the time she climbed back down, the board was perfect—chalked in a print so precise, and yet so fancy at the same time, that it looked like an illuminated manuscript.

"Lovely," W.W.W. said.

"Thank you," Bonnie said and smiled again.

It came to W.W.W., suddenly, that he'd never managed to get a definitive whiff of Bonnie, bliss-wise. He leaned in close and took a deep breath full of the smell of her hair. He caught the scent of coffee brewing, and of worn leather, and of breakfast cooking. But it was shot all through with axle grease and diesel fuel. Bonnie's smell was true bliss, but it was someone else's.

"Bonnie and Blue," he whispered to himself. "Blue and Bonnie."

W.W.W. got so caught up in Bonnie, he hardly noticed when the last of the mountain oysters was gone. But when he walked up to the wait-window to pick up the replacement order, he discovered that Kent had noticed plenty.

"You said do it right," Kent said. "I did it right. I went out, and I bought white aprons. Hell, I bought a new chef's hat for Smiley! You said hire music. I hired music. You said advertise. I advertised!"

"Kent," W.W.W. said, "you have to trust me. This is going to work."

"Trust you! 'The biggest night in the history of the Dixie Fish,' you said. You guaranteed this. And now you won't even try the mountain oysters that you talked me into staking a mint on selling? If this thing don't pay out—if you don't make it pay—it's your ass, W.W. I swear to God, it's your ass!"

"I'll sell plenty."

W.W.W. carried out the mountain oysters, feeling the owner/manager *it's your ass* glare from the waitwindow. He papered the tables while the rest of the waitstaff finished eating. Then he and Brave and Alisha and Gladys carried out tartar sauce set-ups, ketchups, Tabascos, vinegars, and hot pepper sauces while Bonnie checked the salts and peppers.

The whole time, W.W.W. felt Kent's eyes on him. If everything wasn't perfect that night, W.W.W. knew it would be all over for him at the Dixie Fish—and as the Dixie Fish went, he knew, so went the Program for Bliss.

"You've been warned," Kent said, once everything was finally ready to go.

"Trust me, Kent," W.W.W. said. "I'm only asking you to trust me."

"How the hell do you expect to be able to sell something that you won't even try yourself? And who the hell do you expect to be able to sell them to?" The mocking half-smile that Kent gave W.W.W. was exactly the same as the one W.W.W.'s daddy had turned on him in the cow pens all those years ago.

But this time, W.W.W. was ready for it. "Women," he said.

14. BALLS

*T*he handsome older woman at table 24, who wore a lavender print dress trimmed with lavender lace and who—after taking up at least a minute and a half of W.W.W.'s precious time convincing her husband to go ahead and splurge on the RAINBOW TROUT $8.95—ordered clam-strips for herself at $3.95, waited until her husband was all the way past the new RESTROOMS sign before she motioned W.W.W. back over to the table with a wave of her handkerchief.

The new RESTROOMS sign was the final touch in W.W.W.'s Valentine's preparations. Remembering the trouble he himself had finding the restrooms on that fateful night when the Strangers brought him to the Dixie Fish, he'd asked Bonnie to draw up a sign to guide other lost souls just before he opened the double front doors and let in the crowd. The sign hung over the passageway to the back bar, just to the left of the stage where Mr. Guitar—the FREE LIVE MUSIC Kent had hired and advertised in the *Living* section of the paper—was belting out a fiery rendition of "Steamroller." Mr. Guitar was really burning it up, like it damn well ought to be done; but he was taking up entirely too much restaurant space in the process. W.W.W. stood next to the stage, checking everything over one more time on the waitfloor that it would be his ass if things didn't go just exactly right on. He waited for Lavender Lace's husband to clear the door-frame, then squeezed back past the stage and headed to the table.

The handkerchief Lavender Lace was waving to catch his attention was white, with a lavender print pattern that matched her corsage. But all she would have needed, really, was to nod in W.W.W.'s direction. The stakes tonight were so high, and his people radar—a kind of sixth sense peculiar to law enforcement officials, con artists, and food and beverage employees—was tuned to such a high pitch, he had known the minute she ordered the clamstrips that Lavender Lace would be calling him back over.

"I want you to be sure," Lavender Lace yelled over Mr. Guitar's gravelly base voice not more than ten or twelve precious seconds after W.W.W. had made it back over, "to give me the ticket for our dinners!"

"Yes, ma'am!" W.W.W. yelled. He was borderline desperate to get back to the rest of his tables, but he could tell she wasn't finished. So he hung back, just the least fraction, before he turned and started slowly back through his section.

"Young man!"

He heard the catch in her voice even over the blare of the amplifier that must have been cranked up as loud as it would go. He saw the flush on Lavender Lace's face as he eased back over. Mr. Guitar had gotten to the part of "Steamroller" where he promised to "roll all over you, baby," and the innuendo—particularly appropriate on a Valentine's evening—was not lost on Lavender Lace. W.W.W. could see her breath come quick and shallow through the handkerchief she held close to her mouth. He squatted next to her and leaned in on the balls of his feet.

"My husband is not much of an oyster eater!" Lavender Lace yelled through the handkerchief that covered the bottom half of her face. "Would those . . . mountain oysters . . . have the same . . . you know, the same . . . effect . . . as regular oysters?"

"Some cultures," W.W.W. yelled, "believe that eating the, um, sensitive parts of an animal will . . . endow . . . a man with that animal's particular qualities!"

"And what sort of . . ." she lowered her voice and leaned close enough for W.W.W. to smell the lavender water at the base of her throat, "sensitive parts . . . are these?"

W.W.W.'s lips brushed Lavender Lace's ear. "A bull's," he said in his best imitation of Mr. Guitar's gravelly base voice.

"We'll try an order," she said. "As an appetizer."

"Yes ma'am," W.W.W. said. "Right away." He stopped to drop the check on table 25, pulled two empty paper plates off 23, took a styrofoam dessert dish off 22, stacked it on top of the two plates from 23, and then put all four of the forks onto the dessert dish. He took the empty wine glass off 21, made eye contact with the blonde in the red miniskirt sitting behind it, and raised his eyebrows.

She nodded.

Then W.W.W. ducked into the waitstation, dumped the silverware into the silverbucket and the plates into the trash, stepped through the far side of the waitstation to the bar, slapped 21's ticket face-down on the countertop, wrote C.W.W. on the back, then rang the bell. All that was left was to duck back into the waitstation, tear a yellow appetizer ticket off the pad over by the waitwindow, scrawl BALLS on it in big black letters and put it up in the window, head back to the bar, and then—over the string of Smiley's "Sweet Jesuses" and "Goddamns" that came out of the kitchen— yell at Tommy to hurry the hell up with that cheap white wine.

It had been that kind of night all night long—not so much busy as crazy, and getting crazier as the shift went on. Right from the start, mountain oysters had sold and sold. It was W.W.W. who did most of the selling. He pushed order after order to table after table, promising anything: longer life, better love, loaves and fishes. People were eating Kent out of RAINBOW TROUT $8.95 and BANANA PUDDING $1.25. People were drinking Tommy out of domestic beer. People were ordering mountain oysters and pulling W.W.W.'s fat out of Kent's fryer. They came mostly in dress clothes and mostly in pairs. Older couples—Lavender Lace being no exception—with the older women squandering W.W.W.'s precious time, making sure he made a big deal out of their "paying the ticket" for the older men. Younger couples with the younger men trying W.W.W.'s precious patience, making sure he made every bit as big a deal out of their "picking up the tab" for the younger women. Couples poured in until they filled all the tables. They filled the bar while they waited for tables. Then they filled the spaces between the tables, young and old alike, dressed to the teeth and drinking hard. The main difference between the old and the young couples had to do with the mountain oysters: the Lavender Lace set, at least, knew what mountain oysters were.

"Tommy!" W.W.W. yelled again. "Wine!"

Tommy drooped. He stood at the far end of the bar, breathing heavy, filling four pint glasses with draft beer. His white pinpoint Oxford shirt was stained with beer and sweat. His face was spattered with pink suds from the sink, which W.W.W. could see was overflowing with dirty pint glasses.

"Tommy!" W.W.W. yelled.

Tommy didn't even look up.

W.W.W. glanced back at the waitfloor. He saw another younger couple settle into his now-empty—but still dirty—table 25. It now needed to be bussed, and a drink order needed to be taken. He saw Lavender Lace's husband sit back down at 24.

Even worse, the wineglass woman at 21 was starting to look around for the wine that was still not in the empty glass that was still sitting on Tommy's bar. W.W.W. felt an overwhelming urge to shake Tommy until the teeth rattled in his pink-suds-spattered face.

But instead, W.W.W. took a deep breath. He took another. Then he hurdled the bar, found the cheap white wine, and filled the empty wine glass himself. Next he jumped back over the bar, cut through the waitstation, tore off a clean sheet of tablepaper, and grabbed a couple of powder-blue menus and the mountain oyster order for 24. Finally, he picked up the glass of wine from the bar, set it down on 21, and headed back through his section.

W.W.W. had just finished handing menus to the new couple at 25 and was busy folding up the dirty tablepaper from the couple that had just left when he caught the stultifying stink of bloody chicken feathers that meant misfortune lurking near. He could hardly believe his nose. As the evening had worn on, the Dixie Fish had slowly filled up with a strange and wonderful scent that W.W.W. had never smelled before: a mix of the hot-body-odory, cheap-perfumey reek of potential bliss and the first-pot-of-coffee, eggs-in-bacon-greasy aroma of true bliss that he guessed must've come from the interaction of Valentine's-enhanced pheromones and fried mountain oysters. He had been too busy to do much more than take note of the scent—the most favorable omen imaginable on a night when he planned to take his relationship with Shine to the next level—and be vastly encouraged by it. But now, suddenly, the only thing he could smell was bloody chicken feathers; and the heady feeling of confidence that had been building all evening was tinged with doubt and dread.

"*Garçon!*" the younger man at table 25 called out when W.W.W. finished placing the fresh tablepaper, along with crayons and freshly wiped condiment set-ups, on the table. "What are mountain oysters?"

The man's close-clipped blonde hair was concreted into place with as much mousse as there was starch on his buttondown. His tie was as bright as his crayons. With the perfectly manicured hand that wasn't draped across the hand of the perfectly manicured younger woman beside him, he drew a bright red heart and cleaved a yellow arrow through it. It was one of the Strangers. In fact, it was the same Stranger who had given W.W.W. the ride to buy the maroon metal-flake and chrome motorcycle that first Monday morning after he'd arrived in Columbia, South Carolina—and the same Stranger that Shine had come over to break things off with on the Sunday night before the Monday morning ride. He was pretending not to know W.W.W.

"Tasty," W.W.W. yelled, "like you wouldn't believe!"

"I'll be the judge of that!" the Stranger barked, and the veneers on his teeth flashed. "That is, assuming I deign to place an order. But first, what are they?"

W.W.W. realized that his distaste for the blue-blooded Stranger at the table—despite the smell of bloody chicken feathers and the lurking misfortune it portended—outweighed his dread that the Stranger might somehow screw up his Valentine's plans with Shine. This realization was immediately followed by another: that duping the Stranger into eating fried hogs' balls would be a nice way to bring his blue-blooded ass down a couple of pegs.

"Right there," W.W.W. yelled as deferentially as possible, "sir!" He bowed his head in the direction of table 24, where Lavender Lace had just slid her chair around practically into her husband's lap and was now handfeeding him mountain oysters in between sips of cheap white wine. "Those are mountain oysters."

"We'll try an order!" the Stranger barked. "Chop, chop! And the lady," he squeezed the perfectly manicured hand of the bleach-blonde beside him, "and I will each have a glass of your finest Chablis."

W.W.W. yes-sirred and headed back through his section. He stopped off at the waitwindow to hand Smiley the mountain oyster order before cutting through the waitstation and hurdling the bar. The string of expletives started just as W.W.W. started to pour the wine.

"Sweet Jesus! Goddamn them nasty things!"

Through the window between the kitchen and the bar, W.W.W. caught sight of Smiley—sweating, weaving, drunker than sin, trying to cut whole hog's balls up into mountain oyster orders without having to touch them. Kent had been pouring beer down him since 6 p.m. when the Valentine's onslaught had begun.

W.W.W. re-hopped the bar and took the wine and mountain oysters out to the Stranger's table, dropping checks on 22 and 23 along the way.

The couple at 22 looked a little funny when the check hit the table, like they'd maybe been thinking about banana pudding. And W.W.W. could probably have squeezed another round of beers out of 23. But Shine would be in, any minute now, to start their Valentine's evening together. He needed time before Shine came in to get the clean-up work started—and to make a crucial Valentine's arrangement with Mr. Guitar. It had only been a month and a half since W.W.W. had first caught the scent of potential bliss at the Dixie Fish, and the Program for Bliss was so close to bearing fruit he could taste its skin. The right two or three gifts, the right song, and the right timing, and by the end of Valentine's night, he would finally achieve true bliss.

The first thing W.W.W. did to get the close-out started was have Bonnie draw up a NO LONGER SEATING FOR DINNER sign and tape it up on the double front doors. Then he waded into the sections of the other Valentine's waitpeople and started bussing and seating, bussing and seating, until all of the couples who had been standing and waiting for tables were sitting and waiting on drink orders. Finally, while finishing up his own tables, he got the clean-up effort going—a matter of leading by example and dropping a word or two about free draft beer once close-out was finished up.

So despite the bloody-chicken-feather stink of misfortune that now lurked over the waitfloor in an almost perfect balance with the mix of potential bliss and true bliss that still wafted over the bar, things seemed to be swinging W.W.W.'s way. But Mr. Guitar was still untalked-to. W.W.W. was still stuck behind the faded green fish net, pouring "drawn butter" set-ups back into buttery-flavored vegetable oil jugs. And it was beginning to get late.

Then, suddenly, Shine walked in. The world's heart skipped a beat. And for an endless second, everything in the Dixie Fish ground to a halt—even Mr. Guitar.

Silence spread out in front of Shine in a long smooth wave from the front door all the way to the back bar as though even the people who couldn't see Shine could feel that she was there. No one moved. No one breathed except Shine as she passed by the register. Her eyes were gold, her skin pale ivory. Her hair was down, her head held high. And it came to W.W.W. as she reached the waitstation that it wasn't only Shine's pale skin that reminded him of his mother—Shine had the same slight, perfect cleft of the chin.

The cleft is the grace of the chin.

This was a phrase of Plutarch's that W.W.W. remembered his daddy saying sometimes to his mother—usually late in the evening as W.W.W. was headed for bed—and just about the only positive comment that he could remember the old man ever making about anything except the ground. W.W.W. remembered the way his mother's eyes had lit up when his daddy said it all those years ago. It came to W.W.W. that he needed to say it to Shine in the here and now of the Dixie Fish.

"The cleft is the grace of the chin," he said, stepping out from behind the faded green fish net as Shine walked up and lightly touching that perfect indentation just below her lovely lips. He saw her eyes light up, just the way his mother's eyes used to light up. Then he glanced away at Tommy, who stood behind the bar with his mouth open, not moving—looking pretty much like he always looked—and said, "Tommy, a bottle of Kent's best champagne."

"What a lovely way to say hello," Shine said and kissed W.W.W.'s cheek.

"If bliss could be personified, she would look exactly like you do at this moment." He pulled out a barstool and held it for Shine. "I have closing work to do right now. I'll be back as soon as I'm done."

Things started to move again at the bar and on the waitfloor. People started to breathe. W.W.W. walked back into the waitstation feeling six inches taller and a foot thicker through the chest.

Then he caught sight of the Stranger staring at Shine. W.W.W. had seen the Stranger catch sight of Shine when she walked in. But it struck W.W.W. only now how caught up in Shine he must've been to have missed the look on the Stranger's face like he'd just been disemboweled.

The smell of bloody chicken feathers seemed to explode into W.W.W.'s nostrils. He watched as the Stranger left the Perfectly Manicured Younger Woman at their table and moved toward Shine. There was a look about the Stranger's body of unbelievable suffering—his shoulders hunched beneath his buttondown, his lips clenched against his perfect teeth—as though he were literally dragging his guts across the bare concrete floor as he limped toward the bar.

W.W.W. took off his apron as the Stranger reached the barstool where Shine was just taking her first sip of champagne. W.W.W. saw the Stranger grab Shine's arm, and saw him shake her. W.W.W. saw champagne splash the bar, and Shine.

But by that time, W.W.W. was there.

He peeled the Stranger's fingers off Shine's arm. Then W.W.W. caught the pressure point in the Stranger's soft palm and twisted it—getting leverage on the thumb—away up behind the Stranger's back almost to the base of his neck. The arm followed, like it had to follow, and W.W.W. grabbed the Stranger's other shoulder and squeezed.

"Are you ready to calm down?" W.W.W. asked, studying what he could see of the Stranger's face.

"You . . . redneck!" the Stranger choked out.

"Careful." W.W.W. twisted the Stranger's arm higher, almost dislocating the shoulder and thumb. "Those were hogs' balls you were eating," he stage-whispered, just loud enough for Shine to hear. "You wouldn't want to have to eat your own."

W.W.W. used his leverage on the almost-dislocated shoulder joint to walk the Stranger away from the bar and steer him toward the exit. The Perfectly Manicured Younger Woman met them at the double front doors and followed them out into the cold.

"You trailer trash son of a bitch!" the Stranger said, throwing his head back and trying to twist around and fight.

W.W.W. popped the Stranger's thumb out of its socket, hearing the Stranger gasp in pain at the sudden and unexpected dislocation. "Careful," W.W.W. said as he shifted his grip to the Stranger's wrist. "For the first time in more than a decade, I can think about my mother and see something besides hands on bars in a burning window. Shine is the reason for that." W.W.W. realized, hearing himself speak the words, how completely true they were—and what a relief it had been. "One more move, one more word, and I'll cripple you."

The Stranger stood very still and said nothing at all.

"That's better." W.W.W. shifted around to where he could make eye contact with the Perfectly Manicured Younger Woman. "Ma'am, if you would, please reach into this gentleman's pocket very slowly and carefully, and take his keys."

"I've got them," she said after a long, fumbling moment.

"Then could you please open up that passenger side door?" W.W.W. nodded at the Stranger's red sports coupe that was parked in front of the plate glass windows next to where they were standing. "Your date is not going to be doing any more driving this evening."

W.W.W. swung the Stranger down into the passenger seat of the red sports coupe and slammed the door. He watched the car back out and pull away past the fire station. Then he headed back into the Dixie Fish and got a standing ovation.

It started as W.W.W. walked in the door, with scattered people standing and clapping. The ovation picked up steam as he walked past the register and around the waitstation where the crowd was thicker, and where some of the actual witnesses to his rescue of Shine started slapping him on the back. Then the crowd sucked him in and channeled him like a hummingbird into a trumpeter vine straight at Shine, who sat and sipped her champagne just like nothing had happened—but who had a look like love in her eyes.

Finally, Shine stood up and kissed W.W.W. on the lips.

It was a sensory explosion, and the taste of her was pure bliss. The scent of her—of the two of them together—was that heady mix of the hot-body-odory, cheap-perfumey scent of potential bliss and the first-pot-of-coffee, eggs-in-bacon-greasy aroma of true bliss that W.W.W. had been smelling all evening. It welled up so strong now all around him that it took his breath away.

But then they yanked him back, the crowd—not that big as crowds go, but enthusiastic and well-fed—even though W.W.W. was nowhere near finished kissing Shine and probably never would be. Everything was clapping and back-slapping for quite a while. Until somehow, in the middle of it all, he found himself in an eddy at the foot of the stage right in front of Kent's FREE LIVE ENTERTAINMENT for the evening; and W.W.W. realized that he had still not made his crucial Valentine's arrangements with Mr. Guitar.

"Mr. Guitar?" W.W.W. said. "Could I have a word with you?"

Mr. Guitar wasn't listening. He wasn't singing. He wasn't playing the six-string Gibson that was slung, right-handed and low, on a hand-tooled leather strap across his shoulder. Instead, he just stood there on the stage with his white hair and his skin the color of melted chocolate, and stared at Shine.

"Mr. Guitar?" W.W.W. said again, louder.

"Eb," Mr. Guitar said. "Eb Etheridge."

"W.W.," W.W.W. said. He shook Eb's hand that, despite the calluses covering it, was rubbed raw at the fingertips. "That was some serious 'Steamroller' you did a while ago."

"Beautiful."

"Yeah. That's real powerful stuff, Eb."

"The girl," Eb said, "more than the song."

W.W.W. couldn't argue with that. "Eb," he said, "there's a semi-jazzy tune that Nat King Cole recorded back in the 40's called 'For All We Know.' Do you know it?"

Eb nodded yeah.

"I need to sing it to her. Will you play it?"

Eb looked away from Shine, down at the raw skin that covered the tips of his fingers. "Now?"

"Well, first I'd like to give her some things."

Eb was still looking at the tips of his fingers. "What do you want to sing her that song for?" he asked.

"Does it matter?"

"Damn straight. Before I scrape the rest of the skin off my fingertips, I want to know why."

"Fair enough," W.W.W. said. "When I was little, I used to lie in bed and listen to my mother singing. 'For All We Know' was one of the songs she sang. The sound of her voice made me feel like the world was a rainbow, and I was the pot of gold at the end of it. Then she died. And for a long time, I lost that feeling. When I look at Shine, I feel like gold again."

Eb looked past his fingertips into W.W.W.'s eyes. "I'll play the song for you, W.W. Just let me know when."

The next thing W.W.W. knew, he was back at the bar sitting next to Shine. The crowd of customers was drifting toward the double front doors. The staff was settling onto the barstools the customers were vacating. Except for Shine, who was still sipping Kent's good champagne, they were all drinking the free draft beer that W.W.W. had promised during clean-up and that Kent—who dropped like a rock off the New Year's wagon less than a minute after he'd run the final tape on the register—had delivered for what he had dubbed, "The Mother of All Business Nights at the Dixie Fish."

Kent said this just as he personally served W.W.W. his first free beer of the night. Even though it was just a draft and didn't represent a whole lot of sacrifice on Kent's part, the fact that the whole of Valentine's night had been W.W.W.'s idea made the cheap draft beer taste like Dom Perignon.

"Thanks, Kent," W.W.W. said.

"We sold fifty-one orders of mountain oysters," Kent said. He stood behind the bar between Smiley and Tommy, smiling wistfully into his draft beer.

W.W.W. nodded. His people radar was still up. And it told him to keep his mouth shut, even though the mixed scents of potential bliss and true bliss were exploding like a miracle February springtime into the Valentine's night Dixie Fish.

"That's fifty-one dozen mountain oysters," Kent said. "And out of fifty-one dozen sold, do you know how many you personally accounted for?"

W.W.W.'s people radar told him to shake his head no, even though he knew the answer was thirty-three.

"Thirty-three," Kent said.

"I smell a raise coming," W.W.W. said, sensing that the time to speak had finally come.

"Sure enough," Kent said. "Two dollars extra on your hourly wage, starting now. Provided . . ."

"Provided what?"

"Provided," Kent said, leaning eagerly across the bar, "that you tell me how."

"You mean, how I sold all those mountain oysters?"

"How you sold the mountain oysters, the trout specials, the beer and wine. Hell, the whole idea of Valentine's."

"Women," W.W.W. said and took Shine's hand. "Women and love."

"What about them?" Kent asked.

"Yes," Shine said, arching an eyebrow. "What about them?"

"As for love," W.W.W. said, "it's like I told Kent before: love is a thing of mystery, of rainbows and stars and sweat and hormones all tangled up together."

"I rather like that," Shine said. "Now what about women?"

W.W.W. met Shine's eyes that, even in the red glow/white flash/red glow of the Dixie Fish beer lights, gleamed pure gold. "Men tend to see only the surface of love. Women look clear through into love's bones."

15. What Mozart Heard

𝓔b gave the Dixie Fish staff and their Valentines a little time to settle in at the bar before he picked up his guitar again and started tuning up. Bonnie and Blue were getting Valentinesy over in the shadow of the Trivia Whiz machine. Tommy and Gladys sat looking deep into each other's eyes at the far corner of the bar. Brave, Alisha, Smiley, and Kent were unaccompanied, but pounding enough free draft beer to keep them warm even in the absence of flesh contact. It was, W.W.W. realized, about as friendly an audience as could possibly be got. He raised Shine's hand to his lips, then took Eb's cue and got ready to perform.

W.W.W. edged between barstools and around fake pier pilings and ducked into the waitstation to get his backpack. He knew all too well that his whole life was riding on this moment—his past and present intersecting like the armies at Gettysburg; his future hanging fire, awaiting the outcome. Would he finally achieve true bliss? Or would Shine, the minute he started to sing, laugh him straight out of the Dixie Fish and straight out of the Program for Bliss, all the way back to the kind of helpless despair he'd felt seeing his mother's hands clenched onto the bars in her bedroom window while the house he'd grown up in was engulfed in flames?

W.W.W. waited until he heard Eb start to play. Then he reached down into his worn leather backpack and pulled out a pound of chicory coffee, Mozart's *The Marriage of Figaro*, and the silver bracelet he'd been carrying since he left Southwest Texas. He took a second or two to rub a little more luster onto the bracelet before he put the gifts back into his backpack and headed for the bar.

W.W.W. eased back onto the barstool and clenched his backpack between his feet, feeling like Robert E. Lee must've felt watching Pickett's Charge. Cold fingers of fear reached into his belly and knotted everything up around the beer. He had just finished freezing up completely when he heard Eb start into "What a Wonderful World." Eb sang it warm, like Satchmo with that gravelly voice. And before Eb had even made it through the first stanza, W.W.W. felt his insides start to thaw. There was life in the music like the sap in new leaves. With every verse Eb sang, W.W.W.'s confidence grew until he felt like he was riding a spring-green wave of Louis Armstrong straight at Shine.

W.W.W. gave her the coffee first, a pound of ground chicory just like his mother used to make. But Shine wrinkled her nose at the scent of it.

"Trust me," he said, riding the wave. "It's an acquired taste, but you'll love the smell of it brewing in the morning."

When they saw him giving Shine the coffee, the Dixie Fish staff gave W.W.W. a look like the one they'd all given the Opera People wielding their crab bats. But it didn't matter. After all, W.W.W. thought, it was his encounter with the Opera People that had given him the idea for Shine's second gift.

He reached again into his backpack, pulled out *The Marriage of Figaro*, and gave the CD to Shine. But she looked at him with gold eyes full of unspoken questions and unmet Valentine's expectations.

"Trust me," he said again. "It's an opera about a commoner who risks everything, including his life, competing with a nobleman for the love of a beautiful woman. In the end, the common man wins."

Then W.W.W. pulled out the bracelet he'd been carrying since he left Southwest Texas. It looked like a looped vine of sterling silver, with leaves and flowers carved in filigreed whorls around a central stem. He took Shine's hand and slid the bracelet onto her wrist.

"It was my mother's," he whispered, too softly for anyone but Shine to hear. "It looks every bit as lovely on your wrist as it did on hers."

"Thank you," Shine said, and her eyes glowed doubt-free.

Eb finished up "What a Wonderful World," and everyone started clapping. The applause was for Mr. Guitar. But W.W.W. knew that the look of love in Shine's eyes was all his.

Just then Brave asked Eb for another song. Gladys said that Eb had to play one more. And W.W.W. had to admire Eb's sense of timing.

"I'll play one more song." Eb paused to take a long pull off his draft beer. "But my voice is kind of worn out. Who wants to sing this last song?"

Everybody looked around at everybody else. But it was just like every other time W.W.W. had heard a singer ask a group of people for one of them to do a tune—everybody wanting like sin to be a singer, but afraid for anybody else to hear them sing.

"W.W.?" Eb asked.

W.W.W. smiled. "Alright."

"'For All We Know?'"

"Absolutely."

Eb put down his beer and started straight into the opening. W.W.W. heard Eb's boot against the concrete, tapping out the rhythm he could feel in his bones. Eb dipped the neck of his guitar when it was time for W.W.W. to come in, but W.W.W. didn't need the cue. He took the deepest breath of his life, looked into Shine's eyes, and sang the words that he had heard his mother sing so many nights.

> *For all we know, we may never meet again.*
> *Before you go, make this moment sweet again.*
> *We won't say good night until the last minute.*
> *I'll hold out my hand and my heart will be in it.*
>
> *For all we know, this may only be a dream.*
> *We come and go like a ripple on a stream.*
> *So love me tonight; tomorrow was made for some.*
> *Tomorrow may never come for all we know.*

W.W.W. paused while Eb played the bridge, note by note echoing with his guitar the words W.W.W. had sung. He felt Shine lean in close, her eyes shining like suns set in the ivory firmament of her skin.

> *So love me tonight; tomorrow was made for some.*
> *Tomorrow may never come for all we know.*

He felt Eb standing now behind him, tapping out the rhythm W.W.W. was feeling, closer than co-op, as they sang the refrain together. Their two voices blended into one, W.W.W. leading and Eb harmonizing—one voice, one guitar, then quiet.

W.W.W. felt Shine melt against him. "Happy Valentine's," he said.

"Kiss me," she said.

The taste of her was pure champagne, his whole world a Valentine's celebration. The Program for Bliss was right up on the edge of finally finished. The only thing W.W.W. lacked would have to wait until he and Shine got home. And then, for after, he had eggs and bacon that would combine with Shine's chicory coffee to produce the eggs-in-bacon-greasy, first-pot-of-coffee scent of true bliss that he hadn't smelled since he was a child.

"You got a gift," Eb said, finally. "I would've sworn that was Nat King Cole singing. And I watched you sing it."

"You really do have a gift," someone said. It sounded like Alisha, and she sounded shocked.

"Wonderful," someone else said, warmly this time. Maybe Bonnie.

W.W.W. nodded yeah. He was focused on Shine.

"Perfect pitch?" Eb asked.

W.W.W. nodded yeah.

"Hey, Hotrod!" Eb barked. "The man who just played his fingers raw would like an out-loud answer."

W.W.W. managed to look away from Shine, finally, over at Eb. "I'm sorry, Eb. You're right. The truth is that every single thing I hear, I remember."

"Word for word?" Eb asked.

"Word for word."

"And you can reproduce it?" Eb asked. "Exactly? After only one time?"

"Precisely, identically. After only one time."

"Like Mozart," Eb said.

"No," W.W.W. said. "What Mozart heard came from God. Or bliss. Or the great beyond. Whatever you want to call it. What I hear is only Mozart."

"You mean like a tape recorder?"

"More like a twenty-four-hour freaking CD spinning around in my head."

"What bullshit," Brave said. "No offense, W.W., but that has got to be the biggest load of crap I ever heard."

"Bullshit," Tommy echoed, nodding his head up and down. He appeared to be holding himself up only by leaning against the bar.

"Sweet Jesus," Smiley said, nodding and swaying next to Tommy. "What a bullshit lie."

W.W.W. looked around the bar at the faces of the staff that were a mixture of bullshit lie and true belief. He looked into Shine's face that it seemed like a doubt had never darkened. He didn't need his people radar to tell him there was no need to reply.

"What did you mean when you said the CD played twenty-four hours?" Eb asked.

"Exactly that. There are times when I can't turn it off."

"Bullshit," Tommy said again, slurring and swaying against the bar.

"Sweet Jesus," Smiley said again, slurring and swaying next to Tommy. "That is indeed a bullshit lie."

"Either shitfaced is catching," Eb said, "or there's one hell of an echo in here."

Alisha pushed Tommy and Smiley back from the bar, then leaned in close and made eye contact with W.W.W. "So what you're saying is that your life is like a tale told over and over again by a pair of drunken idiots?" The look she gave him through her dyed-black bangs was surprisingly sympathetic—especially considering the disgust she'd expressed at the contents of his reading list on his first night at the Dixie Fish, and the general disdain she'd shown for him since.

"Sometimes," W.W.W. said, hearing again the roar of flames and the sound of his mother's screams, "it's worse. Especially when I can't make it stop."

"I don't know about the rest of these folks," Brave said, "but I'd like to see some proof."

"Proof!" Tommy echoed.

"Proof!" Smiley echoed again.

"Alright." W.W.W. looked from Brave to Tommy to Smiley and back again. "Ya'll ever play any games of chance?"

"What do you have in mind?" Brave asked.

"How about a friendly game of trivia-for-beer?"

Four nursery rhymes, two verses from the New Testament, an entire chapter of the Old Testament, an assortment of football and baseball statistics, a Leadbelly tune as old as the blues, and L.B.J.'s Great Society speech later, W.W.W. had finally managed to wipe the last trace of bullshit lie off of every face in the Dixie Fish. But he was beginning to think that ten cases of beer; two bottles of tequila; and an eggs, bacon, toast, and chicory coffee breakfast in bed might be pushing his trivia-for-beer prowess too far. After all, taking unfair advantage of the Strangers had been one thing; but these people were his friends. And the mad-dog glare that Gladys had been giving Tommy ever since W.W.W. had quoted the entire King James version of the Twenty-second Psalm to make it an even ten cases of Shiner Bock had gotten a little bit more rabid with every bet Tommy lost.

The Twenty-second Psalm had been Brave's idea, the Leadbelly Smiley's. But the Bible had proved to be as much a dead-end at beating W.W.W. as the blues. His mother had read the Bible to him when he was a boy, out loud and cover to cover, because his daddy wouldn't let W.W.W. go to Sunday School. And it was jazz and blues his mother had sung late at night when W.W.W. was warm in bed and feeling like the pot of gold at the end of the rainbow. But even though the Bible and the blues had been Brave and Smiley's ideas, it was Tommy who had done the betting and the losing—and it was Tommy who was the focus of Gladys's wrath.

"Tommy?" W.W.W. said. "How about let's forget the beer and tequila, and just settle up in the morning with a little breakfast in bed?"

The expression on Tommy's face was every bit as dazed and confused as he'd looked since Smiley suggested the Great Society speech that W.W.W. had reeled off without a hitch to add on the second bottle of tequila.

"Tommy?" W.W.W. stuck a hand halfway across the bar. "No beer, no booze. Just the breakfast in bed. Let's shake on it. Okay?"

Tommy set down the glass of draft he had just emptied and made a slow handstab in W.W.W.'s direction. The hand felt as wet and cold as it looked unsteady; but it reached, finally, into W.W.W.'s hand that had been patiently waiting.

"Bargain," Tommy said. The dazed and confused look on his face never changed.

Neither did the mad-dog glare on Gladys's. W.W.W. had seen two cow dogs fight to the death once, back on his daddy's ranch. The winning dog was black, with dead black eyes that never blinked even when his jaws locked onto the losing dog's throat. Gladys's eyes looked just like that.

W.W.W. wondered if he should maybe say something—try to redirect Gladys's attention onto something that might be able to stand up to her a little bit better in case she snapped. Like maybe the red brick walls of the Dixie Fish. But just then, he felt a tap on his shoulder. He let go of

Tommy's hand and turned to face Eb.

"Time for me to go on home," Eb said softly. "I'll be talking to you. Remember what I said about that gift."

W.W.W. clasped Eb's strong, callused hand. "Thanks, Eb, for everything."

"It's time for everyone to go home," Kent said. "Come on, lights out."

W.W.W. collected the chicory coffee and the Mozart CD, and he slipped the gifts into his backpack. Then they all headed out into the cold night air. There were no stars in the sky, and no moon, only the glare of the city lights reflected off the ragged cloudbottoms. W.W.W. walked with Shine around the back of the restaurant where the Dixie Fish area light glowed like a blue-green spotlight in the gloom. It shone down on W.W.W.'s maroon metal-flake and chrome motorcycle that was parked over by the dumpster, on Tommy's white import convertible that was parked next to W.W.W.'s bike, and on Gladys and Tommy—who were standing next to Tommy's convertible having what looked to be a garbage-ball fight.

W.W.W. caught Shine tight against him and pulled her back into the shadows just as Gladys dug a double-handful of paper plates and seascraps out of the dumpster, shaped it into a ball, and lobbed the garbageball at Tommy. Tommy didn't even try to dodge. He just stood there and took the seascraps straight in the face. The paper plates, falling short, bounced onto the convertible where they looked like giant blisters that had been burned into the paint.

W.W.W. started forward, feeling like he ought to do something. But Shine held him back.

"Why are you doing this?" Tommy asked, scraping hunks of uneaten fish, shrimp shells, and globs of coleslaw off of his face. "Why?"

Gladys dug back into the dumpster, came up with another double-handful of garbage, and threw it onto Tommy. Then she stomped off out of the area light without saying a word.

"Gladys?" Tommy stood by the car a while, breathing heavy. There were seascraps caked in his hair.

W.W.W. gently disengaged himself from Shine and started toward Tommy. He didn't know what he was going to do, exactly, or say—*It's alright, Tommy*; or *Let her take a walk, it'll do her good*—but he felt like he had to do or say something.

But Tommy swung his legs over the door of the top-down convertible; and before W.W.W. could say anything at all, Tommy started the car and tore off after Gladys. He left a trail of dirty paper plates fluttering in his wake.

W.W.W. walked into the space where Tommy's car had been and stood among the soiled plates and seascraps, not sure whether it was the bloody-chicken-feather stink of misfortune he was smelling or just trash. "Tommy," he said into the empty space, "it'll be alright."

"It will either be alright, or it won't," Shine said softly and took W.W.W.'s hand. "But either way, you're not responsible. You can't be your brother's keeper."

"If I won't be my brother's keeper, who will?"

Shine didn't answer. They stood hand in hand, surrounded by garbage, until the first drops of rain started to fall. Then they climbed onto the motorcycle and headed up the hill toward Hope Street. The rain blew into W.W.W.'s face cold and heavy enough now so that he had to squint to see. They rode slowly around the corner and up onto Assembly Street—and saw Tommy driving along in the convertible even slower, top down in the rain, leaning out over the doorframe and yelling at Gladys.

"Alright, we'll get one!" Tommy yelled.

Gladys stomped along the sidewalk and ignored him.

"Glad? We'll get both! Glad? Glad!"

W.W.W.'s insides felt as cold and heavy as the rain that stung his face. He felt his faith in the imminent completion of the Program for Bliss start to waver. But just then, Shine squeezed her arms tight around him. The feel of her body warm against his back and the reassuring pressure of her hands against his chest pushed the doubts out of his mind.

By the time they pulled into the front yard of the house on Hope Street, Shine's hands had found their way inside W.W.W.'s clothes. They left a trail of wet shoes and socks across the Green Room, wet pants and a wet shirt and dress across the dining room, wet boxers and wet lacy panties up the attic stairs. Until all that remained was the feel of hands on damp skin, the salt-sweet taste of Shine, and the storm that raged all night.

16. Fire

*T*hat night, W.W.W. dreamed of the fire.

The dream centers on sound. In the past that seems always present, flames roar out of control as smoke crinkles his nose like the touch of fire shrivels the skin. The setting sun mashes into the earth and burns. Billowing smoke blackens the sky, turning the burning sun blood-red. The sun spits hellfire onto the rolling plains and scrub brush; and the west wind whips up the fire, driving a wave of flame across the firebreak and up the hill toward the house that should have been safe.

Flames swallow the barn. The wood, weathered almost white, seems to explode. The fire flashes up into the sun as the hay ignites, fueling the conflagration. Then the wave of flame sweeps through the trees around the haybarn; and the leaves, dried brown by the summer drought, detonate like firebombs and feed the inferno that works its way uphill toward the house where it should have been safe.

The wave of flame leaps the road—just two sandy ruts really, with dried grass in between—and sweeps through the horse lot. The grass between the ruts feeds the fire that swallows the tack shed, the stable, the horses. Flame-colored horses with manes of fire run and scream; and now the flames are in the front yard, leaping up onto the house where she should have been safe.

The fire roars like an avenging angel as it eats the roof: *bars on the windows.* Then the flames leap a hundred feet into the air, whipping back down through the windows like an insuck of breath to roar again: *hands on the bars.*

"Jesus."

Nearby, horses scream. And he can make out, fainter and farther away, the screams of his mother.

97

"Jesus Christ," W.W.W. said. "Not again."

Half in/half out of the here and now at the house on Hope Street, W.W.W. smelled smoke. He heard dogs howling and saw the rising sun blood-red in his bedroom window. He felt Shine stir, naked and warm in his bed.

"Stay here," he said.

W.W.W. leaped out of the bed onto the cold wooden floor and felt the attic stairs dropping steeply away beneath his feet as he stumbled down into the kitchen. Smoke filled the bottom floor of the house, and there was the howling of dogs. But nothing, and no one, was moving. There was no angel-roar of fire. There were no screams. There was only the smoke.

He tried taking a breath, but he choked and then couldn't stop coughing. It felt like there were ants stinging his eyes, and W.W.W. couldn't see. He lay flat on his belly, feeling the kitchen tile cold against his cheek and his chest and his knees and the palms of his hands. He breathed deep in the envelope of clear air, and he could see again. He caught sight of Gladys and Tommy lying on the floor. Their heads were propped against the kitchen cabinets. They were not moving.

"Gladys!" W.W.W. choked out. "Tommy!"

They didn't answer, didn't move.

He crawled toward them. But seeing smoke belching out of the oven and up off the burners in clouds, W.W.W. turned aside. He reached up into the heat and shut off the oven and the burners in an arm-searing moment of fumbling. Then he ducked back under the layer of smoke, pressed his burned arms against the cool tile, buried his face between his arms, and breathed.

W.W.W. closed his eyes and stood up. He groped his way forward, edging his hands along the cabinets. The pain in his burned arms as he reached through the heat rising off of the stove made him falter. But at last he found the vent hood, flipped the switch, and heard the hum of the vent kicking on.

When he staggered sideways away from the stove, he stumbled over something soft—no, there were two soft somethings—but W.W.W. knew that he had to keep moving. He found the kitchen door and fumbled for the latch, the handle. Then he threw open the door to the back yard. He heard, through the latched screen door, the howling of dogs just outside.

W.W.W. ducked low again and breathed. Just breathed. Then he forced himself to his feet and felt his way to the sink. He unlatched the windows, flung them open wide, and ducked down once more to breathe. But he couldn't seem to stop coughing. And for a long, choking moment he believed they were all going to die.

Finally, he saw the smoke start to clear. When he felt his lungs start to work again, he realized he was sobbing. He pulled himself across the floor next to Gladys. He held his ear against her chest, and he heard her heart beating and felt her shallow breathing. Then he held his ear against Tommy's chest. Tommy was alive, too.

"Breakfast." W.W.W. pulled himself up to a sitting position and choked out great heaving sobs. "Breakfast in bed."

Next to him, Gladys coughed and rolled over onto her stomach.

Tommy coughed, kicked. Then he sat up a little against the cabinet. "The beer," Tommy choked out. Then, in between coughing, he said, "I'll buy you . . . the beer instead."

"Beer?" W.W.W. caught hold of Tommy's hair and dragged his head over next to the stove. "Our house could've burned. Brave, Reese, Gladys, you—we all could've died!" W.W.W. shook Tommy hard, banging his head against the stove.

Tommy stopped coughing and started throwing up.

"Shine could've burned," W.W.W. said. "Shine could've." He shoved Tommy's head down into the puddle of half-digested bacon and eggs that had just spewed out of Tommy's mouth.

"Walt?"

"Shine," W.W.W. said. Through the smoke that was clearing fast now, he could see her standing at the foot of the attic stairs. She was wearing one of his T-shirts. It was white. Naked underneath it, she stood looking pale and shaken.

"Walt?" she said. "You're hurting him."

Realizing that he was naked, and that he was still pressing Tommy's head down into a puddle of half-digested breakfast, W.W.W. released his grip.

"My mother called me Walt," he said. "And now you."

17. Ass and All

*I*t wasn't easy fixing things after the kitchen fire that was supposed to have been breakfast in bed. The fire, and certain events connected with it, had caused a wide range of physical and emotional damage that threatened at least three of the seven points of W.W.W.'s Program for Bliss, and that threw the possibility of reattaining a state of true bliss—which W.W.W. had achieved for so heartwrenchingly short a time in the moments between the consummation of his relationship with Shine and the outbreak of the fire—into serious doubt.

W.W.W. knew he had to do damage control, and he knew he had to do it fast.

It seemed to W.W.W. that the first part of the Program for Bliss to focus his efforts on was the 5) ROOF OVER HIS HEAD. He had learned from his own long history of healing both physical and emotional damage that emotions were tougher by far to fix. And he figured a quick victory over something purely physical would give him momentum to help deal with the bigger issues that lay ahead.

The oven was no problem really, no problem at all. Just a matter of W.W.W. doing a whole lot of wiping, buying a pair of heavy-duty electrical gloves from K-mart, causing a 220-volt short in the bowels of a major appliance—and risking ass and all in the process.

The repainting was no problem either. Once W.W.W. had cracked the seal on the fire extinguisher and strewn the better part of a box of baking soda across the oven and most of the kitchen, all that was left was to twist his fabricated "evidence" up into the kind of bullshit letter that even his daddy would've been proud to concoct—and then sit back, relax, and let the leasing company do the backwork.

Dear Bob Cratchett:

We have all almost lost our lives. Sometime last night, while we were peacefully asleep in our beds and completely vulnerable, the oven short-circuited. It was a miracle that we managed to escape unharmed. By the Grace of God, one of us woke up smelling smoke in the nick of time to put out the fire that resulted from the short-circuit. The smoke alarm failed to function. The fire extinguisher failed to function. If not for the fact of our being God-fearing, law-abiding citizens who keep a fresh box of baking soda in their refrigerator at all times, the whole house would have gone up in flames, and us with it. We need a new oven. We need a new fire extinguisher. We need our kitchen repainted. And we need someone to check the wiring on our smoke alarm (and on the rest of our major appliances) so we can sleep again at night.

Please hurry.

The Residents, 3426 Hope Street

The new stove arrived early Sunday afternoon, within two hours of W.W.W. delivering the letter to Cratchett (Don't Get Scrooged, Get Cratchett) Properties and calling the emergency number on the office door. A man came out inside of an hour after that to replace the fire alarm and the fire extinguisher, and to check the wiring on all the appliances.

As far as the letter went, the failure of the smoke alarm was the single blot of truth on an otherwise perfectly pure tissue of lies. And W.W.W. figured: Why stop there? On Monday morning, he took a motorcycle ride over to Cratchett (Don't Get Scrooged, Get Cratchett) Properties and dropped three magic words about Tommy's brother, the "personal injury attorney," in Memphis—and by noon, the house on Hope Street was full of painters. Tommy's brother was a CPA in Atlanta.

Once he had finished scrooging Bob Cratchett to the wall and the 5) ROOF OVER HIS HEAD had been dealt with, W.W.W. shifted his focus to the 6) FRIENDS part of the Program. Even after his triumphant victory over the slumlords at Cratchett (Don't Get Scrooged, Get Cratchett) Properties, and the momentum he'd gained as a result, W.W.W. knew that fixing the emotional damage inflicted by the events related to the fire was going to be a much tougher job.

For starters, Brave and Reese were not talking to Tommy because the entire house smelled like burnt breakfast. Well, that and because of the pair of beagles Tommy had never said a word about to anyone except Gladys before the afore-unsaid beagles showed up in the middle of everyone's back yard. It had been the beagles that W.W.W. heard howling out back during the kitchen fire that was supposed to have been breakfast in bed. And it was those same afore-unsaid beagles that—it seemed like to Brave and Reese at least—had done even more howling since the fire than during it.

Then there was the fact that Tommy wasn't talking to W.W.W. While Tommy's refusal to speak made it tough to be absolutely sure, W.W.W. guessed that Tommy's silence probably had a lot to do with W.W.W. banging Tommy's head against the stove, then holding it down in a puddle of half-digested breakfast. Well, that and the fact that the reason Tommy had been cooking the breakfast in the first place was so W.W.W. could eat it in bed with Shine.

Which brought W.W.W. to the 1) WOMAN part of the Program. Shine Solomon, the one and only 1) WOMAN in W.W.W.'s life, was acting as though she thought the whole bunch of them was insane. If he had known that the mere sight of him naked in the kitchen could so have affected Shine, W.W.W. would have stopped and slipped on a pair of slacks, and maybe a dinner jacket, before dashing down the stairs to save all of their lives.

And even 2) SCHOOL—which was the one part of the Program that W.W.W. had worked out even before he got to Columbia, SC—had been going steadily worse as the weeks went by. In two of his three courses, he was doing fine. All he had to do was take tests and give presentations. For someone with a phonographic memory and food and beverage experience, taking tests and giving presentations was even easier than scrooging Bob Cratchett. But his third course, an American History class that he and Reese were taking together, was shaping up to be a disaster. He'd asked Reese for help over and over again, but the help Reese had to offer wasn't the kind that W.W.W. seemed to need. Except for their mutual appreciation of academic freedom, Reese seemed to have a polar opposite view of the whole graduate school experience than W.W.W.'s. Maybe it was because Reese was double-majoring in Graduate English and Graduate History instead of choosing one or the other. Maybe it was because Reese came from a privileged background instead of a dusty piece of Southwest Texas desert. But whatever the cause, Reese seemed perfectly satisfied studying the characteristics of literary movements and the theoretical underpinnings of historical periods instead of the lives of the literary and historic. He didn't seem to care at all about the people who had written the books and made the history, or about applying the lessons of the past to the problems of the present. What possible difference could it make in the long struggle for human survival, for example, what Dr. Jones thought about Dr. Smith's comment about the problematic structure of the transcendental ideal in Thoreau's *Walden*? Wasn't the real question how we could learn to live practically, responsibly, and equally together— instead of how to go it alone?

After years, miles, and the sacrifice of almost everything from his life back west, W.W.W. had finally managed to achieve true bliss; and by achieving it, to feel in control, not only of his life, but of his past. He had then managed to maintain true bliss for what amounted, all told, to less than a single night—and for most of that time, he'd been asleep. He remembered hearing once about a man in Corpus Christi who died in a hurricane with a long-stemmed rose driven all the way through his chest. And W.W.W. had wondered, off and on, ever since he'd heard it: Did that man have time enough to smell the flower?

Probably because of his desperate need to cure the emotional ills that had been caused by the kitchen fire, Tuesday morning found W.W.W. pondering the death-by-rose question again. His most fruitful thinking had always gotten done while he was making green things grow—and as the sun rose over the trees, W.W.W. was bent over his cannabis garden hoping that today would be no exception. He sat in the Green Room taking the cannabis seedlings that had begun to sprout in rows of pale green and white shoots, transplanting them one by one into green plastic cups that he'd filled with damp potting soil, and placing the cups into a six-by-ten foot wooden frame lined with a plastic sheet. The morning sun streamed through the east-facing windows, warming the marijuana plants and W.W.W. along with them. And the death-by-rose question was getting all mixed together with green things growing and the warmth of the sun against his skin, when the plan for fixing everything struck W.W.W. with such simplicity, beauty, and power that it took his breath away.

There was power and beauty in simplicity. Indeed, the most powerful things W.W.W. had ever known were the simplest and most beautiful. After all, bliss was as powerful, and as simply beautiful, as green things growing in the morning sun. Green things growing lay at the heart of W.W.W.'s plan—well, green things that had been grown, harvested, dried, bagged, and then smoked through a waterpipe. The plan was simple, beautiful, and powerful enough to get everyone back together and make them happy with one another again. And in restoring domestic bliss to the house on Hope Street, the plan would repair the emotional damage to the 6) FRIENDS and 1) WOMAN parts of the Program for Bliss. This in turn could induce Reese to give W.W.W. some help that would prove to be of real use with 2) SCHOOL.

If the plan worked, that is. But the plan, W.W.W. knew, could also fail.

In a perfect world, simplicity plus industry adds up to foolproof.

This was a saying that W.W.W. had heard his daddy spout again and again (usually while watching W.W.W. apply the industry to some simply backbreaking task or other). But as the son of a bitch had always gone on to say—and as W.W.W. had had ample opportunity to discover on his own —the world was too full of fools to be proof against anything. This was especially true of any situation that involved the U.S. Government.

And that, W.W.W. knew, posed a potential problem. Except in documented medical cases involving radiation and/or chemotherapy, the use of marijuana was against the law. What with leisure time cut in half, the multiplication of two-income households, and the rise of China, even the least bit too much rest and relaxation—except in those cases where rest was about to become peaceful, and relaxation permanent—might well mean the end of The American Way. To keep this from happening, the U.S. Government was prepared to fill the prisons with slothful, unpatriotic potheads who were probably also Communists.

It wasn't the U.S. Government itself, though, that W.W.W. feared so much as the effect the U.S. Government's statutes might have on certain housemates. Reese and Tommy came from too much money, and too many private schools, to be much bothered by a misdemeanor or two. And he couldn't see Gladys fearing anything except maybe God. But Brave's daddy had named him after the national anthem—and that could prove to be a complicating factor when it came down to putting W.W.W.'s simple, beautiful, and powerful potsmoking plan into action.

But W.W.W. felt like he had to do something. And it was hard to imagine how things could get any worse. At least if they were arguing about marijuana, they'd be talking again.

So W.W.W. climbed up into the attic and brought out the rainbow-colored bong he had bought at a head shop called Onward Through the Fog in New Orleans. He brought out the half-ounce bag of marijuana that was all that remained—besides the seeds he'd saved back and planted—of the cannabis harvest he'd made in Atlanta. He carried the bong and the pot down into the living room and hid them in the corner behind Reese's dried-blood-colored recliner.

Then he drew up three signs and posted them in the three most looked-at areas of the house on Hope Street, or any other American domicile: the television set, the refrigerator door, and the bathroom mirror. They read:

> ROOMMATE MEETING
> 9 P.M.
> FREE REFRESHMENTS

18. The Beginning of the End of Everything

"There are beagles in our back yard," Reese said. "They are raucous, odious creatures. We are not happy."

"Damn straight," Brave said.

W.W.W. had to admit that this was pretty much what he'd been thinking himself. From the time he'd taped up the ROOMMATE MEETING 9 P.M. FREE REFRESHMENTS signs, to the time Brave and Reese had become the first roommates to arrive, the beagles had been howling like fallen angels announcing the Apocalypse. Once he was done admitting it, W.W.W. went to the kitchen and got three beers.

"Those strident canines howl throughout the day," Reese said.

"And the bastards howl all night," Brave said.

Once again, W.W.W. was forced to agree.

Reese and Brave sat with their eyes narrowed, their jaws thrust forward and locked. They looked like a lynch mob about to wreak all manner of havoc on W.W.W.'s plan to restore domestic bliss. He popped open the beers, then reached over and restarted the Beethoven CD that he'd loaded into the CD player earlier in an effort to drown out the howling in the back yard.

"What do you think we should do?" W.W.W. asked.

"I would like to propose that some form of drastic action be taken."

"I say the sons of bitches have to go."

"But there's a lot to be said for compromise," W.W.W. said without missing a beat. Then he paused, as much to collect himself as to let the Beethoven take effect. While "The Emperor Concerto" spun a soothing web of strings and winds, he took a slug of beer. "We all have to live together, don't we? All those creatures want, really, is to come inside. Couldn't we just let them in for a little while? Just into the kitchen." He tried to make eye contact, but both Brave and Reese still had their eyes locked straight ahead. "'Blessed are the peacemakers, for they shall be called the children of God.'"

"Reese, here, is allergic to frigging dog fur."

"I once had a convulsion after petting a great-aunt's Pomeranian."

W.W.W. almost choked on his beer. "I'm terribly sorry," he said once he'd gotten his breath back. And sorry he was—but not so much for Reese as for the dwindling prospects that his simple, powerful, and beautiful plan would restore domestic bliss to the house on Hope Street. W.W.W. had been counting on beer, Beethoven, and the Bible quote to deliver a knock-out blow to the anti-beagle initiative.

"Our problems, however, range far beyond a mere allergic reaction to fur." Reese snorted violently, as though the mere thought of the beagles was enough to send his sinuses running wild. "Even a reaction as violent as my own."

"They hog up the bathroom," Brave said.

"The beagles?" W.W.W. asked.

"Gladys and Tommy," Reese snorted.

"I thought," W.W.W. said, "that we agreed to take turns in the bath-room."

"This was also our understanding."

"But the sons of bitches cheat."

"Cheat?" W.W.W. asked. "How?"

"While the party of the first part—"

"—frigging Tommy—"

"—is still engaged in showering, the party of the second part—"

"—son of a bitching Gladys—"

"—is engaged in sleeping in. Then, after a pre-arranged signal—"

"—frigging Tommy flushes the john—"

"—the party of the second part rushes from bed to shower, while the party of the first part completes his morning toilet—"

"—frigging Tommy brushes his bastard teeth while son of a bitching Gladys uses up the last damn drop of hot water."

"Couldn't they just shower together?" W.W.W. asked.

"I'm afraid that brings up an even larger problem."

"Damn straight."

"Which is?" W.W.W. asked.

"The rhythmic, thumping din which issues from their bedroom throughout all hours of the day and night."

On that note, W.W.W. brought out the bong. He'd been hoping to hold the bong in reserve until Gladys and Tommy arrived; but if things were going to come down to a fight—the beer, the Beethoven, and the Bible having let him down—W.W.W. would rather it happened now, before Tommy and Gladys came home and Gladys waded into the middle of it. After what he'd seen at the Dixie Fish dumpster, W.W.W. didn't want Gladys wading into the middle of anything. Even if Brave had been named after the last word of "The Star-Spangled Banner," it was time to play the marijuana card.

"So we won't let the beagles into the house." W.W.W. didn't even look at Brave as he said it. Instead, he held the bong in his lap, struck a match, and lit the bowl that was already packed. He took a hit, held it for a long moment, then blew a cloud of potsmoke out into the room. Still not looking at Brave, W.W.W. pulled the baggie out from behind the recliner and repacked the bowl. Then he passed the bong and matches to Reese. "But does that necessarily mean that the dogs have to go?"

Reese sat on a charcoal-colored love seat with his legs splayed straight out in front of him. He held the bong in one hand and the matches in the other. He seemed to be lost in thought.

"The carburetor's right there in front," W.W.W. prompted. "Right there where your forefinger is."

But Reese just sat and stared at the bong.

W.W.W. leaned over, finally, and took the matches. "Here you go," he said, striking a match and steadying his hand over the bowl. The flame worked its way steadily up the match while Reese sat and stared. W.W.W. somehow managed to keep his hand steady as he watched his entire lifelong search for true bliss flash and fade in the fire. San Antonio, New Orleans, and Atlanta all went up in the blue and yellow flame that was working its way toward Columbia now. He felt the heat scorch his nails as the heart of the fire reached for his fingertips, and Reese was still not smoking. He thought again about Brave being named after the last word of the national anthem. And he felt the fight coming, felt domestic bliss smoldering, felt the entire Program for Bliss turning to ash—when Brave snatched the bong out of Reese's hand and took the hit himself, "Star Spangled Banner" and all.

Brave drew in potsmoke. Bongwater bubbled. Then Brave held—and held, and held—in the potsmoke, his cheeks reddening and his eyes squinting tight. Finally, he exhaled a great blue-gray cloud and handed the bong back to W.W.W.

"They never even said a word to anybody," Brave said without coughing. "Just went ahead, solo, and stuck them bastard puppies in all of our back yard."

"We'll make sure," W.W.W. said, "that they keep the beagles quiet."

"But what about the hot water monopolization? What about the carnal din?"

"We'll talk to them," W.W.W. said. "I'm sure they'll understand."

"And the house? Tommy damn near burned down our house."

"He was under a lot of pressure," W.W.W. said. Then he repacked the bowl, handed the bong to Reese, and lit another match before Reese had time to say anything about his allergies.

This time, Reese didn't hesitate. His mouth was on the bong even before the match was over the bowl, so that it was all W.W.W. could do to keep the match lit until the coughing started.

"We might all have been horribly injured," Reese said, once the coughing had subsided enough for him to breathe again.

"Injured?" Brave said. "Hell, boy, we almost roasted alive." But then he picked up his beer, took a long encouraging pull, and looked at W.W.W. "What kind of pressure?"

"She hit him in the face with garbage."

"What?"

"Whom?"

"Gladys," W.W.W. said. "Whom do you think? She scooped a double-handful of garbage out of the Dixie Fish dumpster and slung it into Tommy's face. Then she did it again. He was covered with uneaten seafood. She even got it all over his car."

"What the hell did Tommy do?"

"He stood there and took it," W.W.W. said, "until she stomped off."

"What followed?"

"Tommy did. He followed her up the hill in his car."

"The poor dumb bastard."

"Highly, highly unfortunate."

W.W.W. took the bong from Reese, repacked it, and passed it to

Brave.

"They got into it at the bar, too," Brave said. "She called him *pencil dick*. In front of everybody."

"Is it any wonder he tried to burn down the house?" W.W.W. asked.

"A classic manifestation of the Freudian death wish."

"Poor dumb son of a bitch."

"But what can we, as his roommates, do to help rebuild Tommy's shattered self-confidence?" W.W.W. asked.

"Surround him with good fellowship," Reese said.

"Make him feel like a bull instead of a steer," Brave said.

W.W.W. nodded as he repacked the bong, feeling his own self-confidence starting to return. Things were finally going according to plan.

But just as W.W.W. was beginning to bask in a springwarm rush of renewed domestic bliss, Gladys burst in through the front door. She rolled across the Green Room and into the living room like a blue norther across the Southwest Texas plains, howling as she came: "You're smoking pot! You're smoking pot! We could see you all the way out in the street!"

Wind-blown, half-buried in grocery bags, Tommy staggered in just behind Gladys.

It was, W.W.W. knew, another moment of truth. He quickly got up and drew the blinds. He turned the Beethoven up a couple of notches. Then, mouthing a prayer to bliss for compromise that was every bit as fervent as it was silent, he handed the bong to Gladys, took one of the grocery bags from Tommy, and held his breath.

It couldn't have taken any longer than the massacre at Wounded Knee. But it seemed every bit as long as the Trail of Tears—the Indians had tried the peacepipe, too; and look what it had gotten them—before W.W.W. heard the sound of bongwater starting to bubble. He saw Reese change seats to make room for Gladys. He heard Brave offer Gladys a beer. He felt the spirit of compromise settling over the living room like a mother dove onto her nest.

W.W.W. followed Tommy toward the kitchen, looking for the right moment to implement part two of his plan: the apology. But as they set the bags down on the counter, the lingering smell of burnt breakfast was so overpowering that W.W.W. couldn't think straight. This was doubly inconvenient, as it was precisely because of the smell—and, of course, because of his holding Tommy's head in a puddle of half-digested bacon and eggs—that W.W.W. needed to be clearheaded to begin with.

The irony was not lost on W.W.W. "Tommy," he said at last, "why don't we step out back?"

"Yep."

It occurred to W.W.W. as they walked out into the back yard—and were immediately set upon by two black-and-brown-and-white blurs of tongues and claws—that this single syllable was the first word Tommy had said to him since the fire.

"Good boys," W.W.W. said to the dogs, gritting his teeth and thanking his lucky stars that he'd worn jeans. "Or good girls."

"There's one of each," Tommy said.

"Right. Look, Tommy. I'm sorry for holding your head down in vomit."

"It's okay," Tommy said. "I'm sorry for almost burning the house down."

"It's okay," W.W.W. said. He stuck a hand out in Tommy's direction and felt Tommy's hand, covered in dog drool, slide into his own. It wasn't a perfect apology, but at least it was sincere. Satisfied, W.W.W. led Tommy back inside.

"We passed Shine on the way over," Tommy said. "She'll be here any minute."

"Thanks for the heads-up." W.W.W. opened the first of the grocery bags and started putting things away. "Now carry a couple of these beers into the living room, why don't you."

"But Gladys told me to—"

"I've got this," W.W.W. said. "Go."

When W.W.W. walked back into the living room, Tommy was sitting on the floor and drinking whiskey straight out of the bottle. Reese sat in the blood-colored recliner next to the love seat, sipping beer. Brave sat on the floor close to Tommy. Both Brave and Reese were now talking to Tommy—but whether they were rebuilding his self-confidence, surrounding him with good fellowship, or making him feel like a bull instead of a steer was one too many for W.W.W.

He had just caught sight of Shine. She sat on the love seat next to Gladys in a rainbow-colored sweater-dress that exactly matched the rainbow-colored bong in her lap. Seeing Shine, all W.W.W. could do was stop and stare—things having been more than a little awkward between them since the kitchen fire that was supposed to have been breakfast in bed.

"Hello . . ." he started, finally. "Um . . ."

Then Shine looked up at him with eyes that were the color of late afternoon sun, and motioned him over.

As W.W.W. settled onto the arm of the love seat next to Shine, everything went Valentine's all over again. The love seat felt warm as a bed, winter-blanketed. The scent of burnt breakfast faded. He could almost smell the coffee brewing. All around him, he heard the sound of voices that he knew. And it was home, finally. Home and true bliss, after a lifetime spent looking.

"Now that we're all friends again," Gladys said, "let's do something fun."

"What could we do?" Shine asked.

"We could watch *Independence Day* on DVD," Brave said.

"We might listen to my new *Götterdämerung* CD," Reese said.

Gladys leaned forward on the love seat. "Let's play quarters," she said. "Tommy just bought an assload of beer."

Tommy sat quietly on the floor, drinking whiskey and starting to fade.

"*Independence Day.*"

"*Götterdämerung.*"

"Quarters."

"W.W.," Shine said, "what do you think we should do?"

"Go to bed while we still feel good about each other."

"Be serious," Shine said. "Come on."

But W.W.W. was being serious—anyway, about the going to bed part. There was nothing he wanted more at this moment than some quality alone time with Shine. He didn't want to say or do anything, though, that might breathe a chill into the warm air of friendship that permeated the room. He looked again at Tommy, who looked now to be on the verge of passing out.

"It's Tommy's entertainment center," W.W.W. said. "I think we should let him decide."

"Let's play . . ." Tommy said and drooped. "Let's play . . ."

"Poker," Brave said. "Let's play poker."

19. Poker

"*L*et's play poker!" Gladys said.

"Poker!" Tommy said.

"Indeed," Reese said.

Even Shine said she'd like to watch.

"Let's don't," W.W.W. said, feeling a cold wind blow through the warm, fuzzy feelings that had permeated the living room from the time domestic bliss had been restored up to the moment Brave had spoken the word *poker*. W.W.W. knew from long experience that one of the strongest anti-bliss forces on earth was gambling losses. "It's late. We're all tired. And we haven't got any poker chips."

"Hell, you've got poker chips," Brave said. "I watched you carry some in."

"Would you mind running up and fetching them down?" Reese asked. "While you're at it, fetch that deck of cards I saw you carry in as well." Long-blonde-haired and dressed in blue, like Custer, W.W.W. realized that he had been surrounded and cut off by forces inimical to domestic bliss. He cursed whiskey in general. He cursed Brave in particular. Then he tried to come up with an emergency back-up plan to avert the impending massacre. He climbed slowly into the attic, looking for inspiration. But all he saw was rented furniture, old clothes, and history books. He looked again, seeing the same things he'd seen the last frantic look-around.

So he picked up the cards and poker chips, and he headed downstairs to get scalped—when all of a sudden he caught sight of a gray dollar-bill-sized slip of paper with neat black boxes sitting on his desk. It was the deposit slip for the three hundred dollars he'd won off the Strangers, and the sight of it was even lovelier than a cavalry troop riding to his rescue: all that gambling money, won labor-free from rich people who hadn't even felt the loss, was exactly what he needed to save the day for domestic bliss. They would play poker all right. But he himself would play to lose. And that three hundred dollars, spread liberally among his housemates, should buy enough goodwill to counteract the combined anti-bliss forces of poker and whiskey until everyone was ready to go to bed. W.W.W. didn't much like the idea of playing to lose. But he told himself it was the bargain of a lifetime: three hundred pain-free, victim-free dollars for household peace in his time.

W.W.W. carried the poker stuff down to the dining room table; and once they'd all gathered around, he told everyone that he would like to be the banker. He guessed a credit union was closer to what he had mind—spreading economic benefits as equally as possible in the presence of human greed—but he wasn't about to risk his rescue plan on a definition. He sold chips to Brave, Tommy, Gladys, and Reese. W.W.W. drew fifty dollars worth for himself. Then he passed the cards to Tommy, who had put on his lucky Jack Daniels cap; and while Tommy shuffled and dealt, W.W.W. loaded the bong and passed it to Brave. The betting started.

And W.W.W. started to lose.

He was careful to pace himself, spreading his bigger losses around the table as evenly as possible. He dealt five card draw, deuces wild, every time the deck came around. He anted, dealt the first round of cards, and raised the first bet. Then he discarded his deuces, kept anything he had natural just to make it look good, and called every bet up to the show. It was simple. It was beautiful. It was powerful. It was an every-round bailout-sized cash infusion for the other players that would break the credit union incrementally—shortening the game without it being too obvious.

Even though it galled in W.W.W.'s guts gambling and losing, he occupied his mind by finding ways to make losing interesting. He kept the bong moving. He studied pokerfaces, cataloguing tells: Brave never made eye contact when he was holding three of a kind or better; Reese clinched his chin when he was bluffing; Tommy twitched his left cheek when he drew bad cards; and Gladys, who had never played poker for money in her life, telegraphed every hand with an eye-popping variety of facial movements that were like a how-not-to guide for betting on cards. Every couple of times around the table, on top of his regular five card draw, deuces wild, W.W.W. called "Loser has to go change the stereo." So at least he was enjoying the music.

W.W.W. kept the pace smooth and even, syncopating his losses with the cool jazz rhythms of Miles Davis, Gil Evans, and Dave Brubeck. The Strangers' money slowly worked its bliss-rescuing way around the table. The bong went around and around. Everyone looked stoned and happy behind their steadily growing piles of chips, and the aroma of potsmoke covered almost completely the smell of burnt breakfast from the kitchen. Brave won. Reese won. Tommy and Gladys won. Shine sat next to W.W.W. and enjoyed the show. After a couple of hours, W.W.W. switched the music to the sultry torch songs of Billie Holiday. He was now mostly folding his ante and looking forward—with steadily rising anticipation—to the fast-approaching moment when the credit union would go bust and he could go upstairs with Shine, leaving Gladys and Tommy and Brave and Reese to bask in the glow of their winnings while he basked in the glow of true bliss.

But then the people around the table started to look at him funny. Every time he folded his ante, W.W.W. saw the other players' faces tighten a little more. He tried just shrugging it off. But before long, it was obvious that people were getting suspicious.

The only exception was Tommy. He sat at the head of the table behind a pile of blue chips and a smile of complete satisfaction, taking what came.

But next to Tommy sat Gladys, with a look of first-time-poker general mistrust. Next to Gladys sat Brave, with an eyes-creased, just-short-of-outright-accusing glare. And next to Brave sat Reese, whose sour lip-pucker made it clear that he thought he was being suckered.

Finally, there was Shine—who knew how W.W.W. had fared at trivia-for-beers and football with the Strangers; and who had seen W.W.W. take Tommy for ten cases of beer, two bottles of tequila, and a bacon, eggs, and coffee breakfast in bed. She kept leaning against W.W.W. and sliding him sly half-smiles that shouted: *I know what you're doing! You're suckering these people!* to anybody who bothered to look. It happened every time W.W.W. lost a good-sized pot; and every time, it seemed like somebody was looking.

All of a sudden, the air started to get kind of thick.

W.W.W. couldn't believe it. Here he sat giving these people his money, his time, and the last of his marijuana. Here he sat in front of the 1) WOMAN he loved, losing hand after hand like he didn't know any better. And all this was on top of his crawling into an oven with just a pair of wirecutters and 220 volts of electricity for company, and risking ass and all to restore domestic bliss to his housemates on Hope Street—at no cost to them whatsoever. W.W.W. felt less angry than hurt. But hurt has a habit of turning angry, a habit that ingratitude and misplaced suspicion don't exactly hinder.

Just then Shine leaned over, half-smiling, and Judas-kissed his cheek. Faces tightened around the table. The air of suspicion thickened. And W.W.W. felt a little less hurt and a lot more angry.

He tried to keep his mind on the Program for Bliss. Bliss and growing greens, he thought. Three hundred pain-free, victim-free dollars, he thought. *Simplicity plus industry adds up to foolproof.* Between himself and his daddy, W.W.W. was almost convinced.

Anyway, he would've been, if not for Tommy. A change had come over Tommy as his pile of chips had grown into the biggest stack on the table. He had turned his lucky cap around backwards, and now he sat—bleary in a head-backwards Jack Daniels cap—dipping snuff, drinking whiskey, and not letting well enough be.

"No balls," Tommy said. "No, wait." Then he laughed. "Capon balls." He was looking at W.W.W. "Chicken balls."

W.W.W. kept his mouth shut and folded with three aces.

But then Brave started in on the next hand. "I'll raise two more dollars to chickenshit," he said. Then he winked at W.W.W. "You know, chicken-shit never did pay the banker."

At least, W.W.W. thought, it wasn't the eyes-creased, just-short-of-outright-accusing glare that Brave had been turning on him for the last hour. He kept his mouth shut and folded a flush.

But all through the next hand, Gladys wouldn't stop laughing. "Chickenshit," she snorted. "Capon balls."

W.W.W. bit down hard on his tongue and folded a full house.

Then he saw the mocking laughter that had worked its way around the table reflected in Shine's eyes—and that playing to lose crap wore all the way through. W.W.W. had dug himself into a $265.50 hole at quarter-ante poker, and had been about to fold a natural straight-flush in a hand of five card stud, deuces wild. But the look in Shine's eyes changed his mind.

Tommy, who was showing three aces and a king, had dealt W.W.W. the ten, nine, eight, and seven of hearts, face-up. Tommy slugged whiskey, raised five dollars for the second time that hand, and then laughed at

W.W.W. from over a mountain of blue chips that used to be W.W.W.'s.

"See five," W.W.W. said, "raise ten." His hole-card was the jack of hearts.

"Bluff," Tommy said, and laughed. "Bluff, bluff, bluff." He threw ten blue dollar chips into the pot.

Brave piled in twenty blue dollar chips. He was showing two pair. "Raise five more," he said. Then he looked over at the withered stack of chips in front of W.W.W. "Those couple of little pots you won a while ago ain't helping much now. Are they?"

W.W.W. called the bet, flipped the jack of hearts, and watched Brave's and Tommy's faces wilt. "Why don't we up the ante to a dollar?" he said.

From there on out, W.W.W. kept his mouth shut, kept his mind on cards and his eyes on pokerfaces, and kept winning money.

Tommy kept drinking whiskey. And as the chips started to flow back in W.W.W.'s direction, the whiskey bottle started to move around the table. Gladys drank whiskey. Brave drank whiskey. Reese mixed himself a stiff one with a trickle of Perrier. Shine drank whiskey over ice, and she wasn't even in the game.

W.W.W. was drinking water. In an hour, he was back to about seventy-five dollars down. "Why don't we stop right now?" he asked. "It looks like everybody's stack but mine is just about back to where it started, plus a blue chip or two for time and effort."

"Streak," Tommy said. "Streak, streak, streak." Tobacco juice dribbled down his chin. He was too drunk to notice.

Brave, though, had a look about him that was a bleary kind of crafty. "Have a whiskey, W.W.," he whiskeybreath whispered. "C'mon."

"Come on, have some whiskey," they all echoed. "Come on and have a shot of whiskey, W.W."

"I don't want any whiskey," W.W.W. said.

"Chicken shit," Gladys snorted. "Capon balls."

"All right," W.W.W. said. "Let's up the ante to two dollars."

They gave up trying to feed him whiskey. But they didn't slow up any, drinking it themselves. Around 2 a.m., the checkbooks started coming out. W.W.W. was now up $115.75, and the bloody-chicken-feather stink of misfortune had started to creep into the air.

"Let's stop," W.W.W. said. "It's late. And everybody is down except Brave and me."

"Streak!" Tommy said. "Streak! Streak!"

"It's the ante," Gladys said. "Let's up the ante again."

"It's the music," Brave whiskeybreath whispered. "It's just the music. That's all." So they upped the ante to five dollars and changed the music. They went from K.D. Lang to Tchaikovsky to R.E.M. But they went right on drinking whiskey.

The clock went past 3 a.m.

W.W.W.'s winnings went up to $201.25.

The household went to war.

The music got louder, and it got changed faster and faster. There was a new CD with every hand W.W.W. won. Everybody bawled out whoever had just changed whatever to whatever else—Jimi Hendrix to Verdi, Verdi to Little Richard, Little Richard to the Rolling Stones, the Rolling Stones to Hank Williams, Jr.—and the smell of bloody chicken feathers now filled the air.

"Let's stop," W.W.W. said. "I'm going to stop."

"You can't stop," Brave said. "You've got these people's money."

"Can't . . ." Tommy said. "Money . . ."

"Let's raise the ante," Gladys said, "to five dollars."

"We already did," W.W.W. said.

Then Reese put on *Götterdämerung*, and the beagles went insane. Twin fire sirens howled in the back yard, a German diva howled Wagner at 150 watts per channel, and a houseful of whiskey-sodden people howled at each other. Everybody threw down their cards. Gladys and Tommy staggered into the back yard after the beagles. Reese lurched into the living room after the compact disc player. Shine headed up the attic stairs. The music stopped. All the howling, even the fire sirens in the back yard, came to a halt.

W.W.W. sat at the table behind a mound of chips, cash, and personal checks. He had won $322.50. Brave sat to his right, counting chips. Brave was the only one besides W.W.W. who had any chips left to count.

It was Wednesday morning, almost dawn. And it was finally quiet in the house on Hope Street. But sitting there in the silence that was less a relief than a $322.50 kick in the pants, W.W.W. still heard music. It was Beethoven that he heard. "The Emperor Concerto" that had been playing earlier that day—when W.W.W. was piecing back together the domestic bliss that had just exploded again—spun round and round on the twenty-four-hour CD player in his head, weaving a soothing web of strings and winds.

But instead of soothed, W.W.W. felt sick. Especially about the checks. There were seven of them. Tommy had written three, and Gladys and Reese had written two each. They were all made out to W.W. WOOD-COCK. And they ate at his insides like duodenal ulcers.

W.W.W. couldn't understand why he felt so bad about beating his housemates at poker. They had asked for it. No, they had goaded him into it. Every last one of them had practically begged W.W.W. to take their money. Hadn't they?

But Beethoven spun. W.W.W.'s insides burned. And he decided, for the sake of Beethoven and any hope of domestic bliss that might be left, that he would tear up the checks.

It was exactly then that he heard the noise.

The noise wasn't Beethoven. Beethoven had stopped playing "The Emperor Concerto" on the twenty-four-hour CD player in W.W.W.'s head the minute he made up his mind to shred the checks.

The noise was, in fact, absolutely anti-Beethoven. Anti-bliss. Anti-life.

It reminded W.W.W., all of a sudden, of the Opera People with their billy clubs—a hollow thunking sound that he connected, somewhere in the back of his mind, with an axe breaking through bone into soft flesh.

It was coming from the back yard.

20. Snakebit

W.W.W. didn't know what to do. He had a terrible feeling that Gladys was killing Tommy. Or else, that Tommy had finally gotten a bellyful of verbal and physical abuse, and was killing Gladys. Either way, W.W.W. felt like he ought to do something, in a hurry, to put a stop to it.

But Shine was waiting for him upstairs.

And it seemed to W.W.W. that at this crucial juncture, his relationship with the 1) WOMAN in his life had to take priority, Program-wise, even over the 6) FRIENDS he was trying to work with to shape the 5) ROOF OVER HIS HEAD into a home. Besides, as Shine had said back at the Dixie Fish dumpster after the garbageball fight that had resulted from Gladys and Tommy's last run-in, W.W.W. was not his brother's keeper: it wasn't his responsibility to fix other people's problems.

So why, W.W.W. wondered, did he feel so awful sitting there and doing nothing? All he wanted at that moment was to huddle up with people he trusted—like the waitstaff had done on W.W.W.'s first night at the Dixie Fish when the Opera People started wielding those billy clubs— and take comfort in shared human concern over the undeserved awfulness that so often strikes the innocent and unsuspecting. W.W.W. glanced at Brave, hoping to see some shock, some disbelief, a little human concern that he could share.

But Brave's face looked completely calm. Tranquil, unconcerned, unhurried, Brave finished counting his chips. Then he slid three stacks of red, white, and blue poker chips in W.W.W.'s direction.

"Twenty-five even," Brave said.

W.W.W. couldn't believe it. He tried to tell himself that between the whiskey and the marijuana, Brave had drunk and smoked himself numb. But Brave sat there looking clear-eyed—not bleary, as W.W.W. had thought earlier—and crafty. He met W.W.W.'s glance with a steady reptile stare.

The thunking sound came again, like an axe into flesh, from the back yard. Brave's eyes never blinked, never looked away. Black as the eyes of a diamondback rattler, they sized W.W.W. up in a predatory glare.

"Twenty-five even," Brave said again.

The thunking sound came again from the back yard. But this time, the flesh felt like W.W.W.'s. He snatched a twenty-dollar bill and a five from his pile of winnings, and he threw them at Brave. Then W.W.W. ran into the kitchen alone.

Through the big pane of glass in the kitchen door, W.W.W. caught sight of Gladys. She lay on her back in the grass. Tommy, astride Gladys, pinned her arms against the Grecian garage. The area light turned every-thing in the back yard—the Doric columns, the plaster gods, Tommy and Gladys—a sickly blue-green as Tommy brought his face down hard against Gladys's face. It looked more like a head-butt than any kind of intimacy W.W.W. had ever seen. A face-butt. Then Tommy pressed his mouth over Gladys's mouth.

W.W.W. saw Gladys twist her face away. She bucked, barrel-rolled, and swung up astride of Tommy. She pinned his arms into the grass. Then she tore her right arm free of Tommy's grip and brought her fist down hard into Tommy's face. It was a short, tight punch; as good a clip as W.W.W. had ever seen. The sound was like an axe biting into flesh.

The two of them were no more than forty feet from where W.W.W. stood. In the kitchen, the smell of burnt breakfast and the bloody-chicken-feather stink of misfortune blended together with the bile-colored area light from the back yard. The belly-churning mélange perfectly comple-mented the sound of Gladys's fist against Tommy's face.

Then the beagles started to howl. And as if those twin fire sirens were a signal, Tommy wrenched and bucked. He rolled up, knelt astride Gladys, and pinned her arms against the Grecian garage. Next Tommy ripped open the front of Gladys's blouse, baring her breasts. He tore off the blouse and tossed it across the yard. Then Tommy face-butted Gladys again and covered her mouth with his.

Gladys lay still in the grass. Her head, and one arm, were pinned against the Grecian garage. This time, she didn't twist. She didn't wrench or roll. With her free arm, she reached up and tore open the front of

Tommy's shirt. Then she pulled his face down between her breasts.

"I'll take Gladys," Brave whiskeybreath whispered over W.W.W.'s shoulder.

W.W.W. didn't so much as flinch at the sudden and unexpected sound of Brave's voice. He couldn't move, couldn't take his eyes off the scene in the back yard.

"What the hell are you talking about?" W.W.W. managed at last.

"A friendly wager," Brave whiskeybreath whispered, "about who winds up on top. You take Tommy. I'll take Gladys. C'mon, I'll even give you odds. Two to one, for the twenty-five dollars I walked away from the poker table with."

As they were talking, W.W.W. caught sight of Brave's reflection in the pane of glass in the kitchen door. Brave's cold reptile eyes and his whiskey-breath whisper seemed to bore through W.W.W.'s ears and into his skull— tearing through cartilage and flesh until it felt like there was a snake in his head. W.W.W. could feel the snake sinking its fangs into the back of his forehead. He could feel it coiling its tail around the roots of his eyes. He couldn't make out the snake's body there in the dark space behind his retinas, but its face looked just like Brave's.

"You said earlier that Gladys and Tommy got into an argument at the Dixie Fish bar on Valentine's night," W.W.W. said, "just before they went outside and Gladys pelted Tommy with garbage. You said that she called him *pencil dick*. What was it that they were arguing about?"

"Tommy losing ass and all to you at trivia-for-beers. What else?"

"Then why on earth did you suggest that poker game tonight?"

"Why did you win it?" Brave poked a finger over W.W.W.'s shoulder as Gladys, naked and bloody, swung up astride of Tommy and pinned his arms in the grass. "It's not too late to take my friendly wager," Brave whiskeybreath whispered. Then he laughed out loud.

21. My Bucket's Got a Hole in It

*J*t was Thursday night, W.W.W.'s first shift back at the Dixie Fish after Valentine's Saturday, burnt-breakfast Sunday, scrooging-Cratchett Monday, and poker Tuesday. And as much as it pained him to say so, it felt good to be out of the house.

As things wound down toward the close of business, the Dixie Fish waitfloor was running smooth as a Caddy on cruise control. Everbody looked happy to be along for the ride. The mood had been laid-back, the customers had been friendly, and the waitstaff had worked as one. There had been no fires, no beagles, and no poker games. Everyone had made good tips that they were about to share equally, over discount draft beer, once the clean-up was finished. Even Tommy, staring past a pair of split lips and a swollen nose, had performed his duties with what bordered on alacrity. Gladys had the night off.

Everybody looked happy as things wound down, that is, except Kent. Which was strange, because Kent had started out the night looking borderline ecstatic. The first thing W.W.W. had noticed as he walked in the double front doors was that the heater was on—which was strange in and of itself, Kent usually relying on heat from the kitchen to warm the place—and the February Dixie Fish, instead of cold and dank like was normal at the beginning of a shift, felt as warm and toasty as the flushed and friendly look on Kent's face.

Kent had made small talk. He'd asked how things were going at the house on Hope Street. His face had lit up like a kid's face on Christmas morning while he watched, from the corner of the waitwindow, Bonnie's tight red skirt at the top of the stool as she leaned in, reached up over her head, and chalked specials.

But as the night got later and the crowd tapered off, the Christmas slow-leaked out of Kent's face. His head darted back and forth from the cash register to the sparsely peopled waitfloor. His face slowly puckered until it looked as though he'd swallowed a shot of rotten eggnog.

W.W.W., having seen the Old Testament type of devastation the cost-cutting whims of management could visit on the rank and file, spent the last forty-five minutes of his waitshift in the far corner of the waitstation. He combined plastic cups; plastic lids; and shredded, mayonnaise-covered produce to make coleslaw setups for tomorrow's lunch shift. He poured the unused "drawn butter" set-ups back into the jug of buttery-flavored vegetable oil. He asked Bonnie to run his last two food orders. Kent would never in his life, W.W.W. told himself, downsize a woman in a tight red skirt.

Their closing duties done, the waitstaff huddled up in the waitstation corner where W.W.W. had cupped enough slaw set-ups to last through the weekend. Tommy came out from behind the bar and huddled up with them. Last call had been given, and checks were down on the last two tables. The discount draft beer couldn't possibly start flowing too soon. It sounded as though Kent had started throwing things in the kitchen.

W.W.W. felt his stomach churn with every clang and pankle of slamming pans. And Alisha wasn't doing much to soothe the churning. She seemed to think that Kent's pan-throwing was funny.

"Poor old Pillsbury," Alisha snorted. Ever since W.W.W. had told them about the day he'd come in to fill out an application and seen Kent looking like the Pillsbury Doughboy in that dirty red apron, Alisha had taken to calling him *Pillsbury*.

"As busy a Thursday as we've ever had," Bonnie snorted back, "and you'd think Pillsbury was going hungry." It echoed through the Dixie Fish like a P.A. announcement through a deserted bus station at 3 a.m. "YOU'D THINK THAT PILLSBURY WAS GOING HUNGRY! . . . UNGRY! . . . GRY!"

Kent poked his face—all pouty cheeks and puckered lips—out of the waitwindow as Bonnie's echo bounced its way into the kitchen.

When she caught sight of him, Bonnie announced that it wasn't the Pillsbury Doughboy Kent looked like after all, but "A PISSED-OFF MISS PIGGY! . . . IGGY! . . . GY!"

Alisha laughed. Bonnie laughed. Even Tommy laughed through his split lips. Kent jerked his head back into the kitchen. There came again the clang and pankle of slamming pans.

W.W.W.'s stomach stepped up its churning another notch. Then all those bubbles in his belly started to burn.

Just then, Smiley popped out of the kitchen with his glasses hanging low on his nose and his apron hiked up to his armpits. The apron pooched out over his belly like a maternity dress. With his cheeks puffed out and his face puckered up in an imitation of Kent, Smiley pranced around the waitstation pretending to throw pots and pans.

"You look," Alisha said, "like you're about to give birth to a Pillsbury Pigbaby." Alisha, Bonnie, and Tommy all belly-laughed. Then they all looked at W.W.W., expecting him to join in. But his stomach felt like it was about to catch fire.

"What's the matter, W.W.?" Bonnie asked.

"I just don't want anybody to get fired," W.W.W. said.

Except for the slam of pans from the kitchen, the Dixie Fish went quiet.

"Fired?" Smiley asked thoughtfully, pushing the glasses back into place on his nose. "Honey, Kent ain't gonna fire me. I been here four years. And after six months, unless I been caught stealing or ain't been doing my job—and he can prove it—he's got to pay half my unemployment. Can you imagine Kent Bronstein paying anybody to do nothing?" Smiley let the glasses slide back down his nose and batted his eyes at W.W.W. "Course, he can fire you any time he feels like it."

Laughter erupted from Alisha and Bonnie. Then Tommy started. To W.W.W.'s great surprise, he found himself laughing with them. They bussed the last two tables, split the tips, and clocked out. Then the whole staff sat at the bar drinking cheap draft, feeding the jukebox, and blowing off steam.

After a while, Shine came in wearing the silver bangle W.W.W. had given her for Valentine's. And despite the kitchen fire, the beagles, and the poker game, the Dixie Fish felt to W.W.W. like a bucket full of bliss that they were all sitting around inside together. They laughed at the velveteen Elvis that Kent had hung over the jukebox after Valentine's. They laughed at the stiffly dignified face of Robert E. Lee. After a couple of more drafts, they all broke down completely over—Alisha whispered it—"Kent's puckered-up Pillsbury Pigbaby pout."

But Kent wasn't laughing.

While Shine, W.W.W., and the rest of the staff sat drinking cheap draft beer at the jukebox end of the bar, Kent hunched in the gloom at the restroom end, brooding into a non-alcoholic beer. If the Dixie Fish was W.W.W.'s bliss-bucket, then Kent was trying his best to poke the bottom full of holes.

Kent hemmed and hawed. He fidgeted. He poured his near-beer into a go-cup. Little by little, the laughter died. The staff huddled closer at the jukebox end of the bar and badmouthed Kent under the cover of classic country.

Kent checked his watch. He cleared his throat. He got up, walked past the suddenly silent staff, and switched off the jukebox.

The staff huddled even closer and concentrated on their beers.

Kent re-checked his watch. He hawked. Spat. The sound of saliva against bare concrete was like a tick popping under a shoe.

Smiley tipped his glass up and drained the last of his draft. "Ladies and gentlemen," he said, "that is enough for me. Yes sir, that is quite enough for me."

Alisha and Tommy were right behind him.

W.W.W. was downing the last of his own beer when he heard Kent call his name from the far end of the bar.

"Walt Whitman."

W.W.W. froze with his mouth half-full of beer. Kent's voice, coming from the afterhours gloom at the far end of the bar, sounded very much like the voice of W.W.W.'s daddy.

"Walt Whitman!" Kent said again, louder, sounding even more like W.W.W.'s old man than before.

"It's W.W.," W.W.W. managed, once he'd choked down the last of his draft. "What do you want, Kent?"

"Come over here a minute. I want to talk to you. And while you're at it, pour us both a free draft and switch on the jukebox."

"Only if you promise to stop calling me *Walt Whitman*," W.W.W. said. "And only if you let me pour free drafts for everyone who's left at the bar."

"Okay, okay. Just hurry it up."

W.W.W. leaned across the bar and poured free draft beers for Shine, Bonnie, Kent, and himself. He handed full pint glasses to Shine and Bonnie. Then he carried his and Kent's glasses over to the jukebox, switched the power back on, and punched in a song. Finally, W.W.W. walked into the gloom and delivered his and Kent's beers to the restroom end of the bar.

On the jukebox, Hank Williams started into "My Bucket's Got a Hole in It." Not ten minutes earlier, the Dixie Fish had been W.W.W.'s bucket of bliss. Now, the words of the immortal Hank Williams perfectly described the shift in atmosphere. W.W.W. raised his pint glass in memoriam, took a long pull, and turned to face Kent.

"What can I do for you?" W.W.W. asked.

"I'm not happy," Kent said. "All I want is to be happy, but I'm not."

"Kent," W.W.W. said, "you've just told the story of my life."

"I'm not talking about life!" Kent snapped. "I'm talking about business. Life is easy. It's business that's hard."

"For me, it's kind of been the other way around."

"That's exactly why I need your help. If the Dixie Fish was busy, I'd be happy."

W.W.W. glanced longingly over at Shine, who sat at the far end of the bar next to Bonnie. "Kent," he said, "Bonnie told me earlier that this was as busy a Thursday night as there's ever been at the Dixie Fish."

"Bonnie is marrying a diesel mechanic who lives in a trailer."

"What does that have to do with anything?"

"Nothing, I guess," Kent said. "Which is about what I'm going to clear tonight, after overhead."

"Nobody has that kind of overhead," W.W.W. said. "Admit it. You made out."

"I made out on Valentine's. And you made it happen, W. W. Make—"

The restaurant went suddenly quiet as Hank Williams finished up "My Bucket's Got a Hole in It," and Kent paused. He got up, walked over to the jukebox, and punched in another song. Then he came back over and sat next to W.W.W. On the jukebox, Tammy Wynette started into "Stand By Your Man."

"Make what?" W.W.W. asked finally, shifting uncomfortably on his barstool.

"Make what happened on Valentine's happen again."

"Are you kidding? Kent, you don't want another Valentine's. Don't you remember what all happened that night?"

"Hell, yes! I remember singing. I remember excitement. I remember making more money in one night than I usually make in a week."

"But don't you understand that . . ." W.W.W. started, then stopped. How could he bring home to Kent the fact that the warm, welcoming atmosphere they had here at the Dixie Fish was more important than cold, hard cash? How could he make Kent understand the delicate balance that lay at the heart of that warm, welcoming atmosphere—the communal earning? the true democracy? the everybody doing his or her own thing, at his or her own pace, and yet everything still getting done? How could he make a man like Kent truly comprehend what it felt like to be a part of the huddle?

"Let me tell you what I understand," Kent said. "If it was as busy as Valentine's every night, why, my yearly gross would be . . . a million dollars." Kent's voice sounded as wistful as if he were talking about a lost love instead of a pie-in-the-sky revenue stream. "We could make this a million-dollar store if we worked together. Make me a millionaire, W.W., and I'll make it worth your while."

When he heard the M-word float lovingly out of Kent's mouth, W.W.W. knew that he would need some serious help to rescue the warm, friendly atmosphere of the Dixie Fish from Kent's get-rich-quick dreams. But W.W.W. was completely at a loss as to where to find such help in a country as dedicated to the piling-up of personal possessions as the one he lived in.

"Well?" Kent said.

Just then, the jukebox stopped playing "Stand by Your Man." The Dixie Fish went quiet. And exactly like at his triumphant hiring—when Kent had asked a clueless W.W.W. to identify the menacing and mysterious mechanical oyster shucker sitting on the bar—W.W.W. felt what he could only call animal instinct take over. Instinct pulled his eyes up above the jukebox to the velveteen picture of Elvis in his later years that the waitstaff had been laughing at earlier. The King, all pompadour and jowls, stared hungrily out through the red glow/white flash/red glow of Dixie Fish beer lights, straight into the kitchen. He seemed to be saying, *I could eat my weight in fried catfish.*

It was all the help W.W.W. would need. "Alright, Kent," he said. "We'll do an All You Can Eat."

22. Never Mock a Cow Pie

W.W.W. looked out over the red-brick campus, feeling his stomach rumble. He hadn't eaten all day. He stared through the classroom window at the red-brick buildings and red-brick sidewalks of Confederate State University, letting the monotonous drone of Dr. Coupe's lecture wash over him like cocktail sauce as he daydreamed about delicious deep-fried catfish and all the fixings. French fries. Hushpuppies. Cole slaw.

He felt his belly rumble again so strongly it was audible. At the sound of it, he resettled himself in his desk and focused partway back in on Dr. Coupe's lecture.

"Until 1815, the . . . leaders of the . . . infantile republic were still preoccupied with . . . Mother Europe to the . . . east. But by the . . . second quarter of the . . . new century, the . . . focus had shifted dramatically to the . . . occidental side of the . . . Appalachians."

W.W.W. felt his thoughts turning toward catfish again. He was not so much actively listening now as just passively hearing—and recording everything with that freak part of his head that would never let him forget a single sound. At the present moment, Dr. Coupe was droning on and on in nasal multi-syllables, interspersed with pregnant pauses that W.W.W. guessed were meant to emphasize the dazzle of Dr. Coupe's brilliance, about "Manifest Destiny," "the . . . Frontier Ideal," and "the . . . archetypal American movement west."

Dr. Coupe reminded W.W.W. of an overeducated auctioneer. But instead of cows, Dr. Coupe was selling cow pies—and not very fresh ones, either. And here W.W.W. sat, stuck smack in the middle of all that verbal diarrhea, the same way he'd been stuck for three hours every week since the semester started.

This wasn't what W.W.W. had in mind when he'd come to South

Carolina in search of academic freedom. Back at the Crawfish Boil—the bigtip shitjob place where W.W.W. had worked in New Orleans—he had a regular customer who'd been a history professor at Tulane University. The professor's name was Dr. Schry; and he'd come in every Monday, Wednesday, and Friday during happy hour with a couple of books or a stack of papers, and sat drinking discount draft beer while he worked. Anyway, *work* was the word Dr. Schry had used to refer to what he was doing. All the time that he hadn't spent drinking beer or doing whatever else he referred to as *work*, Dr. Schry had spent singing the praises of academe: the nine-month contracts; the semester-long sabbaticals; and the academic freedom, which he'd defined as *the right to think or say or write anything at all, anytime, anywhere.*

It was the promise of academic freedom, as defined by Dr. Schry, that had led W.W.W. to place 2) SCHOOL second on his seven-point plan for achieving bliss, behind only the 1) WOMAN part of the Program. From the way Dr. Schry had described what he'd referred to as the *Ivory Tower*, W.W.W. had come to envision academe as a bastion of liberty and enlightenment like Athens during the Golden Age—a structure founded not on the lust to pile up material possessions, but on the desire to build up practical knowledge that mankind could use to change the world for the better. But instead of world-changing knowledge, what W.W.W. had discovered at Confederate State University was mostly busywork and arcane mumbo-jumbo: stuff that had to do with sociopolitical terminology and the theoretical underpinnings of historical periods, instead of the lives of historic people. And even worse, the purveyor of all this crap had been Dr. Coupe.

And Dr. Coupe? He was . . . well, he was strangely quiet.

"Mr. Woodcock?"

Out of the corner of his eye, W.W.W. made out someone, or something, standing over his desk. W.W.W. sat with his face still pointed out the window. But his excellent peripheral vision was slowly filling in the physical details of the someone, or something, that loomed over him.

"Mr. Woodcock?"

It was a blazer W.W.W. saw. A tan blazer. A tan camel hair blazer that, he saw, was both single-breasted and perfectly pressed. The topmost of two buckskin buttons closed over a green jacquard silk tie. A green silk handkerchief poked out of the breast pocket almost into W.W.W.'s face.

Underneath the blazer, he saw a pair of black and olive houndstooth trousers. Above the blazer, he saw the classic cheekbones of Dr. Coupe's face. They were flushed deep red.

"*Mister* Woodcock!"

"Dr. Coupe?"

"Would you care to . . . join us?"

W.W.W. heard the rest of the class titter at Dr. Coupe's rhetorical sally, complete with pregnant pause. Anyway, *tittered* was the word W.W.W. guessed that Coupe (That's coo-PAY, heh, heh, like the classic automobile) would've used for the sound they made. The laugh was pure Cow Pie.

"I'm right with you, sir."

"In . . . body," Cow Pie said, "in . . . body. But, Mr. *Walt Whitman* Woodcock, what about in . . . spirit?"

"In spirit, too, sir."

"I wonder. Since the . . . semester's beginning, you have not deigned to . . . note down even a . . . single syllable of the . . . lecture."

Sitting next to W.W.W., but dressed almost exactly like Cow Pie, Reese tittered right along with the rest of the class.

"I've noted every word you've said, sir," W.W.W. said.

"I should hope so, Mr. Woodcock. I should hope so. But in the . . . notable, heh, heh, absence of . . . pen and paper on . . . your desk, I find I have certain doubts." Ten perfectly manicured fingers folded themselves together across the green jacquard silk tie. "Tell me, Mr. Woodcock, what was the . . . last thing I said?"

"Doubts," W.W.W. said.

"No, no. Before that. What was the . . . last thing I said before your inattention forced me to . . . interrupt my lecture?"

W.W.W. thought back. "His destiny in his very lifestyle, the hunter/ trapper pushed farther and farther west," W.W.W. repeated, "opening the way for the agrarian settlers, who pushed inexorably after him, clearing the forests, making fruitful the land, establishing the American Democratic Society."

"Hmm . . ." Cow Pie said. "Very good, Mr. Woodcock." But he did not look pleased. "And before that?"

"Disjointed from . . . society because of . . . his resistance to the . . . American Revolution, dissatisfied with . . . Utopia," W.W.W. repeated word for word, trying this time to get it just exactly like Cow Pie, all the way down to the nasal multi-syllables and pregnant pauses, "the . . . hunter /trapper, rather than progressing in . . . American Democratic Society, regressed to . . . Indian Society."

The class had gone completely silent. W.W.W. could hear the hum of the fluorescent lights as he shifted back and forth in his seat that felt now like it had nails sticking up through it.

"Excellent, Mr. Woodcock," Cow Pie said at last. "Verbatim." But his face flushed redder than W.W.W. had ever seen in the two months since the semester had started. "And before that?"

"It was the . . . destiny of the . . . frontier man to . . . bring about his own ruin."

"Precisely. I should remember that, Mr. *Walt Whitman* Woodcock, if I were you. You have something coming . . . due."

23. Coming . . . Due

"W.W.!"

As he shoved his way out of the classroom building and into the light mist that was falling, W.W.W. clearly heard his name called from inside. But he kept walking. There was nobody at Confederate State University—at any university for that matter—that he wanted to talk to right now. He strode along the red-brick sidewalk past red-brick buildings and even a red-brick trash can holder, feeling the mist cool against his skin and hearing it drip softly from the shadowy pines. He wanted to get as far away from Cow Pie and everything associated with him as quickly as possible. But although W.W.W.'s body moved farther away with every step he took, his mind was still trapped in that desk with Cow Pie on one side, the window on the other, and no help in sight.

"W.W.!"

Why was it, W.W.W. wondered as he ignored the name-caller once again, that he spent most of his indoor time looking outdoors, and most of his outdoor time looking in? And what did it matter where he was looking and whether he was engaged in note taking when it was listening that he was supposed to be doing? And how was any of that connected with something coming due? He had done something back there in that classroom to get himself crossways with Dr. Coupe. That much was clear. But just what it was, exactly, that W.W.W. had done wrong, he had no clue. What he needed right now was to get someplace green and peaceful and dry, where he could think this through.

"An essay, W.W.!" The words echoed and re-echoed off of red-brick buildings, red-brick sidewalks, and red-brick trash can holders. "A mid-term essay! Forty percent of your overall grade for the course."

This time, W.W.W. stopped. Even with the weird red-brick echo, he recognized Reese's voice. W.W.W. wasn't exactly happy with Reese right now. Whatever it was that had gone wrong back in class, Reese had been right there in the thick of it, tittering at W.W.W. along with the rest of them. But cold-shouldering Reese here on campus would only complicate things later back on Hope Street.

"I heard all that stuff about the midterm essay back in Dr. Coupe's class," W.W.W. said as Reese sloshed to a stop beside him. The mist was thickening now into rain, and Reese stood in the shelter of a black umbrella. "What about it?"

"You heard what about the essay? What precisely?"

"I heard it all." W.W.W. looked into Reese's face that was difficult to read in the shadow of the umbrella. "The first day of class, when Dr. Coupe read over the syllabus: 'In addition to the . . . readings below, each student shall be required to . . . complete two essays totaling fifteen to . . . twenty pages apiece. Each essay shall comprise forty percent of the . . . student's overall grade for the . . . course. Essays are to . . . address the . . . topic of the . . . student's choice, as said topic pertains to the . . . readings, or some relevant aspect of the . . . class discussion. The . . . midterm essay will come due on the . . . date you see listed on the . . . syllabus; and the . . . final essay will be handed in during the . . . final exam period.'"

"Precisely correct, as to the syllabus," Reese said, having somehow managed to produce, one-handed, a copy of the syllabus from his briefcase without letting the umbrella dip enough to get himself wet. "And what did you hear today?"

"Like I told Dr. Coupe, I heard every word he said."

"Indeed," Reese said. "A point which you managed to drive home with all the subtlety of a sledge and chisel. But getting back to the business at hand, what was the last thing Dr. Coupe said, prior to dismissing the class? Do you remember?"

"You have something coming . . . due."

"Precisely! Now you have it!"

"Now I have what?"

"How is it that a person who is able to remember every word a man says for two months, and able to reproduce those words exactly, can miss so completely what that very same individual made such a point of not saying, only ten minutes before?"

"What?"

"Essay! Midterm essay, W.W.! Dr. Coupe's calculated omission of the words *midterm* and *essay*, and his substitution of the word *something*—most especially in combination with his emphasis of the word *due*—implies a threat. And he directed this threat specifically at you. How can you not see that? Dr. Coupe communicated more nonverbally, ten minutes ago, than he has verbalized all semester."

"I'll be damned."

"Probably," Reese said. "Unless you are able to compose a truly impressive midterm essay, W.W., you will indeed, quite probably, be damned."

They stood at the intersection of Greene and Pickens, the two streets that quartered the main part of the campus. Motorcycle Parking lay due west across Pickens, right next to the most beautiful and vital building at Confederate State University: Financial Aid. As was always the case in the absence of heavy traffic, W.W.W. felt himself drawn so powerfully toward the Financial Aid Building that he crossed against the light.

"Damned how?" W.W.W. asked Reese after a minute or so. It took a minute or so for Reese to catch up. Despite the fact that Pickens was completely empty of traffic, Reese had waited for the light to change before crossing the street. The awkward conversational pause gave W.W.W. time to admire the squat red-brick Financial Aid Building and to get his priorities straight. "I've got A's in both my other classes," W.W.W. continued once Reese had stepped up onto the curb. "But I'm not bucking for an A from Dr. Coupe. All I'm looking to do is pass. That way, I don't lose my financial aid money."

"Oh no," Reese said. "No, in my opinion, you will be fortunate indeed not to receive a grade of F."

"But why?"

"You mocked a professor, and you made him look like a fool in front of students. And these were not just any students, W.W. You made Dr. Coupe look foolish in front of graduate students. To put it simply, Dr. Coupe is looking for an excuse to crucify you."

"But he's a teacher. Isn't he supposed to help me learn?"

Reese shook his head and smiled sadly at W.W.W. Then he started walking again.

"No?" W.W.W. asked, catching up to Reese.

"Dr. Coupe is much more than just a teacher. He is the Whitefield Distinguished Professor of American History for the State of South

Carolina, and he is the Head of the Graduate Program. The last thing he wants to do is teach."

"Then why the hell is he in that classroom?"

"Quite simply, because university policy stipulates that he has to be."

"So what you're saying is that Dr. Coupe can just hand me an F, and there's nothing I can do about it?"

"That is about the extent of it," Reese said.

"Correct me if I'm wrong on this. But doesn't an F mean I'm out of graduate school, automatically?"

The only reply was the drum of rain against Reese's umbrella.

"But couldn't I appeal it? There must be some kind of a committee."

"Dr. Coupe," Reese said, "is the committee."

"Then I really am damned," W.W.W. said.

"Hubris aside, I see no reason why that eventuality should ever be reached." Reese paused as they reached the motorcycle, which was parked directly underneath the STUDENT MOTORCYCLE PARKING sign. "Go to Dr. Coupe's office. Offer him your most sincere apologies. Take a few notes in class. Participate in the class discussion. Work within the system, W.W., instead of working against it."

"So what you're saying is that I should finesse him a little?" W.W.W. asked.

"Precisely! The system is not completely execrable. You jump through the hoops. You pretend to enjoy it. It is as simple as that."

"Simple?" Looking from Reese's bone-dry camel hair coat and houndstooth trousers to his own rain-soaked jacket and jeans, W.W.W. wondered how he could ever bridge the social chasm that separated the two of them.

"Simple indeed," Reese said and smiled warmly at W.W.W. "A certain amount of deference and a deft bit of hoop-jumping are all that is required. But surely you must have learned most of this over the course, heh, heh, of your undergraduate work."

"I never did any."

"Hoop-jumping?" Reese said, his smile fading slightly.

"Undergraduate work," W.W.W. said. "I never really even finished high school. At least, not officially."

"But if this is true, how can you be here?" All traces of Reese's smile had now vanished. "How can you be enrolled in graduate school?"

"I know a guy in Atlanta who knows a lot about computers."

"And?"

"Let's just say that he owed me a favor."

"But that is impossible."

"It was actually very easy. We just finessed the system a little."

"But this is . . . illegal. This is . . . fraud."

"I just skipped a couple of those hoops is all." W.W.W. swung onto the motorcycle and fired it up. "You coming?"

"I made other arrangements."

"Fair enough," W.W.W. said and grinned at Reese. Despite the camel hair coat and the accent that was just like Cow Pie's, there was something fundamentally decent in Reese that W.W.W. had sensed the first time they met. Maybe there was still some hope that the vast gap between them could be bridged.

"W.W.!" Reese called out. Reese's smile was back now. It looked a little lopsided, but genuine. "What was it all about? Why challenge Dr. Coupe?"

"Let's just say I don't like the way he talks."

"Does it by chance have something to do with the way he said your name?"

"I guess maybe it does," W.W.W. said and laughed a little. "Would you like to know precisely what?"

Reese nodded.

"All right, then. Finish each sentence. I am neither a groundbreaking Transcendentalist poet . . ."

"Walt Whitman!" Reese said.

"Excellent. Nor a Southeastern gamebird with a crepuscular mating flight . . ."

"Woodcock!" Reese said.

"Precisely. And since I'm neither of the above, I prefer to be called W.W. It was my father who named me Walt Whitman. And I'm just about as fond of my old man as I am of the way Dr. Coupe says *Mister Walt Whitman Woodcock*."

"I think I understand a little better now. My relationship with my own father has always been problematic at best," Reese said. "But when it comes to your relationship with Dr. Coupe, perhaps the classical English literary translation of the word *woodcock* would be more appropriate."

"I've never heard it."

"Hmm . . . Never mind. It's probably not important," Reese said. "You said that your father named you Walt Whitman, and that the two of you don't get along. What about your mother?"

"I killed my mother," W.W.W. said.

24. Christ Dancing and Billie Holiday

esus danced on the water. Peter walked, but Jesus danced.
Cool and settling softly, his mother's voice echoed in W.W.W.'s memory as he ran straight through the red light at Greene and Pickens, and continued to pick up speed. The falling rain stung his eyes almost blind. The feel of the motorcycle between his legs, as he gunned the engine and the bike leapt forward, was like a horse running. But the horses had burned.

Jesus danced. His mother's voice sounded cool as the feel of her cheek against W.W.W.'s forehead after fever dreams. *The wind and waves danced with him, boisterous, into a storm.*

He passed the SPEED LIMIT 20 sign doing sixty, the red-brick duplexes flying by. He ran the red light at Greene and Gregg, gunning the engine as he crossed the railroad tracks so that the motorcycle left the ground and flew for a long moment through the rain-whipped air. When he slammed back down onto the asphalt, the back tire whipped around and he felt the bike skitter sideways, out of control. He slid through the red light at Greene and Harden, in among swerving cars and the sound of frantic horns, and he turned his front tire into the skid. He felt the back tire catch, felt the bike line out straight and true, and he swung a hard right turn into the flow of traffic that was heavy on Harden.

Peter walked on water to go to Jesus. But Jesus danced the sea into a storm. Peter grew afraid and started sinking. So Jesus caught him up and carried him into the ship.

W.W.W. wove through the traffic now, passing cars on the shoulder as the rain slackened into a drizzle. He passed red-brick bars, red-brick shops, red-brick nightclubs. W.W.W.'s mother had been a dancer and a singer before his daddy came along and married her, and dragged her

143

away from the dark delta soil of New Orleans. But on the sun-baked Southwest Texas plains, there was no water to dance on—just cactus and scrubbrush, and the deadly dry grass.

And when Jesus was come unto the ship, the waves ceased dancing and the sea grew calm.

W.W.W. remembered his mother drinking with the old man, and the yelling that went on late into the hot summer nights. He remembered how, after the yelling died down, she sometimes sang Billie Holiday. He remembered her favorite song was "Body and Soul." And remembering, he hooked a left onto Devine Street. He didn't know why. Maybe it was just a sneaking suspicion, a hint of doubt born from a dark memory. But he gunned the engine and roared up Devine, running the light at Cedar and flying past the big gray church on the corner with its light-up plastic Jesus.

"Christ dancing," he said.

Jesus gleamed softly in the morning gloom. But he wasn't dancing as W.W.W. turned left onto Heathwood Circle and headed into the Strangers' exclusive red-brick neighborhood. W.W.W. wasn't sure why he made the turn. Maybe it was the sound of his mother's voice running round and round on the twenty-four-hour CD player in his head, husky over two-pack-a-day gravel as she sang "Body and Soul." But whatever the reason, there among the high-dollar homes and manicured lawns, the bloody-chicken-feather stink of misfortune filled the air. And as the Strangers' big red-brick house came into view, W.W.W. saw what looked like Shine's red import sedan parked in front of it.

"Christ dancing and Billie Holiday."

But he'd left Jesus standing on a corner back on Devine Street. And as W.W.W. pulled his bike up behind the car that looked so much like Shine's—but couldn't be—the sound of singing ceased. His mind felt as empty and quiet as the Strangers' red-brick neighborhood. He reached out and touched the black-and-white Virginia vanity plated that read: POSSESS. It was Shine's license plate. And it was only a little after 10 a.m., and Shine was anything but an early riser.

"Body and Soul," he said.

W.W.W. gunned the engine and made a loop around Heathwood Circle. And another, and another. Every time he passed Shine's car, he felt the silence and the emptiness spread inside himself. Until finally, he felt sure his heart had stopped beating and his blood no longer flowed.

When he turned onto Hope Street, the white rock house looked cold and lonely in the gray rain. There was a strange car parked out front, a dark green convertible coupe with a cream-colored ragtop. W.W.W. slowed to a stop about halfway up the block and watched someone in a tan camel hair blazer and a green jacquard silk tie climb out of the car. It looked very much like Dr. Coupe.

Sure enough, W.W.W. saw Dr. Coupe snap open a black umbrella. Then Dr. Coupe walked around and held the umbrella over the passenger door as Reese climbed out. Dr. Coupe walked Reese to the front steps, holding the umbrella over both of them as Reese opened the front door and carried his briefcase into the house. It wasn't long before Reese came back out the front door, his soft-sided briefcase filled now almost to bursting. Something red hanging out of a side pocket dragged along the ground as Dr. Coupe escorted Reese back across the front yard. It wasn't until Reese climbed back into the car that W.W.W. recognized the red something as a silk pajama sleeve.

When he finally opened the front door and stepped inside the Green Room, W.W.W. felt as empty inside as the house on Hope Street. He heard no sound of voices that he knew. He felt no warmth, smelled no breakfast frying. But in the living room, there were fish. The fish had appeared like in the Jesus miracle from the Gospels—but without the loaves—atop the entertainment center the day after the poker game. Unlike the Gospel fish, the fish in the living room were tropical. They glowed like rainbows through the aquarium walls.

Home, he mouthed to himself. It was more a question than a statement of fact, and W.W.W. didn't dare say it out loud.

He went into the kitchen to look for an answer. But he found no bliss in the kitchen and no peace in his heart. So W.W.W. went to look for bliss and peace out back. He walked out the back door and into the rain. But there were beagles in his back yard, and it looked like a battlefield after an artillery barrage.

So he went back inside and looked for bliss upstairs. But his attic bedroom was dark and empty. In the gloom, W.W.W. could find no trace of the bliss that had enfolded him there in the presence of Shine. He needed a light, he told himself. He needed warmth. He needed a fire that would light the way to bliss, and all the warmth and peace and good fellowship that accompanied it.

W.W.W. sat in the dark and lit matches, staring into the place where the yellow edge of each flame burned into blue. In the heart of the fire, he saw again the moment when bliss had first ended back in Southwest Texas, with his mother's hands clenched onto the bars in her bedroom window and the house ablaze. And he felt himself carried back.

In the past that seems always present, a man and a boy wait for sunset. They have cut the firebreak already—beginning in the blinding heat of the afternoon with the man on the bright yellow tractor seat, both hands planted firmly on the black circle of wheel; and with the boy seated on a hot green fender, one hand clutching the yellow canopy and the other hand aping the slow, measured movement of the man's hands as he steers the tractor in slow circles around the edge of the field.

They have walked the field already—continuing the whole way around, corner to corner to corner to corner, checking the strip of bare earth they tilled to contain the fire. The man says the grass will grow back thicker and greener after it burns. He explains to the boy about the ground and about firebreaks: how earth is the strongest of elements, blocking fire, channeling water, buoying up air. But the boy, only half listening, thinks instead about the day he will have his own hands on the wheel of the tractor, uprooting the earth and folding the dried grass under.

In the firebreak at the western edge of the field, the man and boy watch the yellow-white point of the sun swell as it falls. The man explains to the boy how the wind always dies with the sun: how the ground, as the fire of the sun cools out of it, calms the air. The boy's eyes are full of the sun falling and fading, coloring the gray rock house atop the eastern hill gold and orange and red in turn. The boy's mind is full of the sound of larks singing the death of the sun, his nose full of the smell of fresh-turned earth, his hands full of matches. Until suddenly, the sun touches the horizon. The wind dies, and the sea of dried grass goes still.

Now, the man says.

The boy kneels and lights a match that blooms yellow-orange as it touches the grass. Then he is off—released by the man's word to sow delicate flowers of flame. The boy runs along the western edge of the field, kneeling to strike matches that burst into flower as they touch the grass. He feels his bare feet dig into the earth and feels the wind of his passing blow back his hair as he runs and kneels and runs again. But he does not notice the breeze springing up from the west despite the setting of the sun.

He does not feel the breeze freshening, despite what the man has said, and fanning the delicate yellow-orange flowers into a wall of flame.

The boy turns the southwest corner of the field and stops, as the man told him to do. He stands for a long moment, perfectly still. For the first time, he feels the wind blowing hard out of the west and sees the wall of flame that he and the wind have sent racing toward the gray rock house atop the eastern hill.

"Home," the boy says, at last.

Then he races away uphill, running as he has never run in his life toward the house that the man said would be safe. And the whole world turns black in the wake of the burning.

25. Little Girls' Dresses on Easter Sunday

*T*he neon-yellow letters spray-painted onto the Dixie Fish dumpster glared:

NO SCAVENGING
(BY PENALTY OF LAW)

W.W.W. sat on his motorcycle and shivered, hoping the sign was just a figment of his half-frozen brain. Over the course of the day, the rain had gone ice-cold. Then the sleet had started. By quarter to five, the streetlights had come on. As W.W.W. pulled up in front of the Dixie Fish dumpster, he couldn't feel his face or hands; and his vision was narrowed to the area lit by his headlamp. But the sign was no figment. The headlamp highlighted the neon-yellow letters on the dumpster, setting them aglow in the wintery gloom like the writing on King Belshazzar's wall in the Book of Daniel.

It was another moment of truth in a day that had been a string of such moments. After being threatened with an F by Dr. Coupe; after Reese's ripping the scab of years and miles off of W.W.W.'s memory of starting the fire that had killed his mother; after having seen Shine's car parked out in front of the Strangers' house at an hour that guaranteed an overnight stay; after having stopped again at the Strangers' house on the way to the Dixie Fish and seen Shine's car still there—then spending forty-five sleet-soaked minutes sneaking around in his own personal Hades, peeping in windows and trying to catch a glimpse of her—seeing that NO SCAVENGING (BY PENALTY OF LAW) sign on the Dixie Fish dumpster was more truth than W.W.W. could take.

He walked into the Dixie Fish feeling numb inside and out, and saw a cloud of steam escape his mouth as he hit what he'd hoped would be warm restaurant air. It was almost as cold inside the Dixie Fish as it was outside. For a long moment, W.W.W. stood inside the double front doors and dripped rainwater mixed with sleet from parts of himself he couldn't feel. Then he caught sight of what looked like a trail of rainwater on the gray concrete floor. The trail stretched around past the cash register and into the dark depths of the Dixie Fish. W.W.W. followed, drawn instinctively as a herd animal toward the warm, welcoming comfort of others like himself. He followed the rainwater trail past the front bar, around past the restrooms, and into Kent's office where the trail ran out in front of a space heater that glowed red-orange next to Kent's desk.

W.W.W. saw Smiley hunched in front of the space heater looking soaked but toasty, and he came to a halt. Here was warmth. Surely welcome and comfort were only seconds away.

"Hello . . . Smiley," W.W.W. said, trying without success to keep his teeth from chattering. "It's good . . . to see you."

"Hello, W.W.," Smiley said in a tone that was neither warm nor welcoming. He he shifted his body, completely blocking the warmth from the space heater. "I'm afraid there's only room enough here for one body to get warm in, and that body is me."

W.W.W. turned and headed for the kitchen, letting the chattering of his teeth serve as his only reply.

"If you're headed for the kitchen," Smiley called out, in the wake of W.W.W.'s passing, "Kent and Brave are already hogging up the broiler oven!"

When W.W.W. walked into the kitchen, not exactly happy with Smiley but grateful for the warning, he saw flames raging blue and orange in the broiler oven. Beneath the broiler, he saw flames roaring up out of all four burners on the stove. Brave and Kent were hunched in front of the flames, their shivering silhouettes pressed against each other as each man tried to push the other away from the fire. W.W.W. didn't even slow down. He headed straight for the spot where both backlit bodies pressed together— and shoved his way in, savoring the luscious heat that washed over his face and hands.

"Shit, W.W.!" Brave said. "You feel like a freaking icicle."

"Stop it, W.W.," Kent said, bracing himself against the electric deep-fryer that sat next to the broiler oven. "Dammit! I was just getting warm, and now I'm wet."

W.W.W. kept right on shoving. He could almost feel his face again. "Paint up another NO SCAVENGING sign," he grunted, "and hang it on the stove."

"It was you that painted the NO SCAVENGING sign on the dumpster, Kent?" Brave hooked one leg underneath a stainless steel expediting table and levered himself back in toward the stove. "I thought it must've been the city."

"You thought wrong." Kent locked an arm around the stove door-handle and shoved back for all he was worth. "Now quit pushing, dammit, and reach over and turn on that heat lamp."

"No way," Brave grunted.

"Why don't you cut on that heat lamp, Kent?" W.W.W. hooked a belt loop onto the stove door-handle, right next to where Kent had his arm-lock, and held on. "You can paint a NO SCAVENGING sign on it while you're there."

"Listen," Kent said, shoving W.W.W. toward Brave. "I came in here Sunday morning, and there was trash all around that dumpster. Some hungry homeless son of a bitch had scattered rotten garbage all the way from the restaurant to the street."

"Sunday?" Brave grunted and strained, shoving W.W.W. back at Kent now as though his life depended on it. "Do you mean . . . the Sunday morning after . . . Valentine's night?"

"Yeah," Kent grunted and strained, shoving W.W.W. back at Brave. "How did . . . you know?"

W.W.W. tried to reply, but he couldn't seem to breathe. The air was being crushed out of him. He twisted and thrashed in an attempt to find a position that would let his lungs suck air without allowing Kent and Brave to block the rest of his body away from the heat. When he finally managed to free one shoulder, W.W.W. saw to his great surprise that Smiley had abandoned the space heater in Kent's office and was now leaning over, wet and shivering, and reaching what looked like a copper penny into the back of the electric deep-fryer.

"Homeless?" Brave grunted. "Hell, Kent . . . that was . . . Gladys and Tommy." Then Brave stopped shoving and started laughing.

As the pressure against his right side disappeared, W.W.W. felt himself thrown against the stove. He bounced hard off the stainless steel door, then banged back against Kent and dangled by the belt loop he'd hooked onto the handle. But W.W.W.'s attention was focused on Smiley. Smiley had reached one arm all the way up into the electric deep-fryer now. And he seemed to be shaking and shivering something awful.

"What do you mean," Kent said, "Gladys and Tommy?"

"I mean that on Valentine's night, Gladys pelted Tommy with half the trash in that dumpster."

"No."

"Hell, yes. W.W. saw the whole thing. And that's not all. Before she covered him with trash, she called Tommy *pencil dick*. In front of every-body."

"W.W.," Kent said, "is that true?"

W.W.W. didn't answer. He was too busy watching Smiley, who was still shoulder-deep in the electric deep-fryer. But now it looked more like Smiley was jerking and spasming instead of just shaking and shivering. And he seemed to be turning strangely white.

"W.W.!" Kent said. "Listen up, dammit! The firechief at the station there across the street says he's seen suspicious people around that dumpster. What if they were to lay for me late one night when I came out with the receipts? W.W.?"

"Smiley?" W.W.W. said. "Smiley! Are you okay?"

Smiley's answer was part moan, part scream. His eyes rolled back in his head. Then he went slack-jawed, and his legs started to jerk and buck.

"Oh no," Kent said.

"Wow!" Brave said.

"Smiley!" W.W.W. said. Still dangling by his belt loop, he couldn't seem to get his boots to catch on the wet concrete floor. "Smiley!" He felt his boot heels slip and skitter; then he felt his belt loop give, and felt him-self drop onto the wet floor. "Help him!" He started toward Smiley, only to have Kent's strong hands clamp down on his shoulders.

"Don't touch him!" Kent said.

"Don't worry," Brave said.

"Let go of me!" W.W.W. said.

"He must've pushed the penny up too far," Kent said. "And the deep-fryer must not have been grounded good."

"It's grounded now," Brave said.

W.W.W. twisted free of Kent finally, and lunged against Smiley's rigid body. For an instant, W.W.W. felt a surge of current rip through him like the wrath of God. Then, too suddenly for him to sense movement, he was all the way across the kitchen slamming against the pan rack. Smiley slammed against the pan rack a second later. He had stopped making that awful sound. Except for Smiley's twitching and the breath that came in short gasps, he looked dead. His hands were open, his fingers spread wide. Both his arms were clenched stiff against his sides. And his face had gone as white as a little girl's dress on Easter Sunday.

It was one hell of a time, W.W.W. realized, to figure out that you really cared about the crazy son of a bitch. Which was why, when W.W.W. saw Kent and Brave still standing over by the stove, and still talking—quick and quiet, like guilty kids trying to get their stories straight—he kind of lost control.

"You!" W.W.W. yelled. "Yes, you!" he yelled even louder, trying to cut through the squint-eyed, drained-blooded, lawsuit look that was pasted all over Kent's face. "Go turn on some heat!"

Kent went. And Brave went, too.

Brave returned carrying a gallon bottle of Tennessee sour mash with what looked to be enough whiskey in it to raise the Gettysburg Rebel dead. "Tommy's stash," Brave said, handing the bottle to W.W.W. "He keeps it in Kent's office."

The bottle felt cold and heavy. As he cracked it open, W.W.W. heard the heater come on. He splashed some whiskey into the bottle cap and held the cap under Smiley's nose.

Smiley's nostrils twitched. His eyelids fluttered.

"Wait," Kent said, running back into the kitchen. "Wait!"

Instead of waiting, W.W.W. dumped the entire capful, all at once, onto Smiley's tongue.

Smiley coughed, then swallowed.

"Good." Encouraged, W.W.W. raised Smiley's head a little and held the mouth of the bottle against Smiley's lips.

Smiley gulped. Then he blinked—or else, his eyes twitched. It was tough to tell through the glasses that were somehow still perfectly in place on Smiley's face.

W.W.W. felt the back of Smiley's neck. "He's getting warmer," W.W.W. said, glancing up at Kent.

Then Smiley's hands came up, caught hold of the bottle, and tipped it back. Smiley sucked at the whiskey like mother's milk. He blinked his eyes. Then he put the bottle down, blinked again, and breathed deep. His lips moved. Then his tongue moved. He seemed to be trying to say something.

W.W.W. felt Kent edge closer, breathing heavy. He saw Brave lean in. Smiley's mouth opened and closed.

"Law . . ." Smiley barely whispered.

W.W.W. saw Kent freeze.

"Law . . ." Smiley said again, louder.

W.W.W. heard Kent's breath catch, then felt Kent's hands take hold of his shoulders and yank him up off of the concrete.

"Lawdy Jesus!" Smiley finally blurted out.

"Did he say *law*?" Kent asked. He looked almost as bad as Smiley. "Did I hear him say *law*?"

Brave didn't look a whole lot better. "Can I talk to you a minute?" he asked Kent.

"He said *Lord*," W.W.W. said.

"*Law*," Kent said.

"He said *Lord*," W.W.W. said. "*Lordy Jesus!*"

"Hallelujah!" Smiley shouted.

"Can I talk to you a minute," Brave said, "in your office?"

"He said *law*."

"He said *Lord. Lordy Jesus!*"

"Hallelujah!"

"I heard *law*."

"Can I talk to you a minute?"

"Don't be ridiculous," W.W.W. said to Kent.

"There is nothing ridiculous about the law."

"There's nothing more ridiculous," W.W.W. said. "Especially when it's keeping the homeless and hungry from taking food out of dumpsters."

"Are we to going to your office, or not?"

"In a minute, Brave!"

"It's your ass," Brave said.

"W.W.?" Smiley said.

W.W.W. knelt and looked closely at Smiley, whose color seemed to be coming back. He had stopped twitching. His breath came slow and regular. Tommy's bottle of Tennessee sour mash, that had been mostly full, was now half-empty. There was a powerful smell of whiskey on Smiley's breath, and he was grinning.

"Why," Kent said, "I believe he's drunk."

"Stinking drunk," Brave said. "Drunker than Gladys on Valentine's."

"W.W.?" The grin faded slowly off Smiley's face. "Did you . . . did you feel . . . Him?"

"Who?" Kent asked.

"Did you, W.W.?" Smiley asked again. "Did you feel the hand of God?"

W.W.W. tried to remember exactly what he had felt as the current surged through him. Something powerful and uncontrollable, that was for sure. Like a tiny foretaste of the Apocalypse. But the hand of God?

"I don't know," W.W.W. said at last. "What did you feel, Smiley?"

"Reborn," Smiley said.

"Does that mean he's okay?" Kent asked.

"He's fine," Brave said. "Hell, he said he felt reborn. Did everybody hear that?"

"He's right as rain!" Kent pounded W.W.W. on the back. He danced around the pot rack. "Thank God."

"Hallelujah!" Smiley said.

"Speaking of rain, you better be thankful the weather's crappy and business will be off," Brave said. "It looks like you're going to be alone in this kitchen."

Kent stopped dancing. "You think business will be off?"

"Ought to be light," Brave said. "Bad weather is bad for business."

"Bad?" Kent said. "W.W.? Do you think business will be bad?"

W.W.W. was thinking about a lot of things: NO SCAVENGING signs, unsafe working conditions, assault and battery. But what he said was that he figured tonight would be painfully slow.

"Painfully slow?" Kent looked like he'd just been punched in the stomach.

"Painfully, agonizingly," W.W.W. said. "Slow, slow, slow." It felt almost as good as an uppercut.

"It's just one night, Kent," Brave said. "And besides, you're short in the kitchen."

"You're going to be short on the waitfloor as well," W.W.W. said.

"On the waitfloor?"

"Don't you think Smiley might need some taking care of?" W.W.W. asked.

"Well . . ."

"I think that's a fine idea, W.W." Brave said. "For starters, why don't you get his drunk ass up off the kitchen floor?"

26. Compensation

Smiley sat at the Dixie Fish bar next to W.W.W., sipping whiskey and looking better and better. W.W.W. couldn't be certain whether it was Tommy's bottle of Tennessee sour mash, an electric surge of God, or the kisses Smiley got from Bonnie and Alisha when they came in that was the cause of Smiley's recovery.

But W.W.W.'s money was on the kisses.

Well, on Bonnie's kiss anyway. Alisha's kiss was sort of a combination pat on the back and cheek-peck that had more peevishness in it than perfume. She stomped through the double front doors dressed all in black, with her dyed-black hair flying and her cheeks flushed red. "Who the hell painted the NO SCAVENGING sign on the dumpster?" she barked at W.W.W. "Was it Kent?"

"It was Kent all right," W.W.W. said.

Then Alisha caught sight of Smiley. "You look awful," she said, her voice softening as she gently patted Smiley's back. "What happened?"

"Smiley had a little accident," Brave said from behind the bar. He was filling in for Tommy, who had the night off. "Everything's fine."

"Nobody asked you, Brave. You, W.W.! What happened?" Alisha's voice reassumed the acid tone she always used to address W.W.W.

He filled her in on the details: wet concrete floor, copper penny, electric deep-fryer, and all. But the whole time he was talking, W.W.W. was trying to figure out what he'd done to get so crossways with Alisha. Except for that first night at the Dixie Fish when she'd asked him about a bunch of novels he'd never heard of, and the night of idiot laughter at the kitchen-tantrums of Kent—which Alisha walked out of almost as soon as the shift had ended and Shine walked in—and that strange, sympathetic look Alisha had given W.W.W. on Valentine's after he told everyone about his phonographic memory, the only emotion she'd ever shown toward him was irritation.

"And you, Smiley! What the hell did you think you were doing, poking a copper penny into an electrical appliance?"

"Just exactly what Kent told me to," he said. "When the old switch busted, Kent said use that penny to switch it on."

That was when Alisha gave Smiley the peck on the cheek and growled, "I'd sue."

No, the kiss that worked the healing magic was definitely Bonnie's. Soft and lingering slightly, Bonnie's kiss looked to W.W.W. like it could've cured the Plague. But it wasn't just the kiss that had been magical. Bonnie had a saintly-yet-sexy air about her, a mix of Mother Teresa and Marilyn Monroe, that made W.W.W. wish it had been him that had gotten zapped instead of Smiley.

"You okay, sweetie?" Bonnie asked Smiley in that low, raspy voice. Then she laid a gentle hand on his shoulder, leaned in close, and smiled that threadbare smile. "You don't look so good."

"Just went a couple rounds with the electric deep-fryer is all," Smiley said, grinning a dreamy half-grin.

"Did it hurt?"

"Like being on fire."

"Maybe this will make up for it a little." That was when Bonnie kissed him—softly, lingeringly—on the forehead just above his glasses. Then she carried a barstool over underneath the special board and started chalking specials.

"Yes, ma'am!" Smiley hooted, swigging whiskey. "That is indeed what I call compensation!"

W.W.W. snatched the whiskey bottle away from Smiley, poured a shot into his draft beer, and gulped down the boilermaker he'd made. Then he mixed himself another boilermaker and sat sipping it slowly, reminding himself over and over that Bonnie was engaged. Smiley sat at the bar next to W.W.W. and watched Bonnie, not drinking boilermakers only because W.W.W. wouldn't hand him back the bottle. Even Kent watched Bonnie as she stood atop her barstool in a damp cotton turtleneck and chalked the specials.

But while most everybody else in the Dixie Fish was admiring the soft curvature of Bonnie, W.W.W. stared into his boilermaker and asked himself hard questions about the character of Shine. What would Shine have done in response to Smiley's near electrocution? Would she have shown as much human concern as Bonnie, forehead-kissing Smiley so softly and lingeringly as to fix what ailed him? If Shine had even been at the Dixie Fish, that is, instead of over in the rich part of town kissing Strangers—all of whom W.W.W. hoped had the Plague.

"Hand me back that sour mash, W.W.," Smiley said after a while.

"You've had enough of that sour mash."

"Now W.W.," Smiley said. "You ain't thinking of drinking all that sour mash whiskey yourself?"

"Actually, I thought I might get a little help from Louis Armstrong." W.W.W. looked over at Brave, who was standing by the sink washing pint glasses. "Brave, would you mind going back and getting the jukebox key from Kent?"

"Sure thing, W.W." Brave dried his hands and went into the kitchen. Between the very intermittent hisses of deep-frying seafood and the sporadic sizzles of frying starches—as Brave had predicted, it was turning out to be as slow a night at the Dixie Fish as W.W.W. had ever seen in a restaurant that was open for business—W.W.W. made out what sounded like whispering. And when Brave came back with the key, after what seemed like too long a time for key-fetching, the look on his face reminded W.W.W. of a cat crossing cut grass toward a baby bird.

"Thanks," W.W.W. said, taking the jukebox key. "Everything okay?"

"Right as rain," Brave said. But the look on his face never changed.

W.W.W. shrugged, put ten free credits on the jukebox, and then punched in every jazz and blues song on the machine. Finally, he sat back down at the bar and listened as Louis Armstrong started into "What a Wonderful World." It took him back to Valentine's and Mr. Guitar, back to Shine and the smell of true bliss.

"C'mon, W.W.," Smiley said. "How about another taste of that sour mash?"

W.W.W. held up the bottle, studying its contents in the red glow/white flash/red glow of the Dixie Fish beer lights. There was whiskey left. So he handed the bottle to Smiley, who swigged straight sour mash without bothering to wipe the rim.

"Now that," Smiley said, "is what I call compensation."

"I thought kissing Bonnie was what you called compensation."

"And you know that's true! But compensations come few and far between in this life. So while I'm living, I plan to grab all the good things I can get."

W.W.W. took back the bottle and slugged whiskey. "Your compensation is my compensation," he said, watching Brave creep back into the kitchen.

"What's she done to you?" Smiley asked.

"Who?"

"That gold-eyed little thing you were singing to."

"I don't much want to talk about her."

"She's real pretty," Smiley said.

"Yeah," W.W.W. said. "Real pretty. On the outside anyway. And like I said, I don't much want to talk about her."

"You're real pretty too, W.W. Even though you ain't talking like it now. Pretty on the inside, you know? You're the only one to sit here and watch over poor old Smiley."

"Yeah," W.W.W. said. "I'm real pretty, too."

They sat for a while and passed the bottle. Around them, the restaurant emptied out completely. Brave returned to the sink and started washing glasses again.

"Seemed like you two had things kind of worked out," Smiley said finally.

W.W.W. hesitated. "Do we really have to talk about this?"

"Let me tell you something. I might not be book-smart, but I've lived a lot of life and learned a bit about living while I was at it. Maybe even something that could help you, W.W., the way you helped me. That is, unless you feel like you know everything already."

"Alright then. I thought we did. Have things worked out, I mean."

"Spoken things?" Smiley asked. "Promise things?"

"Well . . ."

"Things you felt, and things you thought were felt by her, and that she went on ahead and busted like glass."

W.W.W. studied Smiley, who did indeed look like a man who had lived enough life to know something about living—and who sounded like it, too. Maybe it was just the boilermakers, or the surge of electricity that the two of them had shared. But W.W.W. felt a kind of trust connection with Smiley at that moment that he hadn't felt with anybody but Shine in a very long time.

"This morning, I walked around outside the guy's house that she spent the night at last night," W.W.W. said. "I peeped in the windows."

"Hand me that bottle, W.W."

W.W.W. passed the whiskey back to Smiley.

"Sometimes women are like sour mash whiskey," Smiley said. "They make you warm inside, and they keep you feeling warm all night long." Instead of taking a drink, Smiley put the cap back on the bottle and placed it across the bar out of W.W.W.'s reach. "But sometimes, W.W., women are like broken glass, and the best thing you can do is leave them alone."

"Like broken glass?" Brave snorted, over by the sink. Then he laughed out loud. "Broken glass, my ass."

"Have you ever loved a woman, Mister Brave?" Smiley asked. "I mean, have you ever loved a woman so much that the thought of her with another man made you want to curl up and die?"

"I can't say that I have," Brave said.

"Then could you please go away?" Smiley asked. "And could you take that whiskey bottle with you?"

"Do you have anybody, Smiley?" W.W.W. asked once Brave had crept back into the kitchen, whiskey bottle in hand.

"You mean, do I have a woman?"

"Yes."

"No," Smiley said. "But I have a daughter. She's real pretty, too. Inside, like you."

"I didn't know you had children, Smiley. Does your daughter live at home? I mean, does she live with you?"

"She's grown and gone. She's living out west now, in California."

"Does she like it out there?"

"She says she likes it real fine. Sometimes I think about moving out there. Out west, I mean. But for me, home has always been South Carolina."

"Home . . ." W.W.W. said, letting the word trail off. "How do you get there, Smiley?"

"Most nights, I take the bus."

Despite everything, W.W.W. felt himself smile. "Tonight, why don't you ride home with me?"

"On that two-wheeled thing? In the cold? After all that sour mash? No sir."

"I thought you said you wanted to help me."

"You know that's true. But I never said I wanted to die doing it."

"Please," W.W.W. said. "I don't think I can walk out that door alone. And my only other option is Brave."

"I got two conditions," Smiley said after a long moment. "First you promise me, right now, to take it slow and easy. And second, for later, you promise not to go back by that house with them windows you been peeping in."

"Alright," W.W.W. said.

"Ain't no promise in *alright*."

"I think I'm done with promises."

"Whew." Smiley shook his head. "Do you remember what I said earlier about compensations?"

"Promises and compensations are not the same."

"Nobody said so. But they got a lot in common. In this life, you have to be careful about making the first one, and cagey about getting the second." Smiley studied W.W.W., his head cocked sidewise as if he were expecting an answer. "Well? Are you going to promise me or not?"

As he considered, W.W.W. caught sight of a reflection in Smiley's black plastic glasses. The reflection, W.W.W. realized, was of Brave. Brave stood quietly, blackframed, just inside the door that led into the kitchen.

"No promises," W.W.W. said finally. "Are you coming with me, or not?"

"C'mon," Smiley said. "Let's go home."

27. Cradle Song

"This is it." Smiley pointed over W.W.W.'s shoulder at a little red-brick house with bars on the windows. It looked exactly the same as the line of little red-brick, window-barred houses that stretched all the way up the street. "This is home."

W.W.W. edged the bike off the pot-holed asphalt, up into a yard that was mostly mud. "Thanks for riding with me, Smiley."

"Thanks for nursing me." Smiley swung off the back of the bike and stood next to W.W.W. "Don't go peeping in no windows, W.W. Go on home."

"I'm not sure what that means anymore." W.W.W. kicked the bike into gear and headed back the way he had come. He rode around the rain-soaked streets for a long time trying to sort things out before he finally pulled up into the yard of the house on Hope Street and killed the engine. Then he swung off the bike and stood on the front steps, running his fingers over the white rock walls that felt rough as his daddy's hands; and yet, smoothed by the rainwater, soft as the hands of his mother. Did that make them *home*?

What was it, W.W.W. wondered, that made Smiley call the little red-brick, window-barred place he'd stepped off the bike in front of *home*? W.W.W. crept in the front door, edged his way into the pitchblack kitchen, and put on a pot of coffee by feel. He didn't want to wake the beagles. The minute a light went on, the whining would start. Then the howling would get going, and any chance of his reconnecting with the concepts of home and bliss would be all over before it even got started good. He eased into the Green Room and watered his cannabis garden in the dark, one hand caressing the stem of each plant while the other hand wielded the watering can. He climbed up into the attic and fetched the rainbow-colored quilt, the rainbow-colored bong, and what remained of his harvested marijuana. Then he carried it all down to the living room that was lit by the blue-green glow from the aquarium.

He built a fire using kerosene to soak the logs, and for kindling old newspapers from the recycling stack in the Green Room next to Reese's piano. Then W.W.W. spread the quilt on the hardwood floor in front of the fire. He smelled coffee brewing, and kerosene, and damp wood starting to catch. He pulled off his wet clothes and spread them across the backs of Reese's dining room chairs to dry. Then he packed the bong, lit up, drew smoke deep into his lungs, and blew a potsmoke cloud at the rainbow-colored fish gracefully circling their miniature castle. The fish seemed to be floating on air. For a moment, he let himself think back to the circle he'd just made past the Strangers' big red-brick mansion, only to discover that Shine's car was no longer parked out in front of it. Then he turned toward the fire. Maybe *home*, W.W.W. thought, was just a place that helped you hold on.

The heat from the fire welled out into the room enough now so that he had to pull the quilt back a little from the fireplace. Feeling himself drying and warming, he lay down on the quilt and watched the rainbow-colored fish float in fluorescent circles. It felt good lying naked on the living room floor. There were too many memories of Shine in the attic for W.W.W. to feel comfortable upstairs. And if there was one thing the mess with Mary had taught him, it was never to lie down on a couch during a rain.

W.W.W. tried to focus on the prospects for his beleaguered Program for Bliss. He had no 1) WOMAN to share it with, but he still had the 5) ROOF OVER HIS HEAD. The fire felt warm against his skin, and the smell of coffee brewing filled the house. And things with the 4) JOB part of the Program should still be on track, despite his earlier suggestion to Kent about doing an All You Can Eat. Ironically, it was the same busted deep-fryer that had almost killed Smiley that W.W.W. was counting on to be the Dixie Fish's salvation now that Smiley was safe. The busted deep-fryer, that is, and every other piece of worn-out equipment in Kent's second-hand kitchen. It was simple ergonomics: Kent's worn-out kitchen equipment could not possibly supply enough seafood to keep up with the demand of an All You Can Eat. Tomorrow, W.W.W. would slip away into the back yard of the empty house next door—where it was green and quiet, and there were no beagles, no Gladys or Tommy, and no memories of Shine—and he would think of a way to break the no-All-You-Can-Eat news to Kent gently. Thoughtfully. In such a way as to avoid unemployment. Then they could all forget about grossing a million dollars and get back to the more important business of attaining a state of true bliss.

But what W.W.W. needed right now was calm and quiet: the warm fire, the aquarium that glowed blue-green, the rainbow-colored fish swimming their fluorescent circles, the glow of alcohol and THC in his brain, the smell of coffee brewing. In a little while, he was thinking, maybe he would set some breakfast to frying.

Then there came a crash. A thud. A soft scraping noise. And in crawled Gladys and Tommy, covered in reddish-brown mud.

"What are you . . . doing?" Gladys asked, her voice so slurred it was hard to make out where one word ended and the next began.

"I'm lying on the floor," W.W.W. answered. Then he remembered his current nude state. "Naked," he added, sitting up and wrapping the quilt around himself.

"What are you doing lying on the floor . . . naked?" Tommy asked, his voice as slurred as Gladys's.

Both Tommy and Gladys kept crawling straight at W.W.W.

"Actually," W.W.W. said, "I'm not lying naked on the floor anymore. I'm sitting on the floor now, and I'm wrapped in a quilt. And that," he said, raising the hand that wasn't holding the quilt and pointing a warning finger in Tommy and Gladys's direction, "is close enough."

"That doesn't . . . answer my question," Gladys said.

"That doesn't . . . answer my question either," Tommy said.

But they both stopped crawling and half-sat/half-lay in the living room floor surrounded by a puddle of red-brown mud.

W.W.W. took a deep breath and let it out slowly. "I'll make a deal with you," he said. "I'll tell you why I'm here on the living room floor, wrapped only in a quilt, if you'll go to your bedroom and change into some dry clothes. Okay?"

"Okay," Gladys said.

"Deal," Tommy said.

"I'm sitting here on the living room floor because my heart is broken."

"But why . . . on the floor?" Gladys asked.

"Why not . . . on the couch?" Tommy asked.

"Because it's raining outside."

"What?" Gladys asked.

Tommy mumbled something that W.W.W. couldn't quite catch.

"What?" Gladys asked again, louder.

Tommy mumbled something again, then laughed.

"I can't . . . hear you!" Gladys said. Then she pulled her dress up over her head, where it appeared to get stuck. It looked to be an evening gown that was stuck on Gladys's head, one that had been black before it got caked with mud. Anyway, her bra was black—as sheer and black as the lace panties underneath her slip.

"Hey! Take it to the bedroom," W.W.W. said, pulling the quilt up around his neck. "We had a deal."

While Gladys's head was still stuck in the gown, Tommy mumbled, very fast and a little louder than before: "Do dicks make you deaf?"

"What?" Gladys said again, her voice muffled by the dress.

Tommy laughed out loud. Just as Gladys's face came free of the dress, Tommy pulled off his pants, flashed Gladys, and yelled: "Dicks do make you deaf?"

W.W.W. tried to come up with a word to capture what he thought of Tommy at that moment. *Childish? Alcoholic? Insane?*

Gladys wrenched an arm free of her evening gown and swung a ham-sized fist against the side of Tommy's head in a single, graceful motion that would've been beautiful if it hadn't ended with the hollow thunk of knuckles against flesh. Then Gladys leapt onto Tommy.

All of the above, W.W.W. decided. He rolled away from the melee in the direction of the aquarium. All thoughts of home and peace and bliss had been drowned out by sounds of combat. The only thing on his mind at that moment was holding on. There came another thunk of knuckles. It was followed by a thud. Then came a crash from the direction of the entertainment center.

Keeping his eyes on the aquarium and his mind off Gladys and Tommy, W.W.W. watched rainbow-colored fish swim fluorescent circles. He felt very much like one of those fish, but drained of the rainbow colors. Hearing footsteps slap away from him down the hall, and hearing a door slam shut and a dead bolt click, he felt as though he had never seen an arc of rainbow grace the cloud-dappled sky. Looking for bliss, here lately, was like looking for color in a black-and-white world.

There came the sound of something heavy—like maybe Tommy's oak chest of drawers—skidding across the hardwood floor. It was followed by the rhythmic, slapping thunk of naked flesh against wood. W.W.W. could feel the vibrations in the floor.

In the back yard, the beagles went insane. They whined. They howled. They sounded like an entire pack of beagles, a beagle chorus, a bastard beagle choir. And then came the sound of scratching—no, more like a tunneling kind of sound, as though they were trying to bore their way in through the walls.

W.W.W. lay on the living room floor, struggling to hold onto his sanity. Then he found himself wondering whether there was any point in holding on after all. In the absence of home and peace and bliss, what did sanity matter?

He heard the front door bang open, heard it slam shut. "W.W.!" he heard someone yell. It sounded like Reese.

Remembering the red silk pajama sleeve that Reese had trailed across the front yard and into Cow Pie's convertible, W.W.W. turned and faced the fire.

"W.W., are you alright?"

"No," W.W.W. said.

"Are you injured? Has anyone been injured? What is going on?"

"Does it matter?"

In the back yard, the beagles whined, howled, dug. In Tommy and Gladys's bedroom, naked flesh slammed against wood. And suddenly, in the living room fireplace, instead of the soothing fire he'd just built with damp logs and newspapers and kerosene, W.W.W. saw the inferno he had let loose as a child. He saw the flames leap into the sky and remembered racing against them uphill toward home.

"Perhaps some music," Reese said.

W.W.W. heard a couple of slow chords. Next he heard arpeggios. Then he heard Reese start into something slow and sweet. It sounded like Brahms. W.W.W. tried to focus only on the music—to let the slow swell of chords carry him away from the conflagration and help him hold onto the here and now. Reese was playing Brahms all right. It was the "Waltz in A-flat." It was, W.W.W. realized, the first time he had ever heard Reese play.

W.W.W. listened as Reese finished up Brahms's "Waltz in A-flat" and shifted into the "Cradle Song." The music was beautiful. Peaceful. And Reese's playing was lovely. But the lullaby reminded W.W.W. of his mother. He remembered her humming the melody to him when he was very young, and warm, and lying in bed. And try as he might to stay rooted in the present moment, he felt himself carried back into a memory of the fire.

In the past that is always present, the wind howls out of the west and drives the wall of flames uphill straight at everything that matters. Borne by the wind, fed by the blood-red sun that presses on the earth and burns, the fire seems to fly. The flames take to the air as they eat the barn, eat the hay, eat the trees around the barn. There is everywhere smoke and the heat that prickles his skin. And the ash-covered ground scorches his feet as W.W.W. chases the fire uphill toward home.

The flames fly across the road and eat the horse shed. There is the roar of burning, and dogs howling. There are the screams of horses on fire, and the sun setting through the haze of smoke and ash turns the sky the color of blood.

Their manes ablaze, the horses race around and around like the mounts of the four avenging angels in the Book of Revelations. And then flames are in the front yard. W.W.W. feels the blood in the sky pounding now in his ears as he races fiery angels on horseback uphill toward home.

They whisper at him, the angels. *Flames*, they say, as the fire flies up onto the house and eats the roof. *Bars*, the angels say. W.W.W. feels the air sucked out of his lungs as the fire eats the walls. He sees tongues of flame licking the bars now on his mother's bedroom window. *Hands*, the angels say. His mother's hands are clenched onto the bars.

But it is not until he hears her screams that he drops to his knees.

They are not the screams of angels or of horses. He kneels on the hot, ash-covered ground with the book of matches clutched tight in his hand and listens until his mother's screams are silenced. Then he catches the smell of burning flesh, and everything goes black.

28. The Scent of Things to Come

Hammers.

Whiskey hammers.

There were hangover hammers in his head, banging *whis-key, whis-key, whis-key*. W.W.W. wrestled his way out of the quilt and sat up, feeling as though his head would explode. There were ashes in the fireplace. The rays of the early morning sun felt like cactus thorns in his eyes. And the bloody-chicken-feather stench of misfortune was so thick in the air it made him want to gag.

Sitting there on the living room floor and feeling the whiskey hammers pounding in his head, W.W.W. remembered the first time he'd smelled the bloody-chicken-feather stink that wafted so strongly now through the house on Hope Street. It was a bright August morning in Southwest Texas, just after dawn and hot already. He'd walked outside to find chicken feathers blanketing the back porch like blood-spattered ashes, and blood on the muzzle of one of the big black dogs his daddy let run loose to keep strangers and lawmen off the property. Just as W.W.W. caught sight of the blood on the dog's face, his daddy burst out the back door with a twelve-gauge shotgun and opened the dog's head up like a melon with a twin-barreled blast. Then the old man picked up the dead dog, slit the flesh between the tendons of its back legs, and nailed the corpse up over the entrance to the chicken coop. The air was thick with a mélange of gunpowder, blood, chicken feathers, meat that was already starting to turn in the August heat, and something else—something W.W.W. didn't have a name for. He breathed deep, trying to place it. *That's the smell of misfortune*, his daddy said. *It comes from disturbing the natural order of things.* By sunset, the bloody-chicken-feather stink of misfortune stretched from the cow lot to the hay barn. There wasn't a dog within a half-mile of the chicken coop.

W.W.W. pulled on his boxers that had dried overnight and headed down the dark hall of the Hope Street house toward the kitchen. Dark green shades covered the east-facing windows, and the morning sun filled the kitchen with greenish light. He poured himself a cup of coffee, and the steam that rose out of the cup was green. The stove, the refrigerator, the tiles, the cabinets, even the dirty dishes in the sink were all hazy green. It was like being on the inside of Tommy's aquarium. Except for the smell. The bloody-chicken-feather stench of misfortune was even worse in the kitchen than in the living room.

Then an awful thought went through him, sudden as the touch of God or electricity: Gladys had killed Tommy, or Tommy Gladys, and the corpse of the one who had wound up a victim hung upside-down over their bed. W.W.W. set down his coffee and sprinted from the kitchen to Tommy's bedroom door—only to find the door bolted from the inside. He kicked. He punched. He pounded. The only response was a frenzied barking that sounded as though it came from inside the bedroom.

Then the hall was full of red silk pajamas and red, white, and blue boxers.

"Is anything amiss in the hall?" Reese asked.

"What the hell's going on out here?" Brave asked.

"It's not what's out here in the hall that I'm worried about." W.W.W. jerked a thumb at Tommy and Gladys's door. "It's what's in that bedroom."

"Freaking Gladys and son-of-a-bitching Tommy?" Brave asked.

"Are they the source of that awful effluvium?" Reese asked.

"Open up!" W.W.W. pounded again on the bolted door. "Open up right now!" The sound of barking doubled, tripled, until the noise on the far side of the door was almost as bad as the smell.

"The aroma strongly resembles decomposing flesh," Reese said.

"I've heard it told that a hungry dog'll chew on somebody that's dead," Brave said.

That was enough to send W.W.W. running down the hall, through the kitchen, and into the back yard. Outside, the stench was incredible. He heard footsteps behind him as he rounded the corner of the house and then stopped in his tracks at the sight of Tommy and Gladys's bedroom window. The window looked to have been smashed in from the outside, leaving only a jagged fringe of glass around a cracked white frame.

W.W.W. looked inside, feeling Brave and Reese behind him. Shards of glass covered the bedroom floor. He saw the beagles, who had stopped barking now, sniffing at the bedroom door. And in a naked heap on the single bed that was bare of sheets, he saw Gladys and Tommy. They were both snoring.

"Sons of bitches!" Brave yelled.

"It's alright," W.W.W. said. "It's alright, they're alive."

"Indeed. It appears the only issue here is a broken window."

"It's not only a broken window, Reese. And it's not alright, W.W. Ain't nothing right about it at all. We should've killed the sons of bitches to begin with."

"Brave!" Reese said. "These are troubled human beings! What are you thinking about?"

"He's thinking about the beagles," W.W.W. said, noticing only now the pile of dirt next to the bashed-in window. He leaned over dirt pile, feeling sick. There was a pit on the far side that angled down underneath the house. He saw the broken sewer pipe at the bottom. He saw the sludge. And he realized why the bloody-chicken-feather stench of misfortune had been so overwhelming.

"I must admit my confusion," Reese said, still staring into Tommy's bedroom.

"Take a look over here, genius," Brave said, sinking down onto the mound of dirt. "The sons of bitches have dug up the sewer line. The entire basement is filled with raw sewage."

W.W.W. sank down onto the dirtpile next to Brave. Bright needles of sun stabbed his eyes so that his retinas felt like pincushions. His underwear felt damp, and the wet dirt was freezing. But he couldn't seem to find the strength to move. The hammering behind his eyes was so strong now that he felt like ripping out his own hair.

"Whatever," Reese said, "is that awful din?"

"Do you hear it, too?" W.W.W. asked.

"I sure as hell do," Brave said, pointing toward the house next door. "It's coming from over there."

In the back yard of the house next door, that had been so empty and so peaceful and so green just the day before, W.W.W. saw at least a half-dozen men—and a big blue dumpster. The roof of the house next door was covered with at least a half-dozen more men. The men on the roof, wearing boots and white coveralls, tore off shingles and threw them down to the white-coveralled men in the yard, who threw the shingles into the dumpster.

The back yard of the house next door also contained two men in tuxedos and a woman in an evening gown. The three of them walked around into the back yard of the house on Hope Street and approached the dirt pile where W.W.W. and Brave still sat in their underwear and Reese still stood next to them in his red silk pajamas.

One of the men sported a goatee.

It was the Man Without the Goatee, though, who stuck out a hand at W.W.W. "Well, hello again, Walt Whitman," the Man Without the Goatee said.

"It's W.W.," W.W.W. said, wrenching himself up off of the dirt pile and taking the outstretched hand. The hand felt as cold and clammy as the dirt pile.

"Alright then. Hello again, W.W.," the Man Without the Goatee said. He did not let go of W.W.W.'s hand.

"Hello," W.W.W. managed to say.

Brave got up off of the dirt pile and stood next to W.W.W. "Aren't they," he said, "the folks with the crab bats?"

"Yes," W.W.W. said, trying unsuccessfully to disengage his hand from the cold, clammy grip of the Man Without the Goatee. "Yes they are."

"They are . . . whom?" Reese asked.

"My name," the Man Without the Goatee said, turning now to face Brave and Reese, but still not letting go of W.W.W., "as W.W. here well knows, is Dr. Bob Allen. The bearded gentleman is the Reverend Dale Sessions. This is his wife—"

"Norma," W.W.W. broke in. "But what are you doing in our back yard?"

The Man Without the Goatee smiled, let go of W.W.W, and shook his now-free forefinger in W.W.W.'s face as if to chastise him for interrupting.

The Man With the Goatee also smiled and shook his finger at W.W.W.

The Woman in the Evening Gown smiled and shook her finger, too.

"It looks as though we are all going to be neighbors," the Man Without the Goatee said. "At least, for the moment."

29. Up a Creek

*O*wn. That was the word W.W.W. kept coming back to as he tried to make sense of his current dilemma. He'd spent the morning *down* in the dirt. He'd spent most of the afternoon *down* at Cratchett (Don't Get Scrooged, Get Cratchett) Properties. He was *down* on his luck, *down* in the dumps, and hoping against hope that he hadn't been sold *down* the river.

Cratchett had kept them waiting for hours—kept them sinking *down* into the overstuffed chairs in the outer office of Cratchett (Don't Get Scrooged, Get Cratchett) Properties with only soft Muzak, neutral gray walls, and a gray-haired secretary for company. W.W.W. looked over at Reese, who was slumped into the gray leather chair next to him. Reese's eyelids drooped and his head wobbled. In the far corner, Tommy half-sat/half-lay in another gray leather chair, his head thrown back and his mouth open. It was clear that if anybody was going to haul them up out of the hole that the beagles had dug them *down* into, it was going to have to be W.W.W.

How much did Cratchett have on them, W.W.W. wondered? Unlike with the kitchen fire that was supposed to have been breakfast in bed—where W.W.W. had a little time to develop a battle plan before going toe-to-toe with Cratchett—the sewer catastrophe had happened so fast that all W.W.W. could manage was a series of knee-jerk reactions to the situation at hand: finding Gladys and Tommy breathing, finding the dug-up sewer line, finding the sewage in the basement, all the shoveling and wetting and tamping of all that earth, the final smoothing, the hauling of the cannabis garden to a more secluded spot upstairs. And while all of that was going on, the Opera People must have called the city; and the city must have called the owner of the Hope Street house, who must have

173

called Cratchett (Don't Get Scrooged, Get Cratchett) Properties. And then Mr. Bob Cratchett himself had called Hope Street and asked for W.W.W., who would never forget the words Cratchett had barked into his ear.

"Eviction. Office. Now!"

W.W.W. shifted a little in Cratchett's overstuffed chair, trying to focus on the task at hand. But as busy as he was working up contingency plans for Cratchett knowing about beagle-pits and broken sewer lines and marijuana plants, he couldn't seem to keep the Opera People off his mind. A list of crucial questions had been taking shape in his head all day:

2) Who was Dr. Bob Allen, and

3) What was he doing dressed for the evening at eight o'clock in the morning?

4) Was Dr. Bob Allen a practicing psychiatrist or an escaped psychotic? And more importantly,

5) Was he dangerous?

The tactical situation had gotten so complicated—the beagles plus the Opera People plus the whole Program for Bliss gone haywire, plus W.W.W.'s past that would not leave him alone—that he couldn't come up with a workable defense, much less a plan of attack. Then there was the most pressing, most disturbing question by far; the question that had given him not a moment's peace since he had felt the cold, clammy touch of Dr. Bob Allen's hand in the Hope Street back yard:

1) How could the Opera People have learned his name?

The only thing W.W.W. felt sure of at this moment, battle-plan-wise, was that he could use some reinforcements. But since Brave had been called in to the Dixie Fish earlier that afternoon, the only troops available had been Reese and Tommy—one of whom was currently half-conscious and the other half-dead. W.W.W. heaved a sigh of resignation and reached over to shake Reese awake.

And then Cratchett was in among them.

"I'd like to be able to say that I'm sorry to have kept you all waiting," Cratchett said. "But I'm not. So let's get on with this." Cratchett was a big man. He had a booming bass voice, a black three-piece suit that stretched tight across his massive shoulders, and the advantage of surprise.

Reese and Tommy both bolted awake while W.W.W.—caught almost as completely off guard as Reese and Tommy—struggled to frame a reply.

Cratchett waved him off. "Since Mr. Woodcock and I last spoke about your kitchen mishap, I have had the extreme pleasure of compiling this list of complaints—"

"Complaints?" W.W.W. interrupted, hazy-headed in the sudden fog of war and struggling to get his mental feet under himself.

"Why, yes." Cratchett positively beamed at W.W.W., then pulled a sheaf of papers from behind his back. The sheets were an ugly yellow-green, a cross between banana pudding and bile. They were covered, front and back, with nasty slashes of red ink. "This is a list of complaints against all of you. It is a long list. It begins with the woman—or rather, women— who have been living with you in violation of our lease agreement, and," Cratchett paused for effect, "rent-free."

"Rent-free women?" W.W.W. said. "Ridiculous."

"I have detailed physical descriptions."

"There may," W.W.W. said slowly, "have been female visitors."

"I have here—signed and witnessed—an official record of the times of their arrivals and departures. That is, what few departures there have been." Cratchett waved the sheaf of papers like a yellow-green battle flag. "And I also have a report of nudity and lewd behavior involving one of these women, in gross violation of our lease agreement, not to mention moral standards and the law. The incident occurred in your back yard."

"Would you mind defining," Reese said, "exactly what it is that you intend to signify by that term?"

"Which term?"

"*Lewd behavior*. It occurs to me that the term *lewd behavior* could consist of almost anything."

Cratchett pulled a sheet of paper from the yellow-green sheaf. "I was referring to the sado-masochistic sexual relations that took place near your garage on the Tuesday night following Valentine's."

Tommy, who up to now had been sitting ramrod straight in startle-ment at Cratchett's surprise attack, slumped back into his chair and covered his face.

"And since Mr. Thorvaldson here feels it necessary to address this issue," Cratchett continued, "perhaps we had best next address the issue of Mr. Thorvaldson's returned checks."

"What returned checks?" W.W.W. asked.

"Perhaps you should speak with Mr. Thorvaldson about that."

But W.W.W. could see, from the way Reese crumbled at Cratchett's

175

counterattack, that there was no need for further conversation. W.W.W. couldn't believe it. For a minute there, he'd actually been glad that Reese had come.

"There has been complaint after complaint about late night music turned up far in excess of the level agreed to, by you, in Article 15 of our lease agreement."

"Maybe once or twice," W.W.W. said. "But it's been quite a while since—"

"I received a complaint about late-night piano playing just last evening!"

"Brahms."

"What?"

"That was Brahms," W.W.W. said. "Last night on the piano. It was the 'Cradle Song.'"

"Whatever. I received a much more serious complaint from your new neighbors earlier today. It seems that, just this morning, you were all parading around outside in your underwear."

"Actually," W.W.W. said, "Mr. Thorvaldson was wearing pajamas."

"The strength of these complaints alone would serve to evict you," Cratchett said. "But I have just been on the phone with the city crew that is digging out the backed-up sewer line underneath your house. It seems that the ceramic pipe collapsed because a large section of it had been dug up. By animals. Specifically, by canines that have been kept by you in clear violation of the no-pet clause in your lease."

"Mr. Cratchett," W.W.W. said, "it seems to me that I also recall a certain clause. It says that a tenant may not be evicted by a landlord, for any reason, without first receiving a fair and timely warning."

"Why," Cratchett said, "I have telephoned the residence in question not once, but three separate times."

W.W.W. felt sick. "May I ask, sir, with whom you spoke?"

"I spoke with Mr. Black over there!" Cratchett shook the sheaf of papers at Tommy. "Mr. Thomas Black. I have the dates and times recorded right here."

Tommy shifted a little in his corner seat, but kept his face in his hands.

"Letters," W.W.W. said, "there should have been notification letters."

"The receipt of those notification letters was verified by signature at the Hope Street address."

"May I please see the receipts?"

Cratchett handed them over.

W.W.W. thumbed through receipt after thin, green-and-black, date-stamped receipt. Tommy had signed them all.

"You should receive your eviction notice on Monday," Cratchett said, "along with the official summons."

"Official summons?" Reese asked. "Whatever for?"

"I have filed a civil suit against all of you for the damage to the sewer line, and the damage to the house on Hope Street as a result of its collapse," Cratchett said.

Then he smiled again at W.W.W. "And, Mr. Woodcock?"

"Yes?"

"Do you remember, sir, the lawyer you spoke so highly of over the course of our last conversation?"

"Yes sir."

"You're going to need him, Mr. Woodcock. Have a nice day."

30. Down the River

*U*p. That was the word echoing in W.W.W.'s mind as he sat in the back seat of Tommy's convertible trying to put their crushing defeat at Cratchett (Don't Get Scrooged, Get Cratchett) Properties into perspective. The jig was definitely *up* at the House on Hope Street, and it looked as though what was left of the Program for Bliss was about to go *up* in smoke. In the space of an afternoon, the perfidy of his roommates had turned W.W.W.'s world *up*side-down. He was seriously considering open-ing *up* the same can of wh*up*-ass on Reese and Tommy that they'd helped Cratchett open *up* on him. But just then, W.W.W. heard an awful noise from the front seat—a sound like cloth ripping, except that it seemed to be coming from Tommy.

"I'm so sorry," Tommy choked out. "I thought I could stop. Especially after all the calls and letters from Mr. Cratchett. But Gladys wouldn't let me alone, and . . . well, the sex was incredible. I couldn't say anything, and I couldn't stop." The cloth-ripping noise came again, carried back on the wind.

W.W.W. realized that Tommy was sobbing. "Stop it, Tommy," W.W.W. said. "Come on. Stop crying, and stand up for yourself. Stand up, dammit. Be a man."

Tommy stood up. He stood straight up in the driver's seat and leaned over the windshield, sobbing into the onrushing air and sending the car swerving off the road.

"Down!" W.W.W. yelled. "Sit down!"

The car lurched across the grassy shoulder toward the massive pine trees that lined the road. But just when it looked as though all of W.W.W.'s problems were about to be solved by blunt trauma, Reese grabbed the wheel and the car hopped back onto the road. Tommy was thrown back down into the driver's seat. W.W.W. guessed Tommy's feet must have found the pedals, because the car continued to move along in its lane at a steady rate of speed. Reese kept hold of the wheel, and they rode along that way—Tommy working the pedals and sobbing, and Reese steering the car.

Then W.W.W. saw that Reese was sobbing, too.

"I also have deep-seated regrets," Reese said, "about the checks. It was a kind of compulsion. I feel simply loathsome about the entire affair. This sort of behavior seems to run in my family. I once had a great-aunt who—"

"Look," W.W.W. broke in, "we all have reasons to feel awful. But crying and apologizing isn't going to get us diddly. What we need to do is pull together and work through this mess we're in. If we all work together, and agree to be honest with each other from here on out, we'll be okay."

"Do you really think so?" Tommy asked.

"Absolutely," W.W.W. said. "I have a back-up plan."

"What sort of elements does your plan entail?" Reese asked.

It came to W.W.W. that this was probably not the time to mention rainbows and programs for achieving true bliss. "The foolproof sort," he said. "Head for the Dixie Fish."

W.W.W.'s backup plan, which centered on the return of the Dixie Fish to its pre-Valentine's potential bliss level after Kent's shoddy kitchen equipment caused the inevitable failure of the All You Can Eat, was both simple and already well set-up. He realized now that it would be impossible to talk Kent out of doing the All You Can Eat. Instead, W.W.W. would let Kent's big night disintegrate into a disaster. Once Kent had experienced firsthand the human cost of trying to remake the Dixie Fish into a million-dollar store, it should be easy to convince him to go back to the way things were. The real trick would be getting Kent to take his eyes off the cash register—once the kitchen had crashed—long enough to catch a clear glimpse of the human condition. While he was at it, W.W.W. meant to discover what had been so important down at the Dixie Fish as to make Brave abandon the rest of the soon-to-be former residents of the house on Hope Street to the wrath of Bob Cratchett.

When they walked into the Dixie Fish, Brave was still there. Smiley was there, too. But there was no sign of Kent, which W.W.W. took to be a good omen. He also took the presence of Smiley—whose electrical encounter with the deep-fryer had given W.W.W. the idea for his back-up plan in the first place—to be a portent of good things to come. He took an experimental whiff of the Dixie Fish air, hoping to catch just a hint of the first-day-of-springy, cheap-perfumey aroma of potential bliss. But what he caught instead was the stink of bloody chicken feathers that meant misfortune lurking near.

It was exactly then that W.W.W. noticed the kitchen equipment. The deep-fryer that had almost fried Smiley, the over-and-under broiler oven that W.W.W. had hung from by a belt loop—every piece of worn-out equipment in the place had been ripped out by the roots and dragged up next to the double front doors. Hoses and wires jutted in all directions. Even worse, there were huge cardboard appliance boxes lined up in an ominous row underneath the front windows. W.W.W. edged around the uprooted kitchen equipment, past the hoses and wires, and past the wait-station to the corner of the bar where Brave and Smiley were standing.

"Hey, Smiley," W.W.W. said. "How are you feeling?"

"Hey, W.W. I'd be feeling a whole lot better if I had my paycheck. We ain't gonna be open anyway," Smiley said, turning now to face Brave. "I need my check."

Brave was bent over table 11, magic marker in hand, working on what looked to be a piece of white posterboard. "Kent will be here directly," Brave said without looking up. "You'll get it from him."

"I need it now, Brave. I got to pay March rent before five this afternoon. It's already three days late. You don't want Smiley to have to pay late fees, do you?"

"Kent," Brave said, "will be here directly."

"Well, what's up with all this torn-out kitchen equipment and all these appliance boxes?" W.W.W. asked. "And what's this about us not being open?"

Instead of answering, Brave capped the marker and stood up. Then he nodded down at the piece of posterboard he had marked up into a sign. It read:

ATTENTION RESPECTED PATRONS:
The Dixie Fish Will Be Closed for Renovation
Friday March 3rd Thru Tuesday March 7th

Business Will Resume Wednesday March 8th for the:

GRAND INAUGURAL WEDNESDAY NITE FISH SPECTACULAR
ALL U CAN EAT FISH
FREE LIVE ENTERTAINMENT

W.W.W. felt a terrible feeling rise up into him out of the concrete as he realized that his foolproof back-up plan was anything but. No, it was exactly like his daddy always said: *The world is too full of fools to be proof against anything.*

"Will you please tell us what is going on?" W.W.W. asked.

"Kent . . ." Brave started. But then he turned his face away from all of them and looked out the front windows. "Kent will be here directly."

Sure enough, through the plate glass windows, W.W.W. saw Kent come out of the fire station across the street and start toward the Dixie Fish. Kent was not alone. Two blue-uniformed policemen strode alongside Kent. A man in a yellow fireman's coat led the way. He had on a black plastic firechief hat that caught the last glint of sunlight as he burst in through the double front doors and came to a halt among the uprooted appliances.

Kent and the two cops followed the Firechief into the Dixie Fish. But instead of stopping next to the Firechief, the other three kept coming—the two cops in front and Kent behind. Just as they reached the waitstation, the Firechief pointed a finger in the direction of the jukebox.

"That's him!" the Firechief said. "I'd recognize him anywhere."

"Which one?" the two cops asked, closing in. The closer they got, the more it seemed to W.W.W. like there was something about the policemen that wasn't quite right. But things were happening so quickly that he couldn't seem to get his mind wrapped around what the not-quite-right thing might be.

"The black one," the Firechief said.

"But I . . ." Smiley started, "I just come for my pay—"

"Shut up!" one of the cops yelled and pulled out a pair of handcuffs.

W.W.W. didn't know what to say. So instead of talking, he stepped in front of Smiley.

"Back off!" The no-handcuffs cop whipped out his nightstick.

They all backed off—Brave, W.W.W. Tommy, and Reese—and they didn't waste any time doing it. Smiley backed off with them.

"Not you!" Nightstick yelled. Or maybe it was both cops. W.W.W. couldn't be sure. The cops seemed to move in a blue blur, and before W.W.W. could bring himself to believe what he was seeing—much less say, or do, anything to stop it—they had Smiley cuffed and stuffed, face-down over table 22.

"We'll need you to come with us, Mr. Bronstein," Handcuffs said to

Kent, "to sign the list of charges."

"Just a minute!" W.W.W. said, finding his voice at last. He looked hard at the cops, trying desperately to figure out what it was that seemed out of place. "One minute. That's all I ask."

Nightstick looked over at Kent.

Kent nodded at Nightstick.

"Alright," Nightstick said, squaring up to face W.W.W. "You've got one minute."

"What are the charges?" W.W.W. asked. He studied both men's black leather belts with bullets in them, their guns, their polished black boots, their badges, the police insignias sewn onto their dark blue shirts. They certainly looked like cops.

"Theft," Nightstick said.

"What kind of theft?" W.W.W. asked. He looked hard at the way both men puffed out their chests and leaned forward threateningly; he noticed the brutal efficiency with which they wielded the handcuffs and the nightstick. They certainly acted like cops. But something was missing, W.W.W. was almost sure—but not quite sure enough to go toe-to-toe with Nightstick.

"Grand theft," Nightstick said. "Among other things."

"What other things?"

"He's been trading stolen crabmeat for blowjobs," Kent said, "and stolen shrimp for crack cocaine."

"That's a lie!" Smiley grunted, still mashed face-down onto table 22.

"Shut up!" Handcuffs yelled, mashing Smiley down a little harder.

"Let him talk!" W.W.W. said. "If Smiley says that this whole thing is a lie, then I believe him."

"We've got sworn testimony!" Handcuffs barked. "The Firechief witnessed the thefts from across the street. He signed a sworn statement confirming the fact that Mr. George Washington Carver Smith removed cases of shrimp and crabmeat from the dumpster at the Dixie Fish, and made a hell of a mess in the process."

"Well, I have another story about how the parking lot mess got made," W.W.W. said, thinking back to the garbageball fight between Gladys and Tommy. "A very different story, and one I'll swear to right now."

"Careful!" Nightstick took a step toward W.W.W. "We have a sworn statement from the Chief of Police that on Valentine's night, Mr. George

Washington Carver Smith traded shrimp and crabmeat for oral sexual favors and crack cocaine."

"But . . ."

"Is your name George Washington Carver Smith?" Handcuffs barked at Smiley.

"Yes sir," Smiley said.

"Then you're coming with us!"

"Wait a minute!" W.W.W. shouted, realizing at last what it was that the cops were missing.

"Your minute's up!" Handcuffs barked, yanking Smiley up off of table 22.

"Where are your—"

"Shut up!" Nightstick barked. He lunged toward W.W.W., who found himself leaping backward instinctively. Then Nightstick spun on one heel and joined Handcuffs in dragging Smiley out. Kent and the Firechief went with them.

"Nametags," W.W.W. said to himself, feeling sick at his failure to defend Smiley. But as the significance of the fact that the cops weren't wearing nametags sank in, he had another realization. And the nausea in the pit of his stomach turned to rage. "You knew!" W.W.W. spat at Brave.

"I knew what?" Brave asked.

"That this whole thing was a set-up." W.W.W. crept slowly toward Brave, who was standing by the bar. "You son of a bitch. You knew they were coming. You knew Smiley was innocent. And you held him up with that paycheck bullshit until they could get here to haul his ass away."

"It was a setup?" Tommy asked.

"How can you be so certain?" Reese asked.

"Those cops weren't wearing nametags. On-duty officers always wear nametags. It's part of their uniform. Which means that those cops were working off the clock. Or rather, working on Kent's clock."

Tommy and Reese turned on Brave. Together with W.W.W., who kept closing in, they made a loose half-circle around Brave now, with the bar at Brave's back.

"You did know," Tommy said.

"Obviously," Reese said.

"Okay, so I knew." Brave edged away from W.W.W. He slid along the bar, shoved past Reese, then scuttled like a crab past the jukebox, through the back bar, and on around behind the counter. He didn't stop until he'd put the entire width of the Dixie Fish bar between them. "What of it?"

"It's chickenshit." W.W.W. stared across the bar at Brave. "Like you."

"It's chickenshit as hell," Brave said. "But nobody likes to cheat fair, if that's any consolation. Or should I say, *compensation*?"

W.W.W. was looking at Brave, but his thoughts were with Smiley. He thought about Smiley lying on the Dixie Fish kitchen floor, half-dead. He thought about Smiley at the bar with the whiskey bottle Brave had given him, talking about compensation. Then he thought about the way Brave had crept back and forth between the bar and the kitchen, and about all that whispering Brave and Kent had done.

"You sold Smiley down the river," W.W.W. said. "He wasn't just a coworker, he was your friend. Hell, Brave, Smiley was a part of the huddle. What kind of sick son of a bitch does a thing like that?"

"The new general manager," Brave said, "of the Dixie Fish."

31. A Fishtank Full of Ick, and Gladys

*J*t felt like the cops had dragged the last sane bit of W.W.W. out of the Dixie Fish with Smiley and stuffed it into the unmarked car parked out of sight around the corner. He and Tommy and Reese saw the car pull away—cops, Kent, Smiley, sanity, and all—as they walked out the double front doors.

"So what do we do now?" Tommy asked.

"It does indeed seem as though we have reached an impasse," Reese said.

W.W.W. didn't know what to say. He'd spent his whole adult life looking for an alternative to his daddy's vision of Apocalypse, trying to find a way to renovate the house of society instead of burning it down and rebuilding on the ashes. He'd envisioned the Program for Bliss as the key transition in that renewal effort—kind of like spring after winter or Easter after Lent. But as the prospects of the Program for Bliss dwindled, and the power of the rich and privileged yet again loomed large, W.W.W. found himself thinking about starting fires.

"Let's get out of here," he said finally, "before I do something I'll regret."

What to do? That was what W.W.W. was thinking as they climbed into Tommy's car. It seemed to W.W.W. that life—especially his life—was essentially a poker game, and he'd been pot-committed since he got to Columbia, SC. It looked as though his sole remaining play was to go all-in. After all, he had a pocket ace: his cannabis garden was growing so fast it was almost time to cull the males. And he still had a couple of chances to make a backdoor hand. He was still in 2) SCHOOL, if only barely. He still had 3) TRANSPORTATION; a 4) JOB, even though it looked as though true democracy at the Dixie Fish had been overthrown by Brave; 6)

FRIENDS; and, of course, 7) SOMETHING TO DO. Maybe, W.W.W. thought, he could still pull off a backdoor miracle with his river card if he just pushed the rest of his chips into the pot.

"Leave the top down!" W.W.W. yelled. "And head for a beer store! It's time for another roommate meeting."

"Are you not forgetting something?" Reese asked.

"Not a chance!" W.W.W. yelled. "I've got it all under control." Despite everything, he had this crazy reborn feeling that it would all work out if he could just work some life back into Reese and Tommy.

"What about Mr. George Washington Carver Smith?"

"Well, it—"

"It'll take them a while," Tommy broke in, "to process him. Since it's Friday, and it's after five o'clock, and these are very serious charges. Felonies. That means he won't even be formally arraigned until Monday."

"And?" Reese asked, glancing back at W.W.W.

W.W.W. was too stunned to speak. He couldn't have summed up Smiley's situation any better himself.

"That means," Tommy went on, "his bail won't be set until Monday, either. Until he's been arraigned, and his bail has been set, there isn't much we can do."

Both Reese and W.W.W. sat staring open-mouthed at Tommy.

Tommy shrugged limply. "It took me a year and a half to wash out of law school."

"Indeed," Reese said. "Well then. What about Brave?"

"I can't speak for you all's choice of roommates," W.W.W. said. "But for my money, Brave is out."

"My funds," Reese said, "are with your funds."

"My money, too," Tommy said. "I think. I'll have to ask Gladys."

They found Gladys in the living room when they got back to Hope Street with the beer. She was curled up in the love seat, hugging her legs tight against her chest and staring into the aquarium. Her eyes looked red and swollen, and her cheeks were wet.

The sight stopped W.W.W. in his tracks. He had seen Gladys drunk and laughing, working and sober, naked and bloody, mad as hell. But it was the first time he had ever seen her cry.

"What's the matter, baby?" Tommy asked. He pulled a beer from the bag, popped it open, and carried it over to Gladys.

"One of our . . . f-f-fish is . . . d-d-dead," Gladys sobbed. She sounded like a little girl.

Tommy handed the bag of beer to W.W.W., then they all walked over and took a closer look at the contents of the aquarium. One of Tommy and Gladys's rainbow-colored fish floated sideways on the surface of the water. Its variegated scales were covered with white fuzz.

"Looks like that rainbow tetra there has got the Ick," Tommy said. "They'll probably all get it." He thumped the front wall of the tank and pointed. "See? That one there has got it, too."

The other rainbow tetra was also mostly white-covered. It hung head-down next to the white and gold ceramic castle that W.W.W. had watched both fish swim circles around the night before. The healthy fish stayed well away from the Ick-infected tetra. Tommy thumped the glass again, and all of the healthy fish scattered. But the other mostly white rainbow tetra just hung there next to the castle as though it might be seeking sanctuary inside.

"Will they all . . . d-d-die?" Gladys sobbed.

"I don't know, baby," Tommy said. "Probably most of them." He took a long-handled green fish net out of a drawer in the entertainment center and scooped the dead fish out of the water, holding his arm out straight in front of him with the dripping fish net clenched in his fingertips.

"Are you going to bury it?" Gladys asked and sniffed.

"I'm not gonna touch it," Tommy said.

"I myself have an aversion to cadavers of any sort," Reese said, wrinkling his nose at the dead fish that dangled limply in the fish net three feet from Tommy's chest.

"Did they finish fixing that sewer line?" W.W.W. asked Gladys.

"Yes," she said. "And then some men came by in a big blue van and vacuumed out the basement."

"Give me the fish," W.W.W. said.

Tommy passed W.W.W. the fish net, and he carried the dead fish and the bag of beer down the hall to the bathroom. Then he dropped the fish in the toilet and tested out the new sewer line, which seemed to be working just fine. Once he was done flushing the fish, he took the beer to the kitchen and started stacking it into the fridge. They were, W.W.W. noticed, a little short on fridge space. So he took what was left of Brave's bologna and stacked it between the last couple of slices of Brave's bread. W.W.W.

ate the sandwich quickly, washing it down with one of the beers. Then he tossed the rest of Brave's groceries into the trash and used the newly emptied fridge space to finish the beer-stacking.

When W.W.W. got back to the living room, Tommy was just finishing up telling Gladys what Brave had done at the Dixie Fish.

"I'll kill the son of a bitch," she said. She sniffled a little at the sight of the empty fish net, which W.W.W. had brought with him. "Poor old Smiley. He never stole a shrimp in his life."

"We'd all like to kill Brave," W.W.W. said, handing the fish net back to Tommy. "But we're going to have to come up with some form of punishment that doesn't put us in a cell with Smiley."

"Like what?" Gladys asked.

"I think it should involve Brave's personal possessions," W.W.W. said. "That seems to be what he values most."

"Hmm . . ." Tommy said.

"Hmm . . ." Gladys said.

"Might I offer a suggestion?" Reese asked.

They all heard Reese out. And they liked what they heard. So after a couple more beers, they carried all of Brave's bedroom furniture out piece by piece and rearranged it on the front lawn exactly the way Brave had had it set up in the bedroom—from the solid walnut bookshelf, bed, and chest of drawers to the hand-woven blue-green throw rug. It was the first productive thing that they had all done together in a long while, and it felt good.

The whole time they were carrying out and rearranging Brave's furniture, W.W.W. tried to stay one mental step ahead of the rest of the group. He could feel the positive energy that was in all of them, the newly reborn spirit of co-op, even if it did happen to be employed in punishing a former member of the group. What he needed to do now was find some way to re-direct that positive energy into a channel where it might help fix some of their other problems. As they walked back into the living room, their faces flushed from shared physical activity and the spirit of co-op that went with it, W.W.W.'s eyes were drawn to that little white and gold castle in Tommy and Gladys's aquarium. And it came to W.W.W. in a rainbow-colored flash—one that was not covered, like the sole remaining rainbow tetra, in a white fuzz of contagion—what they needed to do.

"I have a great idea," W.W.W. said as they settled into seats and popped open fresh beers. "We have two weeks, by law, before Cratchett can evict us. Let's find another house together. A three-bedroom place with two or three bathrooms and a fenced back yard. What do you say?"

To W.W.W.'s surprise, no one said anything at all. They wouldn't even look at him.

"Well?" he persisted.

They all started to edge slowly away from W.W.W., who sat cross-legged on the living room floor next to the aquarium. It reminded him, all of a sudden, of the way all the healthy fish in the tank had treated the rainbow tetra that was infected with the Ick.

"Come on," W.W.W. said. "I'll go out and get a newspaper. We can look through the FOR RENT listings and see if we can find a new place that will suit all of our wants and needs."

"I regret to say," Reese said, edging a little farther away, "that I have already made other arrangements."

"You mean about tonight?"

"Yes," Reese said, still not looking at W.W.W. "About tonight."

"Gladys?" W.W.W. said. "Tommy?"

"I think Glad and me are headed across town to watch a movie with a friend of hers," Tommy said. They were edging toward the door now.

"Might I catch a lift?" Reese asked.

"Sure," Gladys said.

"We need to talk about this soon," W.W.W. said.

"Right," they all said. "Soon."

Inside of a minute later, W.W.W. was alone in the living room with the fish.

32. Three Days of Therapy, Free Refreshments

riday:

It was dark in Group Therapy, but not completely. No, W.W.W. guessed what it was, once you'd been there a while, was more dim—dim and indistinct, kind of like his life had become—all beer lights and bodies and problems packed in and pressing against him. But even among all those bodies, he was alone.

W.W.W. sat beneath a television whose screen had been painted over into permanent waves, drinking draft beer between shots of whiskey and listening to angry grunge blasting over speakers mounted on the wall next to the dead TV. It seemed like he had been drinking that way forever, ever since they had left him alone in the living room with that rainbow tetra and the Ick, and he had tried calling Shine—and tried, and tried—and come into contact with nothing but her voice-mail:

"Hi! This is Shine. I'm sorry I missed your call, and I really want to talk to you. Just leave your name and message, and I'll get back to you as soon as I can."

It wasn't much of a message. It wasn't even Shine's voice. Not really. Only a digitized imitation. But he'd called back over and over just to listen to the little piece of Shine that was in it. Until finally, he had gotten tired and left a message. It was an awful thing, W.W.W. thought, becoming a recording—just another part of some machine.

After a long time of waiting and beer-drinking, he had gone out looking for Shine. He'd tried the Strangers' place first, but found no one home. So W.W.W. had trolled every upscale bar in Columbia and most of the dives, hoping to catch a flash of ivory skin and gold eyes. He'd seen nothing but beer lights and bodies that weren't Shine's.

Now here he was in Group Therapy, still looking, but without much hope left of finding Shine. He'd put his back into the first empty corner he'd found a stool in and started looking out into the Group—into the people passing—but it didn't feel much like Therapy. And when he tried sliding his stool a little farther into the corner, away from the bodies pressing against him, he found that the stool was nailed to the floor.

"You looking?"

Startled, W.W.W. looked up from the stool and saw a face in front of him. The face had detached itself from the people passing and was staring into his. It was, he saw, a woman's face. And it looked familiar. But even in the dimness of the corner, and after all the whiskey and beer, he could see that the face wasn't Shine's. The woman in front of him, whoever she was, had bushy died-black bangs and pale skin and dark serious eyes—eyes that he was sure he'd looked into before.

"You looking?" she yelled again. "W.W.?"

"Alisha?" he asked, placing the voice finally. "I'm looking for Shine."

"Let's look outside."

Out front the March wind was cold, and W.W.W. felt a little unsteady. He felt Alisha slide an arm around his waist. In the area lights from the Post Office parking lot across the street, he could see the wind blow back Alisha's hair. It was dark like Shine's, but shorter and thicker. He had never noticed that before. She was wearing make-up—something else W.W.W. had never seen Alisha do—and her low-cut shirt didn't leave much to the imagination. Underneath her short black leather skirt, Alisha's legs looked long and lean.

"You look . . . different," W.W.W. said.

"Thanks," she said. "I think. I'm parked over here."

It was a battered red Mustang they climbed into. "A '65 fastback," W.W.W. murmured.

"You certainly know more about Mustangs than literature," Alisha said and laughed in the half-mocking way that W.W.W. had heard so many times at the Dixie Fish. She drove a couple of blocks, then pulled into a dark spot on the edge of a park.

"I grew up around horses," W.W.W. shot back. But he wasn't laughing. He sat up very straight in the passenger seat, trying to hold himself together as he watched the wind lash at the trees. The trees looked like they were hunkered down, their branches flailing. They looked like they were just trying to hold on. "Back in Southwest Texas," he said, "this is the kind of wind that howls in on the front edge of a norther."

"What's a norther?"

"A cold front."

"This isn't Southwest Texas," she said.

"No. But with everything that's happened the last couple of days, it's starting to feel that way."

"I heard about Smiley," she said. "What are we going to do?"

"I don't know," W.W.W. said. He was thinking about Shine. "Bail him out, I guess. But we'll have to wait until Monday."

"In the meantime, have you got someplace we can go? I live with my mother. She's pretty laid-back, but not that laid-back. You know?"

There was something in Alisha's voice that made W.W.W. look away from the shadows of flailing branches and over at her. Alisha had kicked off her shoes, he saw, and was now peeling off her hose. Feeling almost like he was outside among the trees, instead of inside the car with Alisha who was leaning toward him now, W.W.W. watched himself press his mouth against hers.

Saturday:

The whiskey hammers came back with the sun. And the hangover with them. W.W.W.'s tongue had a furry coat on it; and there was the taste of whiskey, and of the woman who had sounded and looked so much like Alisha—but hadn't acted like Alisha at all. He squinted up into Tommy's aquarium and saw the rainbow tetra that had been mostly white with the Ick the night before. It was now completely covered. It floated belly-up, a still white patch of finality on the calm green surface of the water. There was no sign of Alisha except for her taste on his tongue and the smell of her in the quilt his mother had patchworked. Recalling in hangover-bleared details what had happened there on the quilt in the blue-green light of the aquarium the night before, W.W.W. pulled the quilt over his head.

When he finally crawled up off the floor, he went into the Green Room. Through the windows, he saw carpenters in white coveralls on the roof of the Opera People's house next door. W.W.W. couldn't see anything besides the roof. A wooden privacy fence seemed to have sprung up overnight between the two houses. He walked out into the front yard in his underwear to take a closer look at the goings-on next door, but all he could make out was the fence that extended all the way out to street. He also noticed that Brave's things were gone from the front lawn. W.W.W. found himself hoping that they'd all been stolen.

It wasn't until he turned to go back into the house that W.W.W. saw the message that Brave must have left when he came to get his things. The message had been scrawled in black magic marker onto the front door that had once been pure white. It read:

MANDATORY EMPLOYEE MEETING
DIXIE FISH
4 P.M.

Mandatory, W.W.W. thought, was such an ugly word. Especially on his kind of a hangover. He went back into the house, found a magic marker, then came back out in his underwear and made a little addition:

MANDATORY EMPLOYEE MEETING
DIXIE FISH
4 P.M.
FREE REFRESHMENTS

Then he went back inside, scooped the dead tetra out of Tommy's aquarium, and carried it to the bathroom. By the time W.W.W. finished brushing the hangover coat off of his tongue, the toilet had finished running and the bowl was empty. Another fish down the sewer. He wished it could've been Brave.

But when W.W.W. walked into the Dixie Fish at 4:05 p.m., Brave was sitting next to Kent at the head of tables 41 and 42, which had been pushed together. Brave looked pink and healthy, instead of white and Ick-covered. All Brave's things that had been on the front lawn—and that W.W.W. hoped had been stolen and resold at pennies on the dollar—were now stacked around the Dixie Fish dining room in among the kitchen equipment.

W.W.W. was the last employee to arrive. And when he walked in, everyone went quiet. He could feel them looking at him. It made him feel suddenly guilty—guilty about being late; guilty about not saving Smiley; but most of all, guilty about what had happened last night with Alisha.

Finally, Kent motioned to an empty seat at the foot of the table in between Tommy and Alisha. W.W.W. collapsed down into it. Doing his best not to meet Alisha's eyes, he looked away at Brave's blue-green throw-rug that had been draped across the over-and-under broiler oven.

"I'm sure all of you are aware by now," Kent said, "of the incident that occurred here yesterday involving Mr. George Washington Carver Smith."

The sound of Kent's voice drew W.W.W.'s eyes to the head of the table, where Kent was now standing.

There were nods from around the table.

"Alright then," Kent said. "We're going to talk about this one time, and one time only. Anyone who wants to talk about it further may do so in someone else's employ. Is that clear?" Kent was now staring straight down the table at W.W.W.

W.W.W. felt himself nod. Out of the corners of his eyes, which were still locked on Kent, W.W.W. saw other people doing the same.

"All charges against Mr. George Washington Carver Smith have been dropped. Mr. Smith is now a free man. And no part of this matter, not a single spot, will appear on Mr. Smith's record. Therefore, any reason to speak of this matter, or about Mr. Smith, is now in the past."

"Then where is Smiley?"

The question came from so close beside W.W.W., and Kent's eyes were still locked so tight onto his, that W.W.W. thought for a second it was he himself who had spoken.

"What was that?" Kent asked.

"Where is Smiley?" Alisha asked again.

W.W.W. clearly recognized the sound of Alisha's voice now. Relieved that it had not been he himself who had challenged Kent, W.W.W. let his eyes roam across the other faces at the table. He saw what looked like serious expressions of human concern in every pair of eyes except Brave's, and saw that every eye in the place was now fixed on Kent. It was almost like being a part of the huddle. And deep inside himself, W.W.W. felt a stubborn hope raise its battered but unbeaten head. Maybe everything might yet work out for the best.

"If Smiley is a free man," Alisha continued, "without a spot on his record, then why isn't he here?"

Kent hemmed. He hawed. He shifted the weight of his doughy, white-aproned body from one foot to the other.

"Well?" Alisha asked.

"Alright. Just this once, I'll explain the situation in detail. The charges against Mr. Smith were dropped conditionally. That is, I agreed to drop all the charges on the condition that Mr. Smith agree to leave the city." Kent shifted his stance. "In fact, the condition may have been that Mr. Smith agree to leave the state of South Carolina altogether." Kent shifted back. "At any rate, he left this morning. I believe he said something about California."

W.W.W. saw relief flash across every face at the table except Brave's.

Kent saw it, too. He settled firmly back onto both feet. "The matter of Mr. George Washington Carver Smith is now closed. Any further discussion of this matter in my establishment will result in immediate unemployment. Is that clear?" He was staring straight down the table at Alisha and W.W.W. "Yes or no?"

"Yes," W.W.W. heard someone say. It sounded like Alisha.

"Yes." He heard it come from all around the table.

"Yes." He heard himself saying it, too.

"Alright then," Kent said, "let's get down to business. I believe that all of you know by now about the Wednesday Nite Fish Spectacular."

There were nods from around the table.

"Good. Then I'd like to make some announcements. No, skip that." Kent cleared his throat and started again more forcefully. "I'm going to make some announcements. Anyone who doesn't want to listen can leave right now."

Heads nodded again around the table.

"One," Kent said. "Renovation: we're going to remodel the whole interior. Help if you want, on the clock. If not, fine. If you don't like it, quit. Any takers?"

There were no takers.

"Two," Kent said. "New directorship: the Dixie Fish is now under the directorship of Mr. Brave McSwain, your new general manager. Brave will be in charge of the staff, the front-end operations, everything outside of the kitchen. I believe he will be hiring some new personnel. How about a nice round of applause for Mr. Brave McSwain!"

There was some scattered clapping, mostly from Bonnie and Tommy and Kent.

"Three," Kent said. "Discounts: as of right now, we are launching a fifty-percent-off discount plan for all police and fire personnel. They must, of course, be in uniform. Now, is there any discussion?"

There was hardly any sign of life. W.W.W. himself was barely breathing. He was too busy remembering his first night at the Dixie Fish when they had all huddled up and made a group decision about him taking tables. He was remembering Valentine's and singing to Shine—a memory made all the more awkward and painful by the presence of Alisha beside him. He was remembering policemen without nametags, but with handcuffs and nightsticks and unmarked cars. He felt hope lower its head again as the warm and welcoming atmosphere of the Dixie Fish was swallowed up by Kent's get-rich-quick dreams.

"Good," Kent said. "You're free to go. Work starts Monday morning at eight."

After a while, Alisha stood up. Then they all stood up, and she kind of herded them toward the double front doors. It felt to W.W.W. like trying to wade through a concrete swamp. But Alisha herded him right along with the rest of them until they got outside. Then she caught hold of his arm and led him around by the dumpster, out of sight of the windows.

"Where are you headed?" Alisha asked.

"I don't know," W.W.W. said. He was looking at the NO SCAVENGING (BY PENALTY OF LAW) sign that Kent had painted, and thinking about Smiley.

"Head over to J.D. Stickey's."

"What for?"

"Just head over to J.D. Stickey's. If anybody is going to do anything about this, it has to be the two of us. Now head on over there and get us a table."

Sunday:

It was early Sunday morning, somewhere between twelve and two a.m. W.W.W. and Alisha were sitting at a picnic table out in back of Group Therapy. They were very drunk, which was understandable—when they'd started out, it was still late Saturday afternoon.

Over pitchers of beer at J.D. Stickey's, they'd worked through exactly what it was that had happened to Smiley—beginning with Kent's desperate fear of a deep-fryer-related lawsuit and ending with Kent's, Brave's, the Firechief's, and the cops' despicable response—and then they'd started trying to figure out what to do. They'd talked in great detail about the character of every person on the Dixie Fish staff, and what could be expected from each of them in various scenarios. While Alisha and W.W.W. sat there trying to figure every angle, drinking pitcher after pitcher and studiously avoiding any mention of their hook-up the night before, it had gotten dark. So they'd walked over to Group Therapy.

"But we've got to do something," Alisha said for the dozenth time as she poured the last drops of beer out of their dozenth pitcher of the night.

"Sure," W.W.W. said again. "But what can we do? I mean, Kent owns the place, and now Brave manages it. You and me, we just work there."

"We have to strike."

"I'd like to strike Kent and Brave both. Right between the eyes."

"No," she said. "Go out on strike. You know what I mean. All of us. Right there in the middle of the Wednesday Nite Fish Spectacular."

W.W.W. imagined the panic on Kent's face as he looked through the waitwindow and saw the entire waitstaff put down their trays. Next W.W.W. imagined the way Brave's face would melt as they all walked out the double front doors and left the restaurant in chaos. But then he imagined Brave rushing out onto the waitfloor and offering the customers free beer while Kent rushed over to the telephone and called up every Bronstein in the city. And then he imagined the Dixie Fish carrying on.

"It would never work," W.W.W. said at last.

"It could work."

"No," he said. "Not now. Not ever."

"Why not?"

"Because inside of five minutes after we all walked out," W.W.W. said, "Brave would make the free beer announcement. Because inside of five minutes after that, Kent would have every Bronstein in Columbia there carrying a tray. Because we would all be fired, even before they got there." He emptied his glass and looked at Alisha. "And the real hell of it is that those Bronsteins would make better tips than we would, because every customer in the place would be on their side."

"My God," Alisha said, "you're right." She emptied her own glass and looked back at W.W.W. "But there must be something."

"There is," W.W.W. said. "We can get another pitcher."

It had gotten colder as the night got later, and he and Alisha kept getting closer and closer together. And the closer he got to Alisha, the guiltier W.W.W. felt about what had happened the night before. It was crazy, he knew. As crazy as everything in his life seemed to have gone lately with the Program for Bliss falling apart all around him. As crazy as he felt himself going, still stubbornly hoping for bliss. But the guilt had been building ever since he'd woken up on the living room floor with the taste of Alisha on his tongue. He'd spent the whole afternoon before the employee meeting trying to call up Shine and confess. Just then, Alisha reached over and touched the inside of W.W.W.'s leg—and it was like she had taken a straight razor and opened a femoral artery.

"What's the matter?" Alisha asked.

"We slept together last night on my living room floor."

"Yes," she said. "I rather enjoyed it." He felt her start to rub the inside of his thigh. "And?"

"And what about Shine?"

"Correct me if I'm wrong," Alisha said, and he felt her hand stop. "But hasn't Shine been spending a lot of nights with another man?"

"Who told you that?"

"Come on, W.W.," she said. "We know each other."

"You and Shine?"

"No," Alisha said, and he felt her hand start to move again on the inside of his leg. "You and me."

"Have you ever looked at someone and felt the world spin out from under you?"

"Yes," Alisha said, looking at W.W.W.

"That's the way it is for me," he said, "every time I see Shine."

"She's too young, W.W. That's what Smiley would say. What he would have said, I mean, if he were here. Too young, too full of nothing but herself, and no good when it comes to you."

"Do you really think so?" Remembering what Smiley had said about Shine being like broken glass, W.W.W. gently removed Alisha's hand from his leg and clasped her hand tightly in both of his. "What would you say?"

"I'd say you needed somebody older," she said. "Steadier. More like yourself. I'm going to move down to Charleston and try to make a new start. Now that the weather is getting warmer, the tourists will be returning in droves. That'll mean an awful lot of jobs in food and beverage. Jobs that pay a living wage. I would like it very much if you'd come and make that new start with me."

"Until last night, you acted like you couldn't stand me. Now you're asking me to move away with you and start a new life."

"It was Shine that I couldn't stand," Alisha said. "I've always rather liked you, despite your taste in literature." There was no hint of mockery in Alisha's voice, or in the smile she gave W.W.W. "And I've always felt a connection with you that Shine kept us from exploring until last night. Today at the Dixie Fish and this evening, I felt a confirmation of that connection. Come with me to Charleston, W.W. If we leave right now, we can watch the sun rise over the sea."

"I don't know," W.W.W. said. "That's a giant step. I need some time to think about it. Can I tell you Wednesday night at the Dixie Fish?"

"I'm through with the Dixie Fish," she said. "I thought you were, too."

"I don't know that I'm ready to quit just yet."

"You don't seem to know about a lot of things," she said.

"No," he said. "I don't guess I do."

"Goodbye, W.W." Alisha said. Then she stood up and walked away from the table.

33. Papers

W.W.W. spent the motorcycle ride across town thinking about Shine, about the Dixie Fish, and about the midterm paper he had coming due on Tuesday for Dr. Coupe. But as he turned onto Hope Street, W.W.W.'s thoughts shifted to the talk he was planning to have with Reese and Gladys and Tommy about the four of them finding a new house together that they could all call home. After the way everyone had fled when he tried to bring the subject up before, W.W.W. knew that it was going to take some serious convincing to get his remaining housemates to give the co-op idea another go. Which made it all that much luckier for W.W.W. that his cannabis garden was coming into flower. He would cull the male plants this evening, then hit the females with a dose of grow lights that would set their buds to popping like fireworks on the Fourth of July. With Brave out of the house and a garden of pot about ready to harvest, W.W.W. figured he still had an outside shot at true bliss if he could just keep enough of his 6) FRIENDS together and locate a new 7) ROOF OVER HIS HEAD. After all, the vernal equinox was just a little more than two weeks away—a date which happened to coincide exactly with their eviction from the house on Hope Street. He couldn't think of a more auspicious date possible for them all to move into their new co-op together than the first official day of spring.

Thoughts of spring and bliss were still echoing in W.W.W.'s mind when he caught sight of what looked like a trailer in the Hope Street back yard. He cut the power switch on his bike, killing the headlight and the engine, and coasted silently toward the house. The kitchen light was on. And he could see someone moving in and out of the kitchen door, loading things into the trailer—a U-Haul, he saw now—hitched onto the back of a small white car.

W.W.W. felt a surge of pure adrenaline. A burglar was something simple for him deal with for a change, a much-needed outlet of physical violence for some of his pent-up emotional steam. He parked the bike across the street and slipped into the back yard, creeping along the side of the house toward the small white car that he could see now was a convertible with a trailer hitch special-rigged onto the frame. It was Tommy's white import convertible, W.W.W. realized. And it was just going through his head that the burglar must also be a car-thief when he saw someone stagger out of the kitchen carrying what looked like the box springs from Tommy and Gladys's bed.

W.W.W. crept into the shadow of the back steps, praying that the thieving bastard he was about to beat senseless might somehow turn out to be Brave. But as the suspicious someone stuffed the box springs into the U-Haul, W.W.W. got a good look at his face. It was Tommy. And it looked as though Tommy had been beaten up already. Both of his lips were split, there was a huge purple knot on his jaw, and one eye was swollen completely shut.

"Tommy?" W.W.W. felt the adrenaline drain out of him. "What's going on? And what the heck happened to your face?"

"Gladys," Tommy mumbled. "Whiskey bottle. Moving to Atlanta." Then he ran back into the house.

"Tommy? Hold up! Let's talk about this." W.W.W. walked into the kitchen, through the dining room and into the living room, only to discover that the living room was already empty except for Tommy's entertainment center cabinet, the telephone that sat on the floor next to the aquarium, and Reese's recliner that was the color of dried blood. Just then, W.W.W. saw Tommy stagger down the hall with a mattress—and it came to W.W.W. that his last chance at true bliss was slipping away with Tommy, at a rate of speed he'd never seen Tommy achieve. If he was going to salvage any hope at all for achieving bliss, W.W.W. knew that he had to slow Tommy down.

"I think that's it, W.W.," Tommy said as he charged back into the living room. "You can keep the entertainment center cabinet. It's too heavy for the two of us to lift. And anyway, it won't fit in the U-Haul."

"Okay, Tommy. But wouldn't you like me to walk through the house with you, just to make sure you haven't forgotten anything?" W.W.W. spoke slowly. Calmly. But his thoughts were racing. The only thing he could think of that might slow Tommy down, while at the same time heading him away from Atlanta and back in the direction of domestic bliss, was the marijuana stash upstairs. "We'll start in the attic."

"But I don't have anything in the attic."

"No," W.W.W. said. "But I have something up there that I'd like to share."

"I don't know. My brother's expecting me in Atlanta, and it's a four-hour drive."

"It'll just take a minute. Then we can walk through the rest of the house together." As W.W.W. was talking, he took Tommy's arm and led him into the dining room, around Reese's table and chairs, to the base of the attic stairs. It was dark at the top. "Wait right here," W.W.W. said, "while I switch on the light."

"Alright, W.W."

W.W.W. felt his way to the top of the steps, caught the string to the overhead light bulb, and popped it on. Then he sat down hard on the floor.

"No," he said. "Oh no."

But there it was, right in front of him. The rainbow-colored bong he'd been carrying with him since New Orleans lay in pieces on the floor. His last crumbs of smokeable marijuana, which he'd been planning to share with Tommy, were missing. And his entire cannabis garden had been razed. The stalks had been chopped off an inch or so above the soil. The tops of the plants—the shoots and leaves, the delicate buds—were gone. Someone had taken them. All that was left of W.W.W.'s last hope for re-building the Program for Bliss was bare stalks poking up out of the soil like dead men's fingers.

"W.W.?" Tommy called from downstairs. "Are you ready for me to come up?"

"No," W.W.W. managed to choke out. "Never mind."

"Then could we walk through the house now?"

"Sure." W.W.W. staggered to his feet and down the stairs, and then he walked through the house with Tommy. But while Tommy was looking for things he'd forgotten, the only thing W.W.W. could see was Brave. In his mind's eye, W.W.W. saw Brave cutting down the cannabis garden. He saw Brave stuffing the newly flowering plants into garbage bags. He saw Brave carrying them away and tossing them into the Dixie Fish dumpster. He saw Brave beaten bloody and crucified upside-down.

"The telephone belongs to Gladys," Tommy said as they made their way back into the living room. "I'm leaving it for her. And I'm leaving her the fish."

"That's good, Tommy."

"But I'm taking the beagles. My brother in Atlanta has a fenced-in back yard. This is his address." Tommy handed W.W.W. a slip of paper. "Please don't give it to Gladys. Please don't tell her where I am."

"Alright, Tommy." W.W.W. said. He felt himself shivering.

"W.W.? Are you okay?"

"I feel cold inside."

"I'll leave you the stuff for the fireplace. Maybe that will help."

"What stuff?" W.W.W. asked. He heard a sound that he recognized after a long moment as his teeth chattering.

"There's some wood. And those long matches. And the kerosene. I'll leave them for you. And you can have all the beer in the fridge."

"Do you mind if I ask you something personal, Tommy?"

"Sure," Tommy said. "I guess I owe you. More than just the entertainment center cabinet, the fireplace stuff, and the beer, I mean."

"When I first met you, you seemed really slow. And not just slow-moving, but slow-thinking. Like maybe you were . . . well, not very smart. You don't seem that way now. Why the act?"

"When people think you're a little bit slow," Tommy said wistfully, "they sort of look out for you. They give you things, expect less from you at work, treat you nicer. It's a self-protection mechanism, I guess. Although it didn't work very well with Gladys. Hell, W.W., you do it yourself. I mean, you didn't exactly fall all over yourself telling us about that memory of yours."

"Thanks for being honest. You've given me a lot to think about."

"There's something else," Tommy said. "Reese says he's moving out, too."

"I kind of figured that," W.W.W. said. "The co-op idea was a bust anyway. I guess it made about as much sense as a program for achieving bliss."

"Excuse me?"

"Nothing," W.W.W. said. "Good luck in Atlanta, Tommy. I hope you find happiness there."

Reese pulled out later that morning, not long after first light. It was hard for W.W.W. to believe that it was still only Sunday. He'd been up all night, and the cold place inside him felt as deep and dark as the grave.

"I truly regret doing this, W.W.," Reese said. "I would like you to know that."

"I know."

"I would also like you to know that my moving out has nothing to do with you personally. I simply cannot bear any sort of litigation. It is such an ugly process."

"Yes, it is," W.W.W. said. He was thinking about Smiley.

"Here is the address at which I will be staying." Reese slipped a tightly folded piece of paper into W.W.W.'s hand. "I can be reached there by phone as well. But please do not tell Mr. Cratchett where I am."

W.W.W. stuck the paper into his jeans pocket next to the slip of paper he'd gotten from Tommy. Then he sat down in a corner, out of the way, and watched the movers carry out Reese's furniture and boxes of books. Another person was there from the university helping Reese carry out the lighter stuff. That person was Dr. Coupe. Who better, W.W.W. wondered, than Cow Pie? Reese might as well have brought Brave along while he was at it.

Cow Pie carried boxes of papers out of Reese's bedroom. He lugged the boxes down through the hallway, through the living room, and into the Green Room where he set them down. Then Reese picked the boxes up and carried them outside. The good doctor, W.W.W. noticed, had dressed for the occasion. He wore a bright blue designer sweatsuit and a pair of brand new running shoes.

"You look a . . . trifle doleful, Mr. Woodcock," Cow Pie said after another of his passes through. "Having a bit of . . . hard luck with . . . that midterm essay, no doubt."

W.W.W. hadn't had time to think much about his paper yet. And he hadn't written a single word. Since Tommy left, W.W.W. had been sitting next to the telephone and waiting for it to get late enough to call Shine.

"No," W.W.W. said. "That's all finished. I've just been sitting here admiring your sweatsuit and shoes." He felt his hatred for Cow Pie starting to warm his insides a little, raising his spirit from the grave it had sunk into when he saw the cannabis garden razed.

"Indeed? Perhaps you would like to . . . hand it in now."

"Oh, you'll get it," W.W.W. said, feeling his hate for Cow Pie melt the cold place inside him a little more—enough now so that he began to see the outline of a bold new plan. "But you'll have to wait for it until Tuesday. I've got a couple of things I need to take care of between now and then."

By the time the last of Reese's things were gone, and Reese and Cow Pie with them, W.W.W.'s new plan was starting to take shape. It was not a plan for happiness. No, based as it was on hatred and a desire to inflict pain, it was a plan for revenge—and rescue. It was a plan to rub Dr. Coupe's nose in Cow Pie. It was a plan to ruin Brave. It was a plan that reminded W.W.W. of something his daddy had said once: *Hate might be an ugly thing to live with, but it's a damned sight better than dead and buried.*

The key to putting Cow Pie in his place was to write the best midterm essay that Dr. Coupe had ever seen. And the key to writing that midterm essay was the phonographic memory—or rather, the lack thereof. W.W.W.'s whole life had been spent as not much more than a wingless parrot, a two-legged tape recorder who was great at trivia-for-beers, or taking drink orders, or singing someone else's songs. But re-writing someone else's paper wouldn't play for Dr. Coupe. No, it was time for W.W.W. to sing some music of his own. To do it, he would have to put the twenty-four-hour CD player in his head out of working order for a while. He was counting on lack of sleep and a lot of alcohol.

After all, back in New Orleans, it was the last weekend of Mardi Gras—the final booze-fueled blowout before the beginning of Lent on Wednesday. W.W.W. would carry on that tradition here in Columbia, but with a twist. Instead of celebrating, he would use booze to get writing done. He went first to the kitchen, fetched a beer out of the refrigerator, and got out the phone book. Then he walked back to the living room and started dialing. It was just like he'd told Dr. Coupe. He had a couple of things to take care of first.

Then the serious drinking began.

W.W.W. drank every beer that Tommy had left in the refrigerator. He stayed awake for days. He read books aloud and listened to the music he heard in them, then he wrote the things that he heard down on the page. He heard Robert E. Lee as a steady staccato in baritone, with moonlit leit-motifs that burned in minor keys. W.W.W. put that in the paper. He heard Ulysses S. Grant as a dark movement in bass adagio, with an occasional crescendo that set the South ablaze. W.W.W. put that in, too. He heard William Tecumseh Sherman as a strident decrescendo in a minor key, interspersed with heavy drumbeats and woodwind screams. When he was done putting that in the paper, W.W.W. was through. What he had written was a sort of Civil War symphony, and it was unlike anything he had ever read—or heard, or seen—before.

He was only interrupted twice.

The first time was on Monday morning when a man in a gray tweed sport-jacket, blue jeans, and boots pounded long and hard enough on the front door to draw W.W.W. away from the page. The man who had knocked was big, with dark curly hair and a nose that had been broken too many times to re-set. He left his car running at the curb.

"W.W. Woodcock?" the man barked.

"Yeah," W.W.W. mumbled, feeling papers pressed into his hands.

"You're served."

W.W.W. dropped the papers on the floor, shut the door, and went back to writing.

The second time was on Monday night when the phone rang. "Walt?" a familiar voice said on the other end of the line. It was the voice he'd been waiting to hear for days.

W.W.W. said, "Shine."

"Walt? Is that you?"

"It's me. The one and only me. Is this the one and only you?"

There was a long pause. "You sound awful. Is it you that's been calling me and hanging up?"

"Thanks," he said. "I don't know," he said. And then he said, "Will you see me?"

"What?"

"Will you see me? I need to talk to you. I need to ask you something."

"You are talking to me," Shine said. "Ask me now."

"I need to see you in person," he said, "face to face. It's important."

"I could come over there tonight."

"Not tonight. I have a paper due tomorrow. I haven't slept in . . . two days?"

"Then when?"

"Will you see me Wednesday night at the Dixie Fish?"

"No, Walt. Not there. I'll meet you out somewhere."

"It has to be at the Dixie Fish," he said. "Please."

There was another pause. "Oh, Walt," Shine said. "Alright. I'll be there

Wednesday night."

W.W.W. watched the sun rise Tuesday morning over the red bricks of the Confederate State University campus. When he shut his eyes, he saw light. And when he opened them again, the sun was music. There was music in the light creeping up the trunks of the pines. Everything was music. He had just slid a finished midterm essay underneath Dr. Coupe's office door.

34. Effed by Cow Pie

W.W.W. opened his eyes to see Reese standing over by the fishtank, studying him. It was early Wednesday morning, and W.W.W. was lying on the living room floor where he'd collapsed the day before—after two days of not sleeping, a fridgeful of beer, and a midterm paper slid under Cow Pie's door.

"Reese!" W.W.W. said, throwing off his rainbow-colored quilt and sitting up. A smile of welcome creased his face. "You've come back!"

"Not exactly," Reese said. He did not return W.W.W.'s smile.

"But you're here," W.W.W. said. "Aren't you?"

"Only momentarily. I have come to inform you that Dr. Coupe would like to have a word with you."

"What?" W.W.W. asked, feeling his smile of welcome fade. "When?"

"This afternoon during regular office hours."

"When are those?"

"Dr. Coupe's office hours are between three and five on Monday and Wednesday afternoons."

"Tell him I'll be there," W.W.W. said. "And Reese? Would you like to stay for breakfast? How about some eggs and bacon and coffee, on me? I'm famished. I can't remember the last time I ate a meal."

"No, thank you," Reese said. "I have other plans."

So W.W.W. headed into the kitchen and cooked up a breakfast feast that he ate alone. When he was done, he climbed into the shower and scrubbed and scraped and shaved, preparing himself to face the trinity of trials by ordeal that lay ahead: Dr. Coupe, the Wednesday Nite Fish Spectacular, and Shine.

3 p.m. found W.W.W. standing outside Dr. Coupe's office and looking at the brass plaque attached to the wall just to the left of the door. It read:

Vanderbilt Coupe, Ph.D.
Whitefield Distinguished Professor of American History
Director of Graduate Studies

W.W.W. hesitated a moment in the face of Dr. Coupe's brass-mounted credentials. Then he took a deep breath, focused everything inside himself on the task at hand, and knocked on the door.

"*Entrez!*"

W.W.W. heard the voice of Cow Pie come faintly from the other side of the door—as though the office were quite large, and filled with expensive overstuffed furnishings that absorbed sound. Sure enough, when W.W.W. swung open the door and walked inside, he found himself in an elegantly furnished office suite. Two of the walls were made up entirely of windows. Original works of art covered the other two walls, and a vast mahogany desk sprinkled with neat stacks of papers dominated the room.

"Mr. Walt Whitman Woodcock," Dr. Coupe said. "*Bienvenue!*"

"Thanks," W.W.W. said. "I guess."

"Please be seated." Dr. Coupe nodded toward an overstuffed leather chair.

W.W.W. sank into the sinuous embrace of the chair and studied Cow Pie. The good doctor slouched at ease behind the vast mahogany desk in his tan camel hair jacket and his green jacquard silk tie. He held a sheaf of yellow loose-leaf papers in one hand.

"Ah, the . . . ease," Dr. Coupe said, fanning himself now with the sheaf of papers, "with which the . . . Woodcock is snared."

"Excuse me?" On the yellow pages that swept slowly back and forth across Cow Pie's face, W.W.W. could make out square black printing. He recognized the square black letters as his own.

"Nothing, Mr. Woodcock. A . . . French Proverb. You have been summoned here," he said, "as you have probably surmised, in . . . response to . . . your midterm essay."

"Yes?"

"Here it comes." Cow Pie extended the sheaf of yellow papers a little way across the desk, but not nearly far enough to cover the space between them.

After a long moment, W.W.W. stood up and reached across the desk. The yellow pages felt dry and heavy in his hands, which were now wet with sweat. He rifled through the pages, studying the marks that the good doctor had made. W.W.W. saw that in places—in a lot of places—there was more red ink on the pages than black. He saw, written in red in the side margins, words like *fascinating, brilliant*, and *indeed*! He couldn't believe it. Then he got to the very end of it all and saw the big red F in the yellow margin at the bottom of the final page.

"Oof," W.W.W. said and sank back down into the chair.

"I see you are dissatisfied with . . . your grade."

"I think this is a hell of a lot better paper than an F," W.W.W. snapped. Then remembering where he was, he tacked on a quick, soft, "sir."

"Hmm . . . Do you know who I am, Mr. Woodcock?"

W.W.W. hesitated, not sure where this was headed. "Dr. Coupe?" he tried.

"Very good, Mr. Woodcock. Now do you know what I am?"

W.W.W. felt the term *Cow Pie* pressing hard against the back of his lips. But sitting there in his worn jeans, his worn jean jacket, and his gray lizard-skin boots with holes in the soles—in front of the mahogany desk the good doctor sat behind dressed in camel hair and silk—W.W.W. knew enough, at least, to let that one alone.

"I am the . . . Graduate Director, Mr. Woodcock. Do you have even the . . . faintest idea what that entails?"

"Not exactly."

"Think of the . . . Graduate Program as an . . . orchestra. I trust that you are able. I gathered from . . . your essay that you are musically inclined. What was the . . . title again? Oh yes . . . 'Civil War Symphony.' How picturesque. Now picture a gathering of . . . single instruments all playing different notes, but all playing together in the . . . same key and under the . . . direction of . . . me. It is an . . . orchestra, Mr. Woodcock, for . . . which very talented people are lined up, waiting to . . . audition."

Cow Pie seemed to expect some kind of answer, but W.W.W. just stared across the desk. He was picturing Cow Pie having this same conversation with Christ come again. *Excuse me, Mr. Christ,* Cow Pie was saying, *but we have very talented people lined up, waiting to . . . be crucified. I don't suppose that you play an . . . instrument?*

"You have written a . . . fine essay, Mr. Woodcock. A truly eloquent and completely original treatment of the . . . Civil War, viewed through the . . . lens of . . . musical language. But the . . . assignment specifically called for a . . . detailed treatment of the . . . thematic topic of the . . . student's choice, as it pertained to the . . . portion of the . . . reading list that we have covered so far."

"Yes sir," W.W.W. said. "I remember."

"I also possess a . . . memory, Mr. Woodcock. Perhaps not so prodigious a . . . memory as your own; however, as I recall, we have not yet covered the . . . Civil War. Your essay becomes then, in the . . . words of the . . . immortal bard, merely a . . . tale told by an . . . idiot. In short, Mr. Woodcock, an . . . F."

"It can't be that bad."

"Bad? Oh, no. It is brilliant. But it is not even typed. And as I said before, it does not fulfill the . . . assignment. No, Mr. Woodcock, you are out of . . . key. Indeed, you are not even playing the . . . same song as the . . . rest of us."

"Dr. Coupe, if you give me this F, you take away my financial aid. And without that financial aid money, I can't afford to stay in school."

"You are about to . . . embark on a . . . solo career, Mr. Woodcock. Think of it as an . . . opportunity."

"What about Reese?" W.W.W. asked. "What does he say about all this?"

"Mr. Thorvaldson?" Cow Pie reached over and eased open a door to the right of the desk. In the bookshelf-lined sitting room that lay behind the door, W.W.W. caught sight of Reese. Reese lay asleep, all pale white flesh and red silk pajamas, on an overstuffed leather couch that perfectly matched the overstuffed leather chair in which W.W.W. sat. "As you can see, Mr. Thorvaldson is my principal first violin."

35. The Wednesday Nite Fish Spectacular

W.W.W. was late getting to the Dixie Fish, even though the only stop he made on his way from Cow Pie's office was at a little florist's shop to buy a single long-stemmed red rose. He didn't let himself think about what had happened on campus. Not yet. He wouldn't know the full extent of the damage to his plan for revenge and rescue until he got to the Dixie Fish.

When he pulled up next to the Dixie Fish dumpster, there was already a line out in front of the restaurant that stretched from the double front doors to the fire station down the street. It struck W.W.W. only then what a brilliant marketing idea it had been for Kent to hold the Wednesday Nite Fish Spectacular on the first day of Lent—it looked as though every person in Columbia who had given up meat until Easter was in line for ALL U CAN EAT FISH. He cut straight to the front of the line, shut his eyes, and stepped inside. Then he took the second deepest breath of his life.

There was everywhere the reek of sawdust and drying latex. Underneath it, W.W.W. caught the homey smell of deep-fried fish and frying starches, the slightly sweet odors of beer and steaming oysters, the rank aromas of cigarette smoke and sweating bodies. But there was not even a hint of the first day of spring, or of cheap perfume. It was as though the scent of potential bliss had never existed at the Dixie Fish.

W.W.W. opened his eyes. There were everywhere new faces, and the Dixie Fish had turned pink and blue. The Styrofoam mannequin heads were still there, and still in their Confederate caps along the top waitstation rail. But the faded green fish net had been replaced by a bright pink nylon weave that had never seen the ocean and never would. Bonnie stood in front of the new pink net on the stool that W.W.W. remembered, beneath a ceiling that was nothing but fluorescent lights and bare pink-and-blue rafters. The rainbow-colored canopy was gone. Even the specials that Bonnie was chalking were new: PACIFIC DRUM $9.95, ALL U CAN EAT FISH & FIXINS $5.95, ANGELS ON HORSEBACK (FOUR TO AN ORDER) $3.95.

"Hey, W.W!" Bonnie said. She stepped down off of the stool wearing the same red and white outfit she had worn on Valentine's night, and W.W.W. saw that same familiar threadbare smile.

"Hey, Bonnie," he said.

"It's so good to see you. After Alisha quit, and then Tommy, I didn't expect to see you back."

"I didn't know whether I'd see you, either," W.W.W. said. "Who's left?"

"Gladys. And Brave, of course. But Brave is . . . well, you know. And there are all these new names I can't remember. Where have you been? Why didn't you come down and help out with the renovation?"

"I think I've given up on renovation," W.W.W. said. "And I had something come due at school. Speaking of Brave, where is the new general manager of the Dixie Fish?"

"In the back, helping Kent work the kinks out of the new kitchen equipment."

"Good," W.W.W. said. "That's good. Now, what's going on with the free live entertainment?"

"Mr. Guitar? Well, Brave says he's supposed to be playing tonight. But I haven't seen him."

"Do you remember what time Mr. Guitar was supposed to come in?"

"I believe Brave said that Mr. Guitar was supposed to have been here at five." Bonnie laughed. "That was at least a half-hour ago. Come to think of it, Brave looked a little bit worried."

"Good," W.W.W. said. "I like Brave worried." He looked up at the clock over the register. It was quarter-to-six. "And Bonnie? What are Angels on Horseback?"

"Oysters," she said, "wrapped in bacon strips and fried."

Bonnie climbed back up onto the stool, and W.W.W. walked around into the waitstation fearing further renovations. But everything in the waitstation looked the same, except for the faces. There was a new face over at the freezer table scooping mounds of slaw into clear plastic cups. Over by the fake pier pilings, a new face was putting together oyster-shucking set-ups. Yet another new face stood at the counter rolling silverware. Gladys was also at the counter, but she was pouring buttery-flavored vegetable oil into tray after tray of "drawn-butter" set-ups. W.W.W. grabbed the cuttingboard and knife from underneath the counter and the bag of lemons from the fridge, and started cutting lemon wedges into a gallon bucket.

W.W.W. had to hand it to Brave: preparations for the onslaught of customers who were waiting outside the double front doors seemed to be in full swing. But all those preparations wouldn't help Brave out with the FREE LIVE ENTERTAINMENT. No, W.W.W. thought, there would be no entertainment this evening. Anyway, not the kind that came from Mr. Guitar. One of the phone calls that W.W.W. had made just before getting drunk enough to write his midterm paper for Cow Pie had been to Eb Etheridge, alias Mr. Guitar. And Eb, who was listed right there in the local directory, now had an earfull of what had happened to Smiley—and a paid night off. The look on Brave's face, W.W.W. told himself, would be worth every cent of the hundred dollars he'd promised to give Eb for not showing up.

"Say, Gladys," W.W.W. said without looking up from cutting. "Tommy left your phone in the living room. I'm all through using it. You can pick it up whenever you like."

"What about the beagles?" she asked. "And the fish?"

"The dogs went with Tommy," W.W.W. said. "All of the fish are dead. And down the toilet, like just about everything else on Hope Street. I dumped the water out of the aquarium and left it on the living room floor next to the phone."

It was true. The house on Hope Street was now as empty of life as the aquarium. The next call W.W.W. had made after he'd hung up with Eb was to cancel his contract with the furniture rental company and arrange a pick-up. With the exception of the night he and Shine had first made love, and the few minutes or so between the first roommate meeting and the poker game, the grand experiment on Hope Street was now officially a total failure. And that wasn't the only thing. He took a quick mental survey of the state of his plan for revenge and rescue in light of the afternoon's developments: the F from Cow Pie had slammed the door shut on graduate school, and the scent of potential bliss had disappeared from the Dixie Fish. There was nothing left to rescue in Columbia, South Carolina. All that remained was revenge. The time had come to put an honorable end to things here in Columbia—to make an unforgettable last stand and then move on.

To make that happen, W.W.W. knew, he had to do two things:

1) Get Brave fired from his manager job; and

2) Get Shine to come away with him.

W.W.W. had made a good beginning on both fronts. As for getting Brave fired from his manager job, the end of the FREE LIVE ENTER-TAINMENT was just for starters. The real fireworks would kick off when the food orders started stacking up in the brand-new kitchen, the drink orders started stacking up in front of the brand-new bartender, and the customers started raising hell with the mostly-brand-new waitstaff. As for getting Shine to come away with him, that was the reason W.W.W. had stopped off at the florist's to get the long-stemmed red rose.

"Alright, folks! Everybody get ready. I'm about to let in the herd."

W.W.W. looked up from lemon-cutting to see Brave stride around the corner of the bar, making a last check through the newly renovated restau-rant—or maybe, W.W.W. thought, just a first test of his new authority. Brave had better not get used to either one.

"Why, W.W.," Brave said, stopping dead in his tracks at the entrance to the waitstation. "I'm surprised to see you. Whatever are you doing here in my restaurant?"

"I believe they call this *cutting lemons*," W.W.W. said.

"You could've done that at home. In fact—"

"In fact," W.W.W. said, raising his voice to a pitch that everyone in the restaurant could hear, "I noticed something funny the other day." He gripped the knife tight in his hand and pictured Brave's head there among the lemons on the cutting board. "I noticed that those two policemen weren't wearing nametags."

"Why, whatever policemen could you mean, W.W.?"

"I mean the two policemen who dragged Smiley out of here in handcuffs. Having trouble remembering? No problem. Reese saw them, too. So did Tommy. Now why, I wonder, would two policemen on official duty neglect wearing their nametags? I was thinking of calling up the folks at the newspaper and asking them. I thought I might also mention the new fifty-percent discount for police and firemen."

"What do you want, W.W.?" Brave stepped in close and whispered. "What are you after?"

"Nothing," W.W.W. said, lowering his own voice now. "Not one damned thing."

"And that," Brave said, stepping away from W.W.W. and out of the waitstation, "is exactly what you'll get. That, and section three."

Brave threw open the double front doors and started welcoming patrons. Then the restaurant was full of new customers. There was not a regular among them. Every table on the waitfloor was filled with the faces of people W.W.W. had never seen. The bar was filled with them, front and back. And they were still lined up outside the double front doors.

W.W.W. took drink orders for every table in his section, from the six-top at table 31 next to the waitstation all the way out to the deuce at 35 up against the plate glass windows. From where he was stationed—in section three, in the middle of everything—he could see, on his left, Bonnie and Gladys holding their own in sections one and two. On his right, the three new waitstaff faces that Brave had divided up sections four and five among seemed to be doing pretty much the same. In among the fake pier pilings, W.W.W. mass-dumped orders for six drafts, three longnecks, two bourbon and gingers, and a dirty martini. He saw Bonnie, Gladys, and the New Waitfaces mass-dump their drink orders as well. He ducked into the waitstation and fixed seven teas, two unsweetened teas, and a water with lemon. Then he went back to the bar to check on his drinks from the New Barface, and saw a stack of tickets and not a drink in sight.

W.W.W. couldn't help but chuckle as he put teas, un-teas, and waters down in front of people at tables 31 through 35. He laughed a little more as he saw only nonalcoholic drinks going down on the waitfloor all around him. Then he pulled out his food tickets. If taking food orders went as smoothly as taking drink orders had gone, they would swamp kinks into the brand new kitchen equipment that would last all the way through into next week—and swamp Brave with it, all the way out of his job as the new general manager of the Dixie Fish.

But just as W.W.W. was starting to think he had Brave beat, the questions started:

"What are angels on horseback?"

"What are fixins?"

"What's a Pacific Drum?"

"Ain't $9.95 a little bit much, boy, for a bass that lives in the sea?"

By the time he got done taking food orders and headed for the waitwindow to mass-dump the tickets, W.W.W. saw that there was already food up in the window. And it wasn't just side-orders, either. He saw plates of steaming seafood waiting to be prepped and run. There were no kinks in the kitchen. There was no back-log of orders. The sons of bitches, it came to W.W.W., must have pre-cooked the stuff. He looked over at the bar, hoping for a continued backlog there. But he saw Brave instead. Behind the bar now, Brave was filling order after order—and digging the New Barface out of the weeds.

Just when W.W.W. thought it couldn't get any worse, he felt someone touch him on the shoulder. He turned and saw Eb Etheridge standing behind him. Eb carried his Martin guitar slung low on a hand-tooled leather strap across one broad shoulder.

"Eb?" W.W.W. said. "What are you doing here? I thought you said Mr. Guitar was going to take the night off."

"I couldn't do it, W.W.," Eb said. "I just couldn't do it. You can keep your hundred dollars."

"But why, Eb?"

"Smiley or no Smiley," Eb said, "I gave your new boss my word."

Food shot out of the kitchen. Drinks shot out of the bar. Waitpeople ran it all out to tables. New customers ate and drank what was put before them and ordered more. W.W.W. tea'd, un-tea'd, and watered his entire section in long passes. The New Waitfaces did the same. Tables started to turn. Bonnie flashed her threadbare smile at each new group that sat in her section. Gladys was as much of a trooper working for Brave as she'd been moving Brave's belongings out onto the front lawn. Brave ran the register. He did the seating. He helped out in the bar. In the corner next to the jukebox, Mr. Guitar played country and blues. The line at the door got shorter and shorter. Finally, near the end of the shift, W.W.W. saw the last three people in line seat themselves at table 34. They were, he saw, wearing tuxedos and an evening gown. They also were wearing lobster bibs. And they were calling him by name.

"Hello, Walt Whitman!" they called. "Walt Whitman, hello! We've missed you!"

"Hello," W.W.W. said. He didn't have the strength left to correct them about his name.

"Since we are no longer going to be neighbors, we would like it very much if you would seat us in your section."

"You're sitting in it already," W.W.W. said.

"Tell us," Dr. Bob Allen said, "about your wine list."

"Tantalize us," the Reverend Dale Sessions said. "Tease us."

"Fill us," Norma said, "with lust for the grape."

Then they all turned and waved at Brave.

W.W.W. looked over at Brave—who was standing at the register with a smile of triumph on his face—and then he looked back down at the Opera People. It was clear that Brave had won. And not only Brave: Kent, Cow Pie, materialism, waste, greed. For the Greeks, Fate took the form of three weaver women who spun, measured, and cut the threads of life. For W.W.W., it seemed that Fate had taken the form of three Opera People who may or may not have been escaped psychotics, but who had certainly turned out to be dangerous. An honorable end was no longer a possibility. His plan for revenge had failed. The only thing that remained for W.W.W. to do was wait for Shine.

When she finally came in, Shine was gold and ivory—her eyes gold, her skin pale ivory that was so much like his mother's skin. W.W.W. caught sight of her through the new pink net that had never seen the sea. He took off his apron and laid it gently on the counter. He had run out of plans and programs, and out of ideas. All he had left was a long-stemmed red rose and a question. They were both for Shine. He stepped out of the waitstation and walked up to her just as she reached the bar.

"Hello, beautiful," W.W.W. said. And he gave her the rose.

"Oh, Walt." The expression on Shine's face was exactly the same as it had been the day after Valentine's when she'd seen W.W.W. naked in the kitchen, pressing Tommy's head down into a pool of vomit. "What's this for?"

"Love," W.W.W. said. "A long-stemmed red rose is a gesture of love."

"You're good at gestures," Shine said. "Especially romantic ones. I'll give you that. But Walt, I only came here to tell you goodbye."

"Wait! You said I was good at gestures. What does that mean?"

"It means that all you and I ever had together was gestures. It means that you never talked to me. Not really. It means that I don't know what your dreams are. It means that you and I come from completely different worlds."

"Just hear me out," W.W.W. said. "Please. I'm leaving Columbia and heading down to Charleston for the tourist season. Alisha says there are big-money jobs down there. I'd like you to come with me. We could live at the beach, get to know each other's dreams, make our own world together. What do you say?"

"Oh, Walt, you . . ." Shine started, then stopped. With tears in her gold eyes and her ivory nose wrinkled, she looked as though she had something left to say.

"I what?" W.W.W. asked. "Go ahead. What?"

"You smell like fish."

"It's bliss," he said. "Bliss."

"No," she said. "It's fish." She handed him back the rose. She gave him back the silver bangle that had been his mother's. Then she walked back out the double front doors.

Through the plate glass windows, W.W.W. watched Shine walk out of the Dixie Fish and climb into the Stranger's red sports coupe. He looked around and saw new faces staring back at him where there had been friends before. He saw the Opera People waving their arms, trying to get his attention. They were all against him, even Mr. Guitar.

He had come to Columbia hoping to renovate the house of society and his own life with it, hoping to plant a seed of bliss that would bloom like Easter Sunday after a long season of Lent. But the house on Hope Street was empty, the feeling of warmth and welcome was dead at the Dixie Fish, and Easter was still more than a month away.

He was through chasing rainbows. It was a crazy, dangerous world.

36. Angels on Horseback

W.W.W. watched the fire spread from the Strangers' spacious red-brick house to the red sports coupe and the red import sedan with its Virginia vanity plates. He had doused both cars with kerosene just before he'd splashed kerosene all around the base of the Strangers' house and inside the front door that he'd broken into. Even from the shadows across the street, he felt the heat of the flames that leapt up into the pine trees and saw sparks swarm like a thousand fireflies into the black Carolina sky. There were no lights yet in the Strangers' windows, and the flames had already covered the walls and spread to the roof.

On the horizon W.W.W. made out the glow from the fire that had now completely engulfed the house on Hope Street. He listed closely to the sirens he heard in the distance. None of them were headed this way yet. In another minute or so, it wouldn't matter. The Strangers' house, like the house on Hope Street, would be fully involved.

Standing there, smelling smoke and Tommy's kerosene, W.W.W. remembered that other fire so far away west and so long ago. He remembered kneeling in the front yard and watching everything that mattered burn to ashes. He remembered his mother's screams. He remembered praying for fire trucks that came too late, for water that wasn't there, for the angels to stop whispering from the flames.

He remembered the last time he talked to his daddy. W.W.W. had just driven in from Dallas to pick up his things. The west wind billowed the leaves on the trees that he and the old man had replanted after the fire; it whipped up waves in the coastal Bermuda that had grown back so thick and green. W.W.W. remembered his daddy saying the grass had grown back that way because of the ashes from the fire they'd made.

Walt Whitman, his daddy had said, *can I count on you?* The afternoon sun was a ball of yellow flame, and the old man looked away west into the wind. *The firestorm is coming. Judgment Day is coming. The day is coming when we will take back what is ours. Can I count on you, son? There is nothing in this world more important.*

"What about my mother?" W.W.W. asked. "Remember? Trapped in that house she couldn't get out of because of those bars you put on the windows to keep out the world." Then he climbed into his ranch truck and headed east.

You'll be back, was the last thing he heard the old man say.

Back in the here and now, smelling the kerosene Tommy had left and watching the flames leap a hundred feet into the sky from the house where the Strangers and Shine were still asleep upstairs, it was as though whatever it was that had been Walt Whitman Woodcock, and then W.W.W., had finally been burned away.

All that remained was an angel on horseback.

He pulled his mother's silver bangle out of his pocket and heaved it with all his strength into the fire. Then he stepped onto the maroon metalflake and chrome motorcycle that was parked beside him, strapped Tommy's kerosene can to the back, and headed out.

He would ride first to the Dixie Fish with its dark alley.

He would ride next to the address that Reese had given him, the address that he knew was Dr. Coupe's.

And then he would ride west, armed with fire, an avenging angel on horseback in search of his daddy and Judgment Day.

Andrew Geyer has been a bartender, a waiter, a busboy, a bellhop, a cashier, a landscaper, a construction worker, a manager at a Birkenstock store, a student, a teacher, and a writer. A lover of the outdoors and an avid runner and canoeist, Geyer has traveled extensively in North America, Central America, South America, Europe, and North Africa. He currently serves as Assistant Professor of Creative Writing and American Literature at the University of South Carolina Aiken.

In addition to *Dixie Fish*, Geyer has published three other books and more than three dozen short stories. His first novel, *Meeting the Dead*, was published in 2007 by University of New Mexico Press. His debut short story cycle, *Whispers in Dust and Bone* (Texas Tech University Press 2003), won the silver medal for short fiction in the *Foreword Magazine* Book of the Year Awards and a Spur Award for short fiction from the Western Writers of America. Ink Brush Press published *Siren Songs from the Heart of Austin*, a short story cycle, in 2010.